The Son

A novel
by
M. Ann Ricks

The Son
Leading Lady Publications
A Division of Anointed Word Media Group
1-800-597-9428
P.O. Box 35, Worton, MD 21678
www.publishyourchristianbook.com
Cover Design by: Tamika Johnson-Hall
ISBN-10: 0-9818753-1-9
ISBN-13: 978-0-9818753-1-6
Copyright © 2008 by M. Ann Ricks

Printed in the United States of America

To order additional copies please contact:
Anointed Word Media Group
1-800-597-9428
info@publishyourchristianbook.com
www.anointedwordbookstore.net

Acknowledgements

Allow me to give my Lord and Savior the highest praise. Hallelujah!!!!

Lord, You provided this story's premise. I thank you God for your faithfulness and limitless mercy. You've blessed me with the ability to write and tell the world how wonderful You are! You provided your Word to incorporate into this project to strengthen not only me, but the reader, and using the same powerful Word, You have validated the victory that we all can have if we just trust and believe in You.

Loyal Ricks Sr.: My love, my friend and my biggest fan. Your encouragement and support keep me going. You always believe in me and I thank you for your constant prayers, (don't stop!! ☺).

Loyal Jr. & William, (my "little loves"): I thank God for both of you. Because you said it and believed it, God did it!! I love you!

My Parents; Dea. Earnest Smith Sr. & Anne Smith: Thank you for being the parents that you are. Look at God!!!

My Entire Family: (Smith and Ricks); I love you all. Many thanks to each and every one of you!

Bernika Simmons & Denessa Brown: God Bless you both. Your unabashed honesty and love is what I count on even after twenty years of friendship. Thank you for loving me for me, (you know what I mean☺).

Toni James, Darnyelle Jervey & Wendi Hayman: my advance readers; Thanks for challenging me. You made me want to create the best story possible.

A great, big Hallelujah shout-out to my pastor, **Rev. Jack Miller and First lady, Teresa Miller.** Many thanks to my entire church family at **Abundant Life Christian Center.**

Thanks to......Leading Lady Publications, (Faith Woodard and Tamika Johnson) and Anointed Word Media Group for their partnership on this project.

As always, I acknowledge and thank you, the reader. I write to exalt my Savior Jesus Christ as I provide information as well as entertainment. It is my hope that all will enjoy what I create with the help of the Holy Spirit. May you be blessed!

The Son

Prologue

*Wherefore, come out from among them, and be ye
separate, saith the Lord, and touch not the unclean thing;
and I will receive you.*
2 Corinthians 6:17

"What in the world am I doing in here?" he asked himself.

The question had begun to echo in his brain. Hands shackled, he held his head as he brooded over how he landed in this situation. He knew one thing; he was not going to call his mother. She would be heartbroken. He was the one son that she said she didn't have to worry about. Until now.

His hands released the braids that covered his head as they found a home over his face. Why had he let that woman put braids in his hair in the first place? Yeah, she was fine and could seem to talk a blind man into thinking that he could see but he had never been that gullible before. Why her? Why him? He couldn't think. He had to think.

"God, I know that you are able to help me and right now, I need your help," he said as he stood and looked out of the window that selfishly allowed a few warm rays of the sun to enter his domicile. Natural light spread itself across the flat and very uncomfortable bed as if it were a makeshift bedspread. He longed to be outside enjoying the inviting warmth. The four puke green walls that surrounded him were dirty and the room smelled of human waste.

"I know that you have been speaking to my heart for some time and I have been running from you. I'm ready to hear you." He'd dropped to his knees in an effort to make his plea more pronounced. The cold, hard cement floor assisted in making him humble. His knees were unaccustomed to the pressure. He'd been praying intermittently for the last two hours, believing that God could hear him.

Why am I still wearing these things? He thought, looking at his wrists. He couldn't believe that they said that handcuffs were still necessary. He'd struggled with the arresting officers initially, but that had been almost five hours ago. He was no longer a threat. The whole situation was a nightmare. Tears threatened to make an appearance.

He closed his eyes again and said, "I will accept your will."

An hour after the words were uttered, he heard the footsteps of someone approaching and turned abruptly toward the bars that held him hostage.

"Daniel Ezekiel Manders?" the tall, dark, chocolate man with a shiny bald head asked as the guard inserted the key into the lock.

"Yes," Daniel said, not recognizing the man. "I'm Daniel. Who are you?"

"I'm Samuel Davidson, an attorney. Your attorney," the man said. His answer, delivered in a baritone voice, was void of emotion.

Daniel was confused. He hadn't called for an attorney, nor had he called anyone to retain one for him. "How did you know that I was in here?" Daniel asked, looking at the man that seemed to command his visual attention. Mr. Davidson's eyes were dark brown, almost black. They were unreadable. His face was smooth without a hint of facial hair. Daniel would have mistaken him for an over-developed pubescent boy except for the fact that his voice was as deep as one would think the voice of God's would be.

"A friend called me and told me that you may need my help," he responded and extended a hand toward Daniel's bed, inviting him to sit down. Mr. Davidson slowly sat in the chair that had been provided by the guard upon his entrance.

"It looks like you have been arrested for drug trafficking," Mr. Davidson said.

"That is what they are saying but it's not true," Daniel pleaded. "I have never consumed any form of narcotic."

Mr. Davidson nodded and scribbled something on a pad that seemed to appear out of the air. "The police report says that they found cocaine and marijuana in your home and that you and a... Ms. Eva Sirens were planning to sell it on the University of Wisconsin campus."

"That is a lie." Daniel enunciated each word. "I frequent the campus every now and then to visit former professors but never with the intention to sell drugs." He tried to use his hands to speak but realized that they were still constrained. He grunted in frustration and leaned forward to engage Mr. Davidson. "There is no way I would have possession of illegal substances. Someone placed them in my home. This is a set up. Please believe me."

Mr. Davidson stood and walked over to Daniel. "I believe you. We will find a way to clear you of these charges but you must be totally honest with me and yourself." Daniel looked up at the man who was clearly 6'5" and extremely intimidating albeit his youthful appearance.

"How?"

"Daniel, how well did you know this Eva Sirens?" Mr. Davidson asked.

"I met her at an office party. She was a friend of one of my co-workers." Daniel stood and walked to the bars and placed his hands on them. "She was from Bergen County, New Jersey and since I grew up not far from there, I thought that I would get to know her. Not long after we met, we started hanging out."

"It didn't hurt that she was quite attractive," Mr. Davidson interjected.

"I guess that made her a little bit more appealing. Man, I knew that I was playing with fire, she was Italian, flashed a lot of money and mentioned to me that she was taking a break from a family business that she didn't want to talk about." Daniel wanted to kick himself for even getting involved with the woman. "She was lonely and she seemed okay in the beginning," Daniel explained, knowing it was a weak attempt.

"What changed?" Mr. Davidson asked.

"After about a month, I noticed that she was susceptible to mood changes. She would also leave the room and go into the bathroom and stay there for prolonged periods of time." Daniel couldn't believe that he was so easy to fool. Why hadn't he seen it sooner?

"I can tell by your facial expression that it is all becoming clear," Davidson said.

Daniel noticed that Davidson had begun staring at his hair. His face continued to be impassive but his eyes, now clear onyx, were fixed on the top of his head. Daniel couldn't be certain but Davidson's brows seemed knitted together. He felt the need to explain.

"She wanted me to change my hair and I let one of her visiting girlfriends braid it." Daniel once again, touched his hair. He hadn't liked it but she was putting it on him something good. He really didn't deny her much of anything. He decided that he wouldn't share that with Davidson. He almost laughed when he recalled the day he walked into work with his new look. He'd received stares that were so penetrating and disapproving that even Stevie Wonder could have seen them.

"This is what we are going to do," Davidson said as if he had heard enough. "The bracelets will come off now." He signaled the guard. The uniformed man entered the cell and immediately removed the handcuffs.

Once the guard left, Davidson motioned again for Daniel to sit. "I have information that the police have been following Ms. Sirens since her arrival in Madison and have confirmed that she is part of a well known cartel in New York. She was sent here to essentially dry out, but her ties to New York have assisted her in getting product sent here so that she could sell it and as you have witnessed, use it. You, my friend, were her patsy." Davidson closed his portfolio and placed it in his briefcase; a briefcase that Daniel hadn't noticed before.

"We have to prove that you were exactly what she wanted you to be, a boy-toy slash flunky, who had nothing to do with the selling of the drugs."

Daniel, not really appreciating the categories that Davidson had placed him in, threw him a look of disdain.

"Don't fault me for what you have essentially proven yourself to be Daniel. I'm here to get you out of this mess and provide a way of escape."

"How do we go about doing that, Mr. Davidson?" Daniel asked, becoming a little wary of his mysterious attorney.

"Continue to pray," Davidson said and looked at Daniel with an unwavering and intense stare. Flames seemed to burn in his eyes as he stated the directive to Daniel.

"Excuse me?" Daniel said, not expecting to hear that type of instruction.

"You heard me," Davidson said. "You know the words of prayer and more importantly, you know the word of God." Davidson produced a bible that had appeared out of thin air. He gave Daniel the bible. "Your mother and father provided you with a foundation that you had the nerve to discard for a pretty face and fornication. It is not His will for you to spend your time in here. He has prepared you for such a time as this. Stop running, repent and pray."

At that instant, the fire left Davidson's eyes and he stood and turned toward the bars. "I'll stop by tomorrow afternoon as I expect to make considerable headway. You simply need to be ready for what comes next."

Daniel followed Davidson as the guard opened the cell door and stared, mouth agape. Finally finding his words, he asked with child-like wonder, "Who are you?"

Davidson turned and for the first time, smiled broadly. He extended his hand to shake Daniel's and said with a tone that conveyed humility and delight, "I am the answer to your prayers." Daniel released Davidson's hand and stood transfixed.

Walking away, Davidson said, "Go home and keep your word."

One

*Wait on the Lord; be of good courage and he shall
strengthen thine heart; wait, I say on the Lord.
Psalms 27:14*

"Are you sure?" The voice was a whisper that revealed a bit of apprehension. This was not lost on Melina. She could tell that her mother was not at all sure that she should be entering into a union with a man that had seemed to cause her so much angst in the past months. Zenia Lawrence, the mother of the bride, had said all she could. She sighed and tried to rest in the confidence that God would take care of her daughter.

Melina refused to face her mother. She slowly nodded her response while lifting her gown to walk over to the long length mirror on the other side of the spacious room provided by the church. It was the pastor's wife's study. Because Mattie and Melina had been friends since Melina was in college, Mattie was happy to provide the space to ensure that Melina would have a private place to prepare mentally, spiritually and physically for her wedding.

"Baby?" Melina's mother asked, "Are you okay?" She walked over to Melina and gently took her child's face into her hands. "Do you know where he is?"

"No, Mom. I don't." She held her mother's gaze and then gingerly removed the hands that had wiped away the many tears shed in her thirty two years.

"He will be here."

She could see that her mother was not assured and Melina knew that she was not as convincing as she wanted to be but had to put up a good front for as long as she could. Melina turned again to her reflection in the mirror. She closed her eyes and pictured the look on Daniel's face as he walked out of her house yesterday afternoon. He was so angry but confusion was also stitched in his countenance. His light brown eyes seemed dark, almost as if he didn't see her as she stated why she disagreed with his decision. To rid herself of the memory and loud accusations, she opened her eyes and saw the beautiful woman looking back at her. The shimmering white brocade strapless gown was the one she wanted as soon as she'd laid eyes on it. Although simple in design, when the light hit the bodice, the material seemed to sparkle. The full skirt provided the right contrast to the cinched waist. Melina looked like a fairy princess awaiting her prince charming.

Where was he? She was supposed to walk down the aisle in thirty minutes and he had not so much as called her since their argument. She could feel the sting that was the prelude to tears but she stubbornly resolved that she was not going to cry. Her make-up was applied with precision and she was determined not to ruin it, not when she had to believe that Daniel was just running late. He had to be. He loved her and wanted to marry her. Their courtship had been shorter than most but she said yes, knowing that she truly loved him without reservation.

Some of the things that were said were definitely uncalled for but they were both aware of the commitment they made to each other.

"Any word?" Cassandra inquired, seemingly out of breath. Her cranberry strapless gown with sheer glistening sleeves and full skirt gracefully settled as she stood in the entranceway of the office.

Melina hadn't even heard her enter the room. She turned and Zenia instinctively picked up the silk and crinoline train and followed Melina to where Cassandra stood with a worried expression. Melina's hand nervously went to her neck as her French manicured fingernails mindlessly fiddled with the pearl and diamond choker that matched her dangling earrings. A curled tendril found its way onto her cheek as she lowered her head in response to Cassandra's question. Her head began to feel heavy. She couldn't blame the weight she was feeling on the exquisite up-do that her stylist, Myra, artistically created. Myra was a true master and Melina knew her hair was fierce.

"What is wrong with him?" Cassandra demanded, almost screaming in frustration. Her patience was waning and she was not one to hold her tongue.

Realizing her maid of honor's minor character flaw, Melina chose not to answer and allowed the question to remain rhetorical.

"I know that you two had some issues to iron out Melina but do you think that those issues would keep him from showing up today?" Cassandra queried.

"He feels strongly about the things we discussed. I just have to believe that he feels stronger about me and our life together," Melina said.

That was it. If we are worth it, then he'll be here, she silently told herself.

Zenia had been quietly sitting in Mattie's chair looking out of the window. The sun shone brightly through. There was not a cloud in the sky. It was an absolutely gorgeous day for a wedding. Family had flown in from all over and because it was the Labor Day weekend, more were able to attend; as was the plan. September still held the joy and frivolity of summer. Zenia could feel the warmth of the sun through glass and anxiously wanted to go out to get Melina's father from the sanctuary to talk to her. She was certainly unsure of what he would say, knowing her husband's misgivings about this wedding. He may negatively escalate matters and she didn't want that. When she heard the conviction in her daughter's voice, she turned the chair around and stood up.

"Melina, from day one you have stood by Daniel and his entire family, knowing how they are. If you want a life of constantly competing with them... and Daniel not knowing who number one should really be, then..." She stopped abruptly and sat. "Accepting their past mistakes is one thing..." She saw the look in her daughter's eyes and bit her lower lip. She silently asked God to forgive her. She'd said too much. "Lord, I have to trust you," she whispered. Zenia didn't want to make her daughter feel any worse and had promised that she wouldn't say anymore but she couldn't help it. .

Stunned by Zenia's words, Cassandra stared but said nothing.

"Mom, I know how you feel, but Daniel is who I want. I prayed about this relationship and I believe that he is the one for me. If he is not, God will have to stop this wedding," Melina said with finality, not wanting to argue anymore.

"Melina, Daniel is a good man but you know what he has been though with his family before and since meeting you. Look, he is not here and it's your wedding day. What does that tell you?" Cassandra asked.

Two

Eighteen months earlier…

.

And the Lord God said, It is not good that the man should be alone; I will make a help meet for him.
Genesis 2:18

"You're new here," a deep baritone voice hummed into Melina's ear.

Acting as if she hadn't heard the comment, she sprayed disinfectant onto a paper towel to wipe down the elliptical machine. She'd just completed her grueling thirty minute workout. Using the sleeve of her t-shirt, and attempting to be as unattractive as she could, without being grossly unladylike, she wiped the perspiration from her brow and grudgingly turned to acknowledge the voice. She really wasn't in the mood to meet anyone. This was her alone time and she wanted to keep it that way.

To her surprise, the voice's owner was as pleasing to the eye as the voice was pleasing to the ear. She was a sucker for a man with a deep, husky voice sprinkled with a gravely timbre.

"I think that you are mistaken sir," Melina said, correcting the handsome stranger. "I have been a member of this gym for some time. You must be the neophyte." With that retort, she smiled coyly and walked away with a little hip action, once completing the task of wiping the equipment. She had planned on running a quick mile on the treadmill but decided against it and saddled the stationary bike. After about a mile, the stranger sat down on the bike adjacent to Melina and began to peddle. He turned and grinned and she couldn't help but chuckle. Not wanting to be rude, she removed one earphone.

"There it is," he said as his smile became wider.

She looked at him quizzically. "What are you talking about?"

"I just wanted to see that smile again. Did you know that you smile with your eyes?" He quizzed, as he continued to peddle.

"I hadn't realized," she responded.

"You do. You have beautiful eyes and an even more gorgeous smile." He hoped that she believed him. He had been watching her as soon as she walked in. She looked so serious when she was vigorously working the elliptical. He couldn't think of anything to say to her when he noticed that she had finished and was making her way to the paper towels. The smile that waited for him behind that mask of stern concentration was like a breath of fresh air. When she corrected him and walked away a few moments ago, he felt strangely blessed and knew that he had to get to know this woman.

"Thank you," Melina said and placed her earphone back into her right ear and continued her bicycle program. She tried not to turn to look in the man's direction. She had to admit that he was attractive but she heard stories about meeting men at fitness centers.

No thank you, she thought.

She completed her route and rose to exit the bike when she felt a tap on her forearm. She quickly looked to the source of the tap and it was the stranger again.

"Are you done? I mean, do you think that you've done enough for today?" he asked. Melina could tell that he was being facetious.

"Yes. I think that is it for today. What? Do you think that I should do something else?" she asked, a smile threatening to emerge.

"I don't think that you need to workout at all. You are absolutely perfect," he confessed. He smiled and to his surprise he blushed a little not realizing that he was coming out his "mack-mode" and was simply being honest. He hadn't been moved to be totally honest with a woman like this in years. "I'm Daniel Manders," he stated as he extended his hand. "You are right. I am a new member. As a matter of fact, I'm just returning to the area. Things have really changed." He kept his eyes fixed on Melina. He could tell that she was completing a mental checklist as she took in his mahogany skin and light brown eyes.

His hair cut was fresh and he was glad he decided to get rid of his braids. That was the old Daniel. His hair was cut in a very short fade. The barber made a point in cleaning up his beard and clipping his mustache. Even his mother mentioned how handsome he looked. "The right hair cut can change your whole look," she'd said when she saw him. "My, my, my, don't you look handsome." She always had a way of making him feel good.

Melina accepted his hand and she could tell that he was not a nail biter. His nails were kept neat but he didn't consult a professional. His hands were not smooth, which was a good sign. Men with smooth hands were a turn off. She believed that a man without rugged hands didn't want to work hard. She knew that that wasn't a good barometer, but so far she had been right.

"Melina Lawrence," she said and a smile was returned under protest.

"It is nice to meet you Miss Lawrence," Daniel said and squeezed her had slightly.

"Same here, Mr. Manders." She removed her hand and decided it was time that she was going. "I'm sure that I'll see you around, being that you are a newbie and all. Take Care."

"I certainly hope that I'll see you again Miss Lawrence," Daniel said and smiled, looking forward to the next time he would see her. He returned to the bike, looking at his hand and realized that he continued to feel her warmth. He watched her as she entered the ladies locker room.

Daniel walked to his car, thankful that his mother had kept it in good condition while he'd been away. She promised him that she would not let any of his brothers use it during his absence. They couldn't be trusted and she knew that. It saddened him that none of his parent's values seemed to have found their way into his siblings. They all seemed to physically resemble each other. All four of the Manders boys looked like carbon copies of their father in different ways but the sense of responsibility and accountability that his father and mother had tried to instill in each of them had not made their way into their gene pool. All except for Daniel.

Shaking his head, he thought of his older brother Naimond. He was MIA, missing in action. No one seemed to know where he was. The last he'd heard, Naimond was living in Portland, Oregon. He'd left home right after their father's funeral.

When his father died, the rumor was that the fatal coronary was brought on by Naimond's illegal dealings with a drug gang in the city. Lila Manders continued to try and raise the boys although three of them were approaching manhood. She would always say that she was going to continue to put her trust in Jesus. She had trained all the boys to follow the right path and make Christ the center of their life. They all had attended Sunday school and Youth Group. Major and Baylor had even been active in the church choir at one time.

As Daniel turned the corner onto the parkway that took him back to his mother's house, he thought of how Major, the second oldest, had become a modern day pimp, without a real source of income, save their mother. Baylor, his baby brother, was what they were calling an "eternal" senior in college. Daniel heard that his grades were not where they should be and he continued to jump in and out of school. This had already resulted in a three year delay in his graduation. Were his brothers stuck on stupid?

Exiting the parkway, Daniel just couldn't seem to understand what the problem was. He had to admit that he was in no way perfect. He had made his share of mistakes and wasn't in any position to throw stones. Daniel knew that it wasn't anything short of a miracle that he had escaped a situation that would have landed him in a world of trouble. That escape had prompted his return home. He rationalized that the mistake could have been made by anyone but the reality was, it happened to him and Daniel knew that it was only God's intervention that caused him to avoid certain destruction. Daniel recalled that in the midst of the trial and when all hell was about to break loose, a certain scripture provided encouragement. As he turned into his parent's driveway, he said it aloud: *"1 Corinthians 10:13 There hath no temptation taken you but such as is common to man: but God is faithful, who will not suffer you to be tempted above that ye are able: but will with the temptation also make a way to escape, that ye may be able to bear it."*

Daniel had truly been tempted by his own desires, knowing that it wasn't God that tempted him because James 1:12 confirmed that God doesn't tempt. He was thankful that God was true to his word, God had provided a way of escape and as a result he had been directed back home. Daniel had to believe that this was God's will and he wanted and needed to be in the will of God. He knew that he could not be successful if he operated outside of it.

The Son

Three

Behold, children are a heritage from the Lord. The fruit of the womb is a reward.
Psalms 127:3

Standing at the door waiting for her son, was Lila Manders. She heard her son's car as it entered the driveway. She was happy to have him living with her. He had not told her why he was home but she knew that he would reveal the reason for his return soon enough. She smiled as she thought of him as a baby. The light brown eyes that were her husband's secret weapon were bequeathed to her cherished baby boy. He was a good baby, only crying when he was hungry or when he needed to be changed. He was unusually peaceful. Smiling, just because. There was a special place in her heart for her third son. He seemed to have inherited not only her husband's physical attributes but his personality as well. Daniel, like his father was very slow to anger. He was always ready to forgive and seemed to be liked by all. Always an excellent student and athlete, she was pleased when he decided to attend college but was disappointed when he wanted to go to school in Wisconsin. She worried about her special boy and did everything she could to dissuade him from going but Obadiah succeeded in convincing her that he needed to go.

As with everything else, Daniel was successful. The potential for failure was not what worried her. His wonderful spirit might be tarnished by those fast white girls that seemed to sniff out promise and monetary potential in a handsome and grounded Black man. She didn't consider herself racist but she didn't want him losing himself with some white gal. Graduating with honors and almost immediately accepting a position in the Madison, Wisconsin area at Alliance Power, he had made it clear that he was going to make Wisconsin his home. She was devastated. His brothers were causing havoc and Obadiah's health was failing. She needed her beloved boy but Obadiah would not allow her to tell him to come home.

"The boy needs to build his life," Obadiah said, through clenched teeth. The pain that he had been experiencing because of the arthritis in his legs was becoming unbearable. "He is doing well and calls every week and even sends us money," he said trying to console Lila.

Daniel came home every other Christmas which brought Lila much joy. Those were the holiday events when she went all out and even invited family over for the feast of a lifetime. He had even sent for Lila and Obadiah to come out to Wisconsin to visit on a couple of occasions.

Much to Lila's dismay, Daniel did introduce them to a blonde, bouncy, all too peppy, white girl. Disappointed, she didn't even bother to remember the girl's name.

"You know how I feel about this, Danny." Lila had told her son when meeting the girl. Her arms were across her chest and she was vexed to a point where concealing her frustration would be useless.

Daniel just smiled and said, "It's not serious, Mom. You know it shouldn't be about color. I'm surprised at you," teasing her in an admonishing tone.

"It's not about the color, it's about the culture Danny. Who wouldn't rather have chocolate?" she sighed.

He smirked and she realized that he would have to make his own mistakes. In the interim, she prayed nightly that he would find the right kind of woman.

The words of Obadiah echoed in her mind as she smiled at Daniel, now ascending the steps of their front porch, "There isn't a woman, black or white that you would approve of. You know that he is your darling son and you won't recognize his soul-mate until God points her out to you and even then you may put up a fight." She laughed at the memory. Her Obie knew her so well. She missed him terribly. Sometimes when she looked at Daniel it was like looking at Obadiah and that brought her comfort. Her much-beloved son was home and she embraced him. Kissing her on her cheek, he looked at her. His eyes told her something had happened. She decided to let it go and led him into the house for lunch.

"So, did you have a good workout?" Lila asked as she placed the hot pastrami and cheese sandwich on a plate. She retrieved the barbeque chips from the cabinet and placed a handful on the side of the plate next to the pickle.

"Yes, that gym right off of Route 27 is nice. It's a shame that I can't find a nice facility closer to the house but it'll do for now. I can't let myself get too out of shape. I think that it's in a nice area and saw a few townhouses for sale. I may look at a few of them next week."

Daniel winced when he heard a quick swoosh of air tipping him off that his mother had turned quickly toward him at the mention of him finding a place to live. He knew that she liked him living with her but it was important that he find a place of his own, especially since he had the feeling that he would be living in the area for a while.

Trying to appear unaffected by Daniel's comment, Lila placed the plate in front of Daniel. "You know that you don't have to move into your own place so soon. Give yourself some time to get reacquainted with the area. After all, you have been gone a while."

Although Lila wanted to say more, she decided that she wouldn't push the subject. He'd see that he was needed and would stay.

"It has changed a lot around here, Mom. I'm glad that the neighborhood has stayed the same. There doesn't seem to be any riffraff hanging around. Making the nearby college a university has brought some prestige to the area as well. I like it." Daniel smiled and remembered how his mother wanted him to apply to Kene College so that he wouldn't have to be far from home. That was entirely too close, he had reasoned. It was now Kene University. He remembered how his mother used every tactic in her arsenal for him to attend. Thankfully, his father was the voice of reason and solved the issue. Wisconsin offered him an academic scholarship so there wasn't a contest.

"Have you seen or heard from Major or Baylor?" Daniel asked as he placed a couple pieces of bacon on his sandwich and brought it to his mouth. He hadn't had a good pastrami and cheese sandwich in what seemed like decades.

"No, I haven't," Lila said and seemed to suck her teeth. "Baylor didn't come home last night and Major is staying with one of his women." She pulled out the wrought iron chair and sat on the charcoal colored cushion. "I don't know why those boys are so trifling. I hate to use that word but that is exactly what they are." She clasped her hands as if she was about to pray. She exhaled and her eyes settled on Daniel. "Finish your lunch so that you can continue your day. Please don't forget that I need you to drop by your Aunt Sienna's house to take her grandson to get his hair cut."

"Okay, Mom, but I have to be back this evening because I have plans to really do some research on a company that has shown some interest in me. I do need to get a job and get my career back on track." He sighed and continued, "I also have to stop by the church." Daniel didn't want to expound on his need to visit the church until he was clear on his next steps. No sense getting the family in an uproar until it was necessary.

"The church?" his mother asked. Her interest was peaked and Daniel noticed that her eyes, the color of black pearls, lit up.

"Uh-huh," he responded affirmatively.

Taking the hint, Lila stood. She removed Daniel's plate and quickly placed it into the dishwasher. She closed the door and pressed the green start button.

"Okay. Well, I'm going to get moving. I'll talk to you later on." She smiled at her son and kissed him on the forehead. "Be safe. I'll have dinner for you at six o'clock."

The Son

Daniel, felt a little uncomfortable with his mother cooking for him at his age and especially kissing him on the forehead. "Thanks for lunch, Mom. Please don't trouble yourself about dinner. I can pick something up."

"It's no trouble son, the chicken is defrosting. I'll make it and have it ready. You know I don't mind cooking for you," she confirmed and headed down the hall, turned and climbed the steps.

Four

We are troubled on every side, yet not distressed; we are
perplexed but not in despair.
2nd Corinthians 4:8

Melina stepped out of the shower and wiped the mirror clean so that she could see her reflection and wondered how she would spend the rest of her day. She'd called out sick. She hadn't really lied. She was sick of her job. She believed she wasn't going anywhere with the company and truth be told, she hadn't any desire to, especially if it meant doing the same thing that she was doing now. She needed more. She had begun to dread hearing the stories from employees that complained about their company everyday. The daily chronicles about how badly they were treated and why the company couldn't invest more into their employees had become old and tired. Working in Human Resources, she was certain that she would be able to make a difference but that was a young idealistic girl with a Mary Tyler Moore complex. Now she was just a burned out administrator waiting for her next gig. She'd moved from Willingboro to northern New Jersey, thinking that she would be closer to the hub-bub of New York. She didn't want to be in the midst of the so-called "fast life" but wanted to make the kind of money and make the contacts that would place her on the fast track toward success. Now, years later, she was tired of it all. She ideally thought that working for Killington Pharmaceuticals, Inc., a large player and one of the premier companies in the industry, would catapult her to where she wanted to be. She'd thought that she had landed on pay dirt.

The company was very parental when it came to their employees. That was good and bad. The people that she worked with were the epitome of clueless. Diversity was just a word. It meant nothing to those that it really should impact and Melina just couldn't see herself painting on a smile to get through another day. Like a punk, she punked out and called out sick.

After throwing on a pink sweatshirt and matching pants, she padded into her kitchen. As she passed her office, her eyes quickly spied that her bible was sitting on her desk open. She really needed to spend some time with God so that she could get some perspective on what she should do. She knew that the only way that she was going to find out God's will for her was to read his word. Still operating in punk mode, she bypassed the office and found her way to the kitchen. She pulled out a frozen pizza and decided that she would have a quick lunch and then take a nap.

"I'll read this evening," she half-promised herself aloud.

As soon as she plopped onto her black leather sofa, her phone rang. Melina quickly turned to look at the clock that sat on her wall unit. It was already one o'clock. She told herself that the caller had to be Alex.

"What's up, Alex?" Melina said into the receiver.

"Hey, you knew it was me, huh?" Alex chuckled.

"Yup, I didn't even have to look at the caller id," Melina responded joining Alex with a little sardonic laughter.

"Why'd you leave me hanging today?" Alex inquired, sounding wounded.

"I just didn't have another performance in me today," Melina confessed.

"I know what you mean. Dina is not happy that you are not here to do her job."

Melina just added that to her list of reasons why she hated her job. Dina was the queen of "pass the buck." There had to be a picture of Dina next to that definition in the dictionary; smiling, totally oblivious of her butter colored teeth and red lipstick smudges. She looked like she had just eaten Ronald McDonald. Melina began to get a little angry just thinking about Dina. Knowing that verbalizing her negative feelings about her direct report would not get her blessed, she decided to change the subject.

"Alex, what do you want, girl?" Melina asked as she extended her legs and placed her feet on the smoky grey glass coffee table. Taking a discriminating look at her feet, she decided that she would forego the nap and get a pedicure.

"I just wanted to make sure that you were okay. You know that it is you and me against the world on this plantation." She laughed at her own joke. "You know that I was the key witness for the mini inquest that took place when you failed to report this morning. They had me in the hot seat," Alex quipped. "No worries, girl. It's all good. I told them that you were feeling a little bit under the weather and they seemed to buy it."

"I needed a day, Alex. My stomach gets tied up in knots when I walk in that place, so in actuality, it is a sick day," Melanie said, trying once again to justify playing hooky.

"Girl, I've to go. Massa D is returning from lunch. Call me tonight if you get a chance, if not I'll catch you up on the drama tomorrow, that's if you grace us with your presence."

"Alright. Thanks for checking on me," Melina said, shaking her head at Alex's description of Dina.

"Take it light."

The oven beeped, alerting Melina that it had reached the desired temperature. She walked over to the oven, opened it up and checked her pizza. Not quite ready.

She poured herself a glass of water and returned to the comfort of her sofa and flicked on the television.

A Different World rerun was on the television and because this was one of her all-time favorite sitcoms, after the exit of Lisa Bonet of course, she decided to watch. The chemistry between Dewayne and Whitley was great. At that moment, the face of the handsome stranger from the gym appeared in her mind's eye. He was a tasty looking man. Nice build, clean and sexy. His mustache and beard were almost perfect. His lips were perfect. Kissable, to say the least, Melina thought. His smile revealed perfect white teeth and the one dimple on his right cheek added to his physical appeal.

He mentioned that he'd just recently returned to the area, hadn't he. Where had he been? Those questions and more flooded Melina's mind as she thought about the man from the gym.

Daniel Manders. That sounded like a nice respectable name. The line he used to get her attention was admittedly lame but she thought it was cute nonetheless. She was doubtful that she would see him again because she wouldn't be at the gym in the morning until the next company day off.

Oh well. He *was* something, she concluded.

Melanie picked at her pizza and continued to watch the next sitcom, *Living Single,* another one of her favorites. She closed her eyes and pulled the lilac comforter that she had dragged off of her messy bed, closer to her chin. Drowsiness swept over her. Determined not to eat and then fall asleep especially after her workout this morning, she removed her feet from the coffee table and placed them soundly on the floor. She remained in a seated position thinking that this would at least impede the onset of slumber. That was not to be. She closed her eyes and told herself that she was going to get mentally prepared to get up and do something but the last thing she remembered was hearing the high pitched "Whoohoo" that signaled the closing credits of the program.

In her dream, she was talking to Alex. They were laughing while exiting the jazz club they frequented, Zenegals. Her cell phone had been ringing and she was searching her purse in an effort to answer the phone but looked up to see Daniel Manders walking in the door they had just exited. He looked at her with those eyes and she forgot all about the phone ringing. His smile, which resulted in the appearance of his lone dimple, succeeded in holding her captive and she decided to let the call go to voice mail. It wasn't until she heard the voice of her mother on her answering machine that she became lucid.

Her mother's strong vibrato was crystal clear. Melina woke up just as she was about to greet Daniel Manders.

"This is your mother. Neici called and told me that you were not at work today. Are you sick or are you just hiding out. I know how you can be child." Her mother's voice had a touch of amusement. "Call me when you want to come out of hiding. I just want to make sure that you are okay. Oh and don't think I won't have your father drive up there to check on you if you don't call me tonight. Bye now."

Neici was such a snitch, Melina thought to herself. Only her older sister would call her mother and tell her that she didn't go to work. Only Alex would be that scandalous to tell her.

Her mother's demand for a return call made Melina feel like she was seventeen again. Being an adult didn't mean squat to her mother. Zenia Lawrence is the queen bee and that was it. Melina made a mental note to call her mother before 9:00 p.m. or she would most assuredly have a visitor from Willingboro by midnight.

Stretching, Melina stood to her feet and consulted the clock. She couldn't believe that it was now 4:18 p.m. She had to rush if she was going to make it to the Nail Salon in Edison. She was definitely going to have to contend with drive- time traffic.

Penny, the only African American nail technician in the area and the best by Melina's standards, would take her without an appointment and it was doubtful that she would have to wait long. She ran to the bathroom, brushed her teeth and pulled her hair back into a ponytail at the nape of her neck. Her ears needed earrings so she quickly placed silver hoops in her holes and slipped on her pink mule sneakers. She patted the pockets of her sweats and realized that her keys were on the entrance way table. She grabbed them and was out of the door.

The Son

Satisfied with her new fluorescent pink toes, Melina decided to get her eyebrows waxed. The salon was almost empty and Penny suggested that she clean them up.

"You never know who you may meet," she warned with a gap tooth smile. Penny's eyes lit up with excitement. She loved to talk about love and the prospect for love. She was a happily married, forty something woman. Melina always wished that she could have her own business like Penny. She wanted to do something that would bring her joy and make money.

Fred Hammond's "You are My Song" was playing and Melina found herself becoming engrossed in the words of the song. *"In the tone of honor………pull my heart strings daily…"* Penny only played inspirational and gospel music in her salon. Melina liked the song and began to hum along. She turned her attention to Penny as she decided whether or not to talk about Mr. Manders. She didn't believe in jinxing the possible love connection but didn't want to talk about someone she may never see again. She threw caution to the wind and responded.

"If that is the case, I think that the waxing is a little late, Penny," Melina confessed.

"What, girl?" Penny asked, grinning mischievously.

"I happened upon a handsome man this morning while I was at The Training Spot," Melina confided with a lilt in her voice. The thought of this morning's encounter made her a little giddy. She had to admit that it was a good feeling. She wiggled her 100 watt pink toes, sprayed them with enamel dryer and then glanced back at Penny.

"You happened upon him, huh?" Penny laughed. "Was he a gentleman?" she asked.

"As a matter of fact, he was. He didn't immediately call me by my first name when I told him my name, he called me Miss Lawrence. I thought that was a sign of good upbringing."

Melina knew that this type of observation would not be overlooked by someone like Penny.

"Good sign," she nodded. "Will you see him again?"

"Doubtful, he was at the gym this morning and I'm not usually there at that time."

Penny noticed that the happiness that was briefly displayed in Melina's dark brown doe eyes dissipated.

"You know that I have been praying that you find a nice young man. You know that the prayers of the righteous availeth much," Penny reminded.

"Penny, I know. You, my mother, father and I have been praying for God to send me a husband. God said the he would give me the desires of my heart. I'm banking on that."

Melina explained to Penny how Daniel Manders approached her earlier that day and she laughed like a high school girl as Penny shaped up her brows.

"I have a feeling that you will be seeing this young man again," Penny predicted.

"I wouldn't mind that," Melina said.

She hugged Penny goodbye and jumped into her car. She turned onto the busy street and began to feel a little better. The day away from Killington and its misfits had done her some good. She decided against stopping for a take out dinner. She was feeling a little adventurous and would make something with the ground chuck that was defrosting in her fridge. Boldly singing the song she had heard in Penny's shop, she thanked God for the day and headed home.

The Son

Five

*O house of Israel, cannot I do with you as this potter?
saith the Lord. Behold as the clay is in the potter's hand,
so are ye in mine hand, O house of Israel.*

Jeremiah 18:6

"Can you explain what you mean when you say
that it has been impressed upon you to seek a mentor in
the ministry?" Pastor Cuffe asked. His large hand rubbed
the salt and pepper hair on his chin. The Holy Spirit was
telling him that although he knew what was being
communicated, he should not jump the gun but patiently
hear the young man's account. He was convinced that if
he allowed Daniel to effectively verbalize what he thought
God was telling him to do, it would aid him and he would
also fully understand it.

"I don't know if I can, but it seems to me that God
wants me to receive guidance from someone who has a
true relationship with Him so that I can learn and as a
result become a pastor." The words he needed to utter
seemed to be jumbled on top of each other in his larynx
like a twelve car pile up. Each syllable felt heavy as he
noisily gulped trying to place them in an orderly fashion
so that they would exit his mouth with some fluency. It
was very difficult for Daniel to articulate what he was
feeling but he felt that he had to. He desperately needed
to get it all out. "I feel that I have been called into the
service of spreading the gospel." Daniel had never
actually said it out loud and hearing it from his own lips
sent a little chill down his spine. It wasn't a chill that
alerted him to fear but it was a chill of excitement.

When he initially came to grips with what he had
been trying to avoid for the last seven years, he likened
himself to Jeremiah. It was like a fire in his belly.

"I, like the prophet Jeremiah, don't feel equipped
to teach, let alone preach but I'm convinced that God

won't leave me alone until I say yes to His will." Daniel wasn't sure if he was clear in his explanation to Pastor Cuffe. He hoped that the learned man of God would be able to read between the lines. In a last ditch effort to make it plain, Daniel stood and walked behind the high backed, suede, cobalt blue chair he was just sitting in and began to speak slowly.

"Pastor Cuffe, in Jeremiah, chapter one, Jeremiah talks about how he feels that he can't speak for the Lord because he didn't feel that he was experienced enough. He says that he was child. That was the excuse that I used all of those years in Wisconsin. When I think of ministers and pastors, I think of gray haired men that have deep thunderous voices." Daniel smiled nervously, not wanting to offend Pastor Cuffe. "In no way, did I feel I was ready to lead anyone."

Daniel let his gaze fall from Pastor Cuffe as he walked to the opposite side of the large pastor's study. He turned and once again achieved eye contact with Pastor Cuffe. "I'm now thirty-three years old and I can't use that excuse anymore. It has been revealed to me that I will not be as successful as I would like to be if I do not answer God's call. On the flight from Wisconsin to Newark, I fell asleep on the plane. This is not a rarity because I can fall asleep at the drop of a dime but...during my nap, I dreamt that I was in a church. The church and its decor were not clear but I was standing at the podium in a brilliant purple robe looking at the congregation. I was supposed to speak but when I began to speak, I couldn't. I looked around and the faces in the room were grim and somber and I became afraid."

Pastor Cuffe, intrigued with the young man's story placed his elbows on his desk, settled his chin on his clasped hands and nodded as if to say, "Go on."

Daniel walked back to the chair and sat. He stared into the Pastor's seemingly small dark almond colored eyes. He noticed that there was a little blue around the circumference. Pastor Elias Cuffe was at least sixty years old, if not older, and Daniel was confident that he would impart some advice or knowledge that would help him.

Daniel cleared his voice and continued. "In the dream, just as I was about to walk back to my seat, I heard, *Thou shalt go to all that I shall send thee and whatsoever I command thee, thou shalt speak. Be not afraid of their faces; for I am with thee to deliver thee.*" Before he told Pastor Cuffe the last part of the dream that had essentially sealed the deal, he looked at the stained wood floor and then the tips of his black and grey Timberland boots, noticing a scuff mark at the toe. He raised his eyes and said, "Pastor, I felt something touch my mouth as if it was burning it," he exhaled loudly. Just remembering the whole experience made Daniel feel honored and just a little keyed up. "My lips felt as if they were scorched. I heard the words just like they were written in Jeremiah, *"Behold, I have put my words in thy mouth.* I awoke with a start and that was it. Last week, your name was placed on my heart and I knew that I had to consult you for direction."

The expression on Pastor's face was that of complete agreement. He believed everything Daniel had disclosed. His calling had not been that dramatic but it was life changing nonetheless. He had been listening intently to everything Daniel said and all the while the Spirit was confirming it and telling him that Daniel was his protégé. A smile slowly made an appearance on Elias' face as he thought of Elijah and Elisha. He had been wondering what would happen to his flock. Although he hadn't received a word from God as to who would take over in his stead, he knew that Daniel would be around for a while.

"Well son, it sounds to me that you are on your way to becoming a fisher of men." Elias stood, walked around his large mahogany desk and embraced the young man. Without warning, he placed his hands on Daniel's head and began to pray. "Father God, we thank you. We thank you for being who you are. We love you for forgiving our disobedience. Thank you for giving us the opportunity to teach and preach the gospel of your son,

Jesus Christ. Daniel now accepts the task that he must fulfill and trusts that you will lead him and guide him. We will seek you first and everything else will fall into place. We know that you sanctified him when he was in the womb. Come what may, we praise and thank you in the magnificent and glorious name of Jesus Christ, Amen."

"Amen," Daniel repeated.

Elias embraced Daniel again. He noticed that Daniel's eyes were moist but didn't call attention to the display of emotion. He knew all too well how the young man felt. He made a mental note to call his wife Madeline to have her invite him over for dinner next week. He was going to need all of the spiritual guidance he could get. He was concerned about the boy's home life. His brothers seemed to be wayward. None of them seem to be getting their lives together. That puzzled Elias because Lila and Obadiah were good parents and provided a loving but stern home environment. He shrugged his shoulders and decided that God knew exactly what he was doing. Since Obadiah had passed on, Lila had not been as involved as she had been in church activities. She continued to attend church regularly but something was missing.

"Thank you, Pastor Cuffe," Daniel said and sat down in the chair. He felt like a burden had been removed from his shoulders.

"Son, it is my pleasure and privilege. You are destined to be great man of God. Rest in that and believe that God has your back." Pastor Cuffe paused, "Isn't that what the kids are saying nowadays?" He chuckled and sat in the seat next to Daniel.

"I don't want to occupy any more of your time. I appreciate you allowing me to share what has been going on with me. I have to get back to Mom's house. She insisted on making me dinner and I'd hate to disappoint her," Daniel stated.

"Please don't rush on my account, Mattie is picking me up and she won't be here for another hour." Elias was cutting Mattie some slack, knowing that Mattie, as hard as she tried, was never on time.

The Son

Mattie was a good woman. The congregation had a hard time accepting her in the beginning. Having a Caucasian first lady in a predominately Black congregation was something they simply had to get used to. That was a trial they had both endured together. He knew he would have to share that story with his new apprentice. The story of his accepting his call to ministry and the hell that seemed to follow would definitely demonstrate how God would certainly give you victory, even when you feel as if everything is about to fall apart.

Daniel walked through the stained glass doors of the church and crazily enough, he felt like he could breathe easier. He clicked his car remote to open the trunk to deposit his bible. When he opened the trunk, he noticed that it had been cleaned out. Only his mother would have done this. When he left the car at his Mom's house, knowing that he would be back in two months once he had closed up things in Madison, he never guessed that she would clean it out. He loved his midnight black Mustang. In Madison, he could open her up and really feel the speed. Unfortunately, in this area, he couldn't enjoy it as much. He noticed he had forgotten to remove his sneakers and almost out of nowhere, the alluring face of Melina Lawrence entered his thoughts. She was beautiful and well put together. She possessed long, toned legs and thighs. Not too small in the waist, but definitely cute in the face. She was the quintessential woman.

He laughed aloud. He had just exited the church and was almost immediately thinking about how Melina's body swayed seductively as she walked from the stationary bike to the locker room. Her smile was captivating and welcoming. She was going to be a challenge but something told him that she was well worth it. "Melina," he said and let her name roll around on his pallet. "I like the way that feels", he decided. He turned the key in the ignition and listened to his engine come to life. "Lord, I hope she is part of your will for me," he prayed earnestly and drove home to sample some of his mother's smothered chicken.

Six

*He that is void of wisdom despiseth his neighbor but a
man of understanding holdeth his peace.*
Proverbs 11:12

Daniel walked into his mother's house and the aroma of chicken, seasoned to perfection, smothered in gravy, attacked his tenses. He welcomed the assault as he followed his nose to the kitchen, the room that had always been the heart of the house. As he neared his destination, he began to hear mumbled voices. They sounded low as if someone was hatching a plot. As he turned the corner, he saw the backs of the people that were doing the talking. They must have heard him because they turned to face Daniel abruptly and their smiles froze. Recognition registered on their faces and although not completely sure, they said in unison, "Daniel?"

Daniel recognized his brothers as soon he saw the backs of their heads. Major and Baylor looked the way they did the last time he saw them. Baylor was a little taller and wore a goatee. His hair was braided neatly going toward the back of his head. His clothes looked as if they were about to fall off of him. Daniel never liked the baggy look. Little brother was always considered the skinny one when they were younger. At their father's funeral, Baylor seemed on the frail side as well. Now, almost a decade later, he looked like he had put on some mass and his face had filled out. He could definitely see the family resemblance clearer now that they were all grown men. Major, Baylor and Daniel all had the trademark Manders dimple. Naimond was the only one that didn't have one.

"Yeah it's me," Daniel said and smiled. He extended his hand and pulled Baylor into a warm and heartfelt embrace. He then grabbed Major and stood directly in front him so that he could get a good look at him as well. His elder brother's eyes held something that

Daniel could not recognize. Truth be told, Daniel didn't want to recognize the cruel and heartless expression Major's eyes revealed. That couldn't be a part of his brother's being, he thought. Daniel hugged Major. Major, however, did not let the hug linger. He pulled out of the embrace and took a couple of steps back so that he was facing Daniel and his back was against the counter and the sink. Daniel noticed that Major's hand's quickly retreated behind his back. Immediately, Daniel knew foul play was afoot.

Major's dark eyes cemented themselves onto Daniel and as a result, Daniel couldn't avert his gaze to see what Major was hiding behind his back. The uncombed hair on the top of Major's head seemed to be going everywhere and in addition to not liking what was going on, although not knowing exactly what was going on, Daniel hated seeing any Black man looking unkempt.

"What's up with your head, man?" Daniel asked his elder brother and chuckled, hoping that it would relax what seemed liked a tense homecoming.

"It's the way I like it," Major retorted. Major never liked how Daniel seemed to always be so critical of him. Daniel was not perfect. Everyone didn't want the corporate cut. Fades were yesterday's news. "Why are you all in my scalp?" Major asked.

"Hey, it's your hair," Daniel said, not wanting to anger his brother. He didn't want their first meeting to be one of vexation. He had been home almost one week and it seemed odd that this was the first time he saw his brothers. Baylor was supposed to be living with their mother but he had been away. He remembered Mom placing some emphasis on the word away. "You are a grown man. Do what you want," Daniel said.

Just as the words exited his mouth, Daniel was able to see what was behind Major's back. It was a patchwork, suede woman's pocketbook. After looking at it for another moment, he realized that it was their mother's pocketbook. Daniel could feel himself becoming unglued and anger seemed to be bubbling up like a volcano just as it was about to spew lava. He heard a scripture in his mind that he allowed to settle over him and as a result, caused him to rethink his actions. "I can get angry but I will sin not", he said in a breathy whisper loud enough for only him to hear.

"What are you doing with Mom's pocketbook?" Daniel asked. "Are you stealing from her?" He found that his feet were moving closer to his brother. Major was older than him but Daniel was about two or three inches taller than him. It was Daniel's turn to stare purposefully at Major.

"Nah man, it was just sitting on the counter and we were moving it. We wanted to straighten up the kitchen so that we could sit down and eat," he said unconvincingly.

"I don't believe you, Major. How can you steal from your own mother?" Daniel was incredulous. "You know she would give it to you. All you have to do is ask her." Daniel stopped walking toward Major and searched for his wallet. "As a matter of fact, I have some money I can lend you," Daniel offered and pulled out five twenty-dollar bills. He placed the money in Major's hand. Major snatched the money from Daniel's hand while contorting his face. "Why do you always think that you have to be the one that comes to the rescue? Everybody don't need you and your superman antics," Major said ungratefully.

"If you have to stoop to stealing from your own mother, it looks like you need what I gave you and possibly much more. I'm not just talking about money," Daniel responded.

"Aww... stop being so self-righteous, golden boy," Major spat.

"If I'm so golden, give me the money back," Daniel said. He stared at Major and knew that he could not accept the money back.

"I should punch the..." Major said, unsure why he exploded with anger.

Baylor stood frozen not knowing if he should break up what seemed to be a scuffle in the making.

Thankfully, Lila appeared from around the corner and entered the kitchen.

"What is going on in here?" she asked as she entered the kitchen, ushering in the scent of lavender. She stopped and stood between Major and Daniel. "Major, did you check the on the chicken? I know you didn't let it burn," she said, making her way to the oven. She opened the door and retrieved the Pyrex covered dish and placed the finished poultry entree onto the lower left eye of the stove. She erected herself and looked at Major, Baylor and Daniel and then back at Major.

"What is going on, I said?" she asked again with added fervor. Major and Daniel stood glaring at each other for almost a full twenty seconds.

"I was just wondering what was going on with these two sons of yours," Daniel said, trying to affect a smile. He didn't want his mother getting upset about them almost coming to blows. He relaxed his posture and let his hands fall to his sides.

Seemingly satisfied with Daniel's answer, she pushed past Major and removed the succotash from the fridge. "Good thing I made this last night. It is too late now to try and make another vegetable. The mashed potatoes will take only 15 minutes."

She removed the boiling pot that held the potatoes, poured the hot water out and then poured cold water into the pot. "I'll just peel those and mix them with some butter and a little milk and we'll be all set."

Baylor seemed to come to life once Lila opened Jiffy corn muffin mix and poured its contents into a bowl.

"Mom, I can do that," he offered.

"No baby, I don't mind doing this. After all, Daniel hasn't been eating this good since he came back home. Only God knows what he was eating in Madison." She stopped and placed her bark colored but smooth hand to Daniel's cheek and smiled at him.

"Thanks for the offer, son," she said to Baylor and gave him an air kiss. "I'll get it all done."

"Mom, thanks for taking such good care of me. It's a good thing that I joined the gym," Daniel said rubbing his abdomen.

Major moved to the entranceway of the kitchen and took in the touching scene. His mother, he knew, loved all her sons but for some reason Daniel was her little favorite. Although, he had come to accept this fact, he had never understood it and would never mention it to his mother. He leaned against the wall and crossed his arms across his toned chest after placing the money that he'd just pilfered from his younger brother into his pocket. He noticed that his black jeans were comfortably loose. He had lost another couple of inches in his waist and was pleased. The black and gray t-shirt he wore was snug across his chest. Just enough to bring attention to his well chiseled pecks. That was exactly the way he liked it. He knew that he looked like a professional trainer. He also liked how his biceps looked in this particular shirt. Although he was considered handsome in a rugged sort of way, he received more compliments on his well-toned body.

Ladies seemed to forego his smile, dimpled visage and untapped intellect. Major knew that he was smart but he was admittedly, too lazy to make a life and a name for himself. He had his women do that for him. He smiled just thinking about how he lured yet another last night. He could talk a good game but he knew it was his body that closed the deal. Thankfully, his current lady was out of town. Being hooked up with a flight attendant had its advantages.

"Mom, I'm not staying for dinner. Baylor and I have to make a run." He looked at Baylor and cocked his head toward the front door. He deliberately let his eyes settle on Daniel and smirked.

Baylor was not aware of any run that had to be made and had decided to stay and eat some of the good food his mother had prepared. Why should Daniel get to eat all of the food by himself? Baylor thought. He was staying.

The Son

"Uh, Major, I'm thinking that run can wait. I'm going to stay here, catch up with Daniel and get my grub-on. I'll catch up to you tomorrow." Baylor's mind was set.

"Alright, stay," Major said in a clipped, flat voice. He was perturbed but he wasn't going to give Daniel the satisfaction. If Baylor wanted to hang-out with Daniel, "the good," then so be it. Daniel will get tired of this town and pack up and leave soon. He just had to be patient. Baylor will see how selfish and self-centered Daniel really was.

"I hope you plan on leaving without that item we talked about," Daniel warned, as he walked over to half-embrace his brother. He felt that he had to be diplomatic about the pocketbook situation for his mother's sake. He glowered at Major. Major blinked to shake off the stare and shrugged his shoulder to remove Daniel's arm.

"Yeah, thanks to you, I don't think I'll need to go that route today." His sinister smile almost made him ugly.

"I hope that you won't ever have to travel that route again," Daniel said as he returned to his seat.

Lila acted as if she was oblivious to the exchange but unbeknownst to her sons, she knew exactly what was going on. Thank God for Daniel, she thought to herself and tasted the mashed potatoes after adding extra butter to the mixture, just the way her Obie and Danny liked it. Baylor was easy to satisfy. She hoped Baylor would spend more time with Daniel while he was around. Her youngest son needed a good male role model. Major, she knew, was up to no good. He was her son and Lord knows, she loved all of her boys. She just couldn't figure out what had gone so wrong with him.

She placed the completed meal on the table. She missed cooking like this for her family. Baylor didn't seem to want to spend much time at home so she had decided that she wouldn't waste her time cooking these simple but soul-filled meals. She turned to look at her boys, and her gaze lingered on Daniel. She never understood why he and Major always seemed to butt heads.

She thought of Major and a picture of her strong son at a young age crossed her mind's eye. He had always seemed so angry. He had become even more so after Obadiah passed. Obadiah, not always pleased with the decisions Major made, seemed to have more patience with him and tried to understand him.

She noticed that Major was a little reluctant to leave, even with all of his "I don't care talk." She walked him to the door and he placed a halfhearted kiss on her cheek.

The Son

Seven

And his brethren said to him, Shalt thou indeed reign over us? Or shalt thou indeed have dominion over us? And they hated him yet the more for his dreams, and for his words.
Genesis 37:8

Lila looked down at her hands as she unclasped them once Daniel completed blessing the food. There was something different about the way he spoke. His voice was sure and without reservation as he talked to God with conviction. It was like he was speaking to someone in the room.

Daniel noticed that his mother's eyes were searching his when their eyes locked. She was watching him as he prayed and when he concluded the blessing, he lifted his head to find her staring at him with what seemed like curiosity and mild amazement.

"What's wrong, Mom?" Daniel asked. He was beginning to feel just a little uncomfortable. He turned his head to his right to pose the question to Baylor. He must have had something in his nose. Did he have a booger? To his surprise, Baylor had a similar expression painted on his face as well.

Baylor noticed the change in Daniel as soon as he looked into his eyes. He was different. He just couldn't put his finger on how. His voice, although it sounded the same, was strangely altered. He had an authoritative quality that didn't demean or condescend.

Baylor likened him to the young Martin Luther King Jr. Not in physical appearance, just the tone and timbre of his voice.

"Why would you think something was wrong, child?" Lila asked. It was hard for her to suppress her smile but she was successful. She could tell, she didn't know how, but she was almost certain that God had called Daniel to do so something special. She didn't know when or to what purpose, but she knew that God had called him. She had mixed feelings but was happy that he would be near her for the time being. She knew that she had selfish reasons but she couldn't help it. She just couldn't help it.

"You and Baylor are staring at me as if I was Jesus or someone magnanimous like that." He smiled nervously.

Lila almost burst out laughing. "No, honey, we certainly know that you are not God."

"That's for dam….. I mean, you are right about that, Mom," Baylor agreed.

"Okay. You guys had me a little scared for a moment," Daniel said and lowered his shoulders and began to relax. Maybe he shouldn't have prayed over the food. Did his thanks and praise unto God give away his secret. He knew that he couldn't keep a lid on this for long. He really didn't want to conceal something like his becoming a minister but he didn't know how his family would take it. His mother, he knew, would be happy. His brothers were the ones he was concerned about.

As he began to cut the chicken and consume his food, he thought about the time he'd told his brothers that he had a dream about becoming a very important man. At that time he couldn't see that he was standing in a church but he knew that he was speaking to a large multitude of people. People were clapping and he thought that they were clapping for him. Now he knew that the people were clapping and praising God.

The dream had inferred that Daniel was dressed to the "nines" in expensive apparel and was surrounded by people of importance and prominence. In the dream, he was standing in front of people and they were kneeling in front of him. It was revealed to him, once he fully understand the dream, that the people were not kneeling before him but were lying prostrate at the foot of the altar. Daniel stood behind the podium. When he communicated his dream to his brothers, they laughed at him and even began to get angry.

"People are going to kneel before you?" Major had asked, sucking his teeth as he dismissed the whole story. Major, older than Daniel, didn't like anyone being placed before him. He had pushed Daniel and said, "You must have drugged those people, like Jim Jones to make them kneel to you. I'll never kneel in front of any man. You better get that through your head." He used the palm of his hand and pushed Daniel's face with it as a gesture to completely humiliate Daniel.

"You had better stop, Major," Naimond warned. "Daniel will remember this and get you back when he becomes that important person," Naimond said sarcastically and laughed. He walked toward Major and they slapped five, dismissing Daniel.

Baylor, too young to really have an opinion, just followed the crowd and laughed at Daniel. Recalling and reliving the hurt from that day, Daniel could feel his face becoming warm.

Disappointment must have shone on his face because hearing his Mom's voice, laced with concern pulled him out of his reverie.

"Daniel, are you okay?" Lila asked. She was standing and looking at him from across the room. When he faced her, she turned toward the sink and resumed placing dishes into the soap-filled water.

"Yes, Mom. I'm okay. You didn't eat much," he said, trying to change the subject. She only took a couple of forkfuls of her dinner.

"I'm just not feeling very hungry, baby," Lila admitted. She was feeling a little tired but wanted to make sure that Daniel had a good meal. She would finish her dishes and lie down for a little while. She reminded herself that she should take it easy. She had to stay healthy enough to witness what God had in store for her son.

"Please eat as much as you want. I will keep the leftovers for you and Baylor. Oh and you never know, Major may come back this way and want something to eat," she reasoned. "I know that he is not always the easiest person to be around, but we still have to look out for him. He is family." Almost immediately, she thought of Naimond and her heart seemed to beat faster. Something had to be done about Naimond, she thought. It was her earnest prayer that somehow, he would surface and find his way home so that they could be a family again.

Daniel noticed the faraway look on his mother's face when she talked about family and told himself that he would continue to try and make peace with Major. He exhaled. A strange feeling coursed through his body and his brother Naimond's face was before him. The visage dissipated and he was thrown a little off kilter as a result of the experience. He looked at his mother. She had her right hand over her left breast.

Naimond, he thought. Where are you? Why haven't you contacted your own mother?

He loved his older brother but always felt that he was way too young to make any inroads with Naimond. He recalled a conversation that they had during their father's funeral. Naimond told him of his plans to leave home and try his luck somewhere else. He had thankfully not been convicted of the charges and said that he needed to get away. He had felt the stares and received verbal attacks by the extended family saying that he was to blame for his father's early demise. The guilt was too much and he said that he had to leave.

It happened the morning after the funeral. Daniel was helping his mother with a big breakfast. No one could talk her out of cooking for fifteen people. As he walked toward Naimond's room, he felt that something was different. Naimond was not an early riser. As a matter of fact, he was a late sleeper because he commonly worked the night shift at the Weekly Journal, an old newspaper that was printed and distributed right in town. He remembered that Naimond had aspirations of becoming a reporter.

It was always difficult to rouse Naimond from slumber. His snores could usually be heard downstairs. Daniel clearly remembered walking into his brother's room and finding all of his clothes gone. His closet was empty and the cherry wood bureau drawers were opened with bits of clothing hanging out. The room was left in disarray. Daniel was not sure what to do. He saw a note scotch taped to the mirror, grabbed it and rushed downstairs.

"Mom," Daniel said in a huff after bounding down the stairs and running into the kitchen, "I found this in Naimond's room." He handed his mom the note, not even thinking to read it. Daniel instinctively stood back and turned his body to face the stove that was warming buttered biscuits and fried ham. The cheese grits were bubbling and eggs were sitting on the counter next to the frying pan that held a pat of butter slipping around the pan. Daniel's mind felt like that pat of butter sizzling and sliding around the pan without an inkling of direction. His mind was out of focus until he heard an exclamation that began with a gurgle and then opened up to a wail.

"Why Naimond!?" she screamed. "*My* son!" The tears on her face were rolling down her cheeks rapidly. Her face became saturated with liquid almost immediately. She looked up at Daniel as if he was Naimond and continued to make the same heartbroken inquiry.

She was beyond consoling and all he could do was hold her. Baylor heard the screaming and crying and rushed into the kitchen and just stood there, gripping the wrought iron chair. His eyes searched Daniel's in an effort to understand what the commotion was about.

"Naimond left and I don't think that he is coming back," Daniel informed Baylor as his mother continued to cry into his chest. Baylor heard the words. His eyes focused on his mother, crying and clutching her chest as if something had been forcibly ripped from her.

"Do you know why he is gone? Did you say anything to make him go?" Major interrogated. He entered the room without making a sound and immediately went to the stove and turned off the food that had begun to burn. "You know how you can be?" He inquired in an accusatory tone.

"No. I haven't said anything to him. We have just been trying to get through the funeral. That has been hard enough don't you think?" Daniel responded, feeling offended that Major would assume that he was the cause for Naimond's departure.

It was at that moment that Major and he had become adversaries. Daniel tried to put an end to the rift but Major would not allow it. No matter how hard Daniel tried, Major would not talk to Daniel about Naimond and after a few years and many more arguments and unanswered letters, he simply stopped trying.

Daniel never knew what the note to his mother said. He could have kicked himself for not reading it before handing it to his mother. The letter was addressed to his mother, so he believed that the words for her eyes only. He now knew that it was better that he hadn't read it.

Removing her hand from her chest, Lila breathed in and out to decrease the pace of her heartbeat. As she thought of her eldest son, her mind took her to her closet and the letter that outlined his goodbye. Lila had kept the note hidden in old envelope with all of the letters she'd had received from Obadiah. The envelope was hidden in the back of her closet on the shelf behind items she couldn't even remember. Her boys never knew where the letter was and Lila planned to keep it that way.

The next morning arrived earlier than expected for Daniel. The sun was almost too bright as it shone through his window, illuminating his old room. He knew that his mother had been in the room and had opened up the drapes. That was just her way. She wanted him to get out of the bed and get his day started. She never believed in a man staying in the bed past seven o'clock. Sleeping in was not allowed unless you had worked the night before or if you were sick.

He really wanted to get to the fitness center. He was looking forward to seeing Melina. He'd dreamed of her during the night and could still see her face. Daniel was determined to have a conversation with her and even ask her out on a date. He smiled at the thought of her and sat up in his bed. He groaned as he realized he missed his old bed and rubbed his back. I'll work out this kink, he thought.

He began his morning ritual as he opened his leather bag and pulled out his bible. His mother had given him his father's bible. From the time the bible was passed on to him, he never went anywhere without it. The bible opened up to the book of Daniel and that made him chuckle.

The story of Daniel was one that had stayed with him since childhood. Initially, he took to the Old Testament book because of its name but as he began to read the book and learned more about Daniel, his interest increased. He tried to make sure that he prayed at least three times a day just like Daniel, feeling that it was important that he stayed in constant communication with God. He needed certainty that he was proceeding in the right direction and only prayer and constantly seeking God would make his instructions clear.

He wanted to achieve the confidence that John talked about in 1 John 5:14-15.

Daniel believed that whatever he asked, Jesus would make petitions for him, provided it was in line with God's will. He hadn't any problem with asking of the Lord because as long he was obedient and looked to God, he would be operating in that will and his requests would be granted. Knowing that his prayers were being answered and angels were being dispatched to act on what he requested, he knew that the situation with his brothers would work out and he would find the strength he needed to tell his family about his call to the ministry. But when? He didn't want to keep this from his family, especially his mother, much longer. Rising from his knees, he put on his robe, tied it securely and headed to the bathroom to bathe.

He smiled as he passed Baylor in the hall. "What are you so happy about?" Baylor asked as he shuffled in the opposite direction. He stopped and turned his body in Daniel's direction, rubbing his eyes.

Daniel kept walking toward the bathroom, the smile had not disappeared but he didn't want to talk to Baylor first thing in the morning. If memory served correctly, Baylor had killer morning breath. For some reason he thought of Pam from the *Martin* sitcom and how the character Martin would always bring Pam's foul breath colorfully to the audience's and Pam's attention. She had really bad halitosis issues. As much as he loved his little brother, he didn't think that even Pam's breath could be as bad as Baylor's in the morning. A snicker escaped his lips and all he could do was shrug his shoulders while looking back in Baylor's direction. He finally entered the bathroom and closed the door.

The Son

Eight

Now unto him that is able to do exceedingly abundantly above what we ask or think according to the power that worketh in us.
Ephesians 3:20

"So you made it in here today?" Alex asked as she stood and stepped from behind her desk and whispered into Melina's ear conspiratorially. "There was a big meeting this morning. The big wigs came in a rush and not long after, Dina was walking out of the office with them. I tried to follow them to find out their destination and all I could tell was that they were headed to the large conference room outside of the office of Carrie Knowland."

Melina's freshly waxed left eyebrow rose curiously as her mind processed the information Alex just shared. Carrie was the VP of the entire Human Resources department. She was responsible for Benefits, Compensation, Training and Development. Melina knew that this meeting was a big deal.

"I wonder what is going down," she whispered to Alex as they entered the employee cafeteria to get their usual beverages before the start of their day. Melina usually filled up her oversized red Big Gulp cup with ice and water and Alex who seemed to never drink water, purchased a large French vanilla flavored coffee.

"Well something is still going down because she just went back in the meeting. Her "dotted line" boss was also called in just a few moments ago." Alex seemed to be enjoying all of the mayhem but Melina knew enough to realize changes were coming. She wasn't sure what the changes were and began to get a little nervous about her job. She realized that she complained about her job but it was a paycheck and she couldn't afford to be without one. She could just hear her mother telling her to move back home until she found something else.

"Okay, Melina, you are getting a little bit ahead of yourself," she whispered to herself as she walked with Alex back to their department.

"Let me get my day started, Alex. If you hear anything, don't e-mail me," she warned, "call me or just come over to my desk." She looked at Alex with a face that silently communicated that people would be on pins and needles and that no additional drama was needed. Alex needed to keep what she learned on the "QT", which meant keeping whatever she found out quiet until they could discuss it.

Fully comprehending the non-verbal message, Alex nodded and walked to the other side of the office. Melina, shifting back into "work-mode" pulled her shoulders back and imagined a book was on her head as she walked over to her desk. She performed this exercise at least three times a day to ensure that she was walking with the absence of a slouch. She believed that posture was important, especially when conversing with her co-workers. It never hurt to try and improve one's outward physical appearance.

Not two minutes after she began to schedule her day, the phone beeped. She could tell by the extension displayed that it was Alex. The day was getting crazier by the minute and according to the computer, it was only 9:45 a.m. "Hey, Massa D is comin' your way. She looks flushed." Before Melina could ask anything, she heard a click. Alex had hung up. This was getting too crazy. Dina breezed by Melina's desk. She saw Dina's mouth open as if to greet her but a murmured "hello" was all that she could decipher as Dina passed.

She opened her e-mail and sighed. Her inbox read fifty three unread messages. How is that possible? She asked herself inaudibly. I was only out one day.

"Melina," said a voice that was not familiar.

Melina looked up into the face of Carrie Knowland. She was an olive colored woman with large hazel eyes and dark brown curly hair, styled into a severe corporate French twist. Carrie's uncharacteristic full lips, with neatly applied blackberry lipstick were turned up into a smile. Although the smile looked genuine, Melina didn't feel the warmth that should accompany such a smile. Carrie was an average height, full-sized woman. She had round hips and a much smaller waist. The black pinstriped skirt suit accentuated her figure.

"Hello Carrie," Melina greeted. "What can I do for you?" Melina stood. She smiled and hoped that Carrie would receive it as genuine because she really wanted it to be.

"I was wondering if I could have a few moments with you," Carrie said, closing the gap between them. Melina could smell Carrie's perfume but she couldn't place the fragrance. It was fruity but soft. Melina liked it. She would use that to make small talk when she needed something to say.

"Sure Carrie," Melina stated. "When would you like to get together?"

"Today is a bit hectic but my schedule is open tomorrow, in the morning. Go ahead and place yourself on my calendar anytime before 11:30 a.m."

Carrie stopped speaking and appraised the young woman. The salmon colored suit with the oxford styled blouse Melina wore accentuated the air of business that seemed to envelope the young administrator. Carrie didn't think that Melina was older than thirty and liked the professional body language Melina used to communicate. She wasn't hard or unyielding and seemed forthright.

Carrie had barely spoken with Melina since interviewing her almost a year ago when Melina applied for the senior Benefits Administrator position. She presented herself well and knew the company and its inner-workings. Carrie was impressed with Melina. She fully endorsed Melina's promotion and since then, she had heard nothing but good things about her. It had become no secret that she was doing Dina's work and doing it very well. Dina had become very passive and the employee rumor mill reached Carrie about it. Melina was the one person that the more vocal employees really liked. They said that she would research their problems and provide solutions and even created programs to alleviate some of the employee unrest and dissatisfaction. She worked with Alexandra Norman closely on health insurance problems and was of great assistance with improving the service that was being provided by the carriers.

Killington offered three different carriers and Carrie couldn't even remember the type of plans being offered. Melina was a smart and conscientious worker but she had heard that there was some concern that Melina was going to be wooed by another company for the same type of position without all of the headaches. She was thankful that she had her outside sources and would beat them to the punch. Carrie was not a fool and knew that it would take some time to bring in another person to take Melina's place. Melina had certainly gained the employees' confidence and that was not easily replaceable.

"I will certainly do that, Carrie," Melina said with a little apprehension. "Is there anything wrong?"

"Not to worry, Melina. I'm just trying to get some feedback and I understand that you are the person that I need to speak with," Carrie responded. She turned to leave and then abruptly turned back to Melina and stared at her as if she had made a definitive decision. Carrie had already concluded that Melina would assume Dina's role and oversee additional areas of Human Resources for Killington. She simply wanted to present Melina with the opportunity during their conversation.

"I'll look out for the invite. Talk to you soon," Carrie said and walked away.

Confused, intrigued and very concerned, Melina watched Carrie as she walked out of the department and then slowly turned to sit in her seat. She slipped off her sling backs, as was her custom, and sat back in the chair.

As her eyes focused on her screen saver that pictured her family, Melina's mind began to think of reasons why Carrie would want to meet with her after they had just had a big pow-wow with her bosses. It obviously didn't end well for Dina based upon her behavior. She was now concerned about what the outcome would be for her.

"Well?" Melina heard Alex's voice coming from behind her. She turned her chair in the direction of the voice and simply stared at Alex with what she knew was a blank expression.

"I don't know girl," Melina said. She really didn't know what to say. "I know you saw me talking with Carrie. She asked me to get on her calendar for tomorrow morning so that she and I could talk." Melina slipped on her beige sling backs and stood. "Come with me to the ladies room," Melina whispered. "Dina has her spies all over the office."

"Come on then," Alex said as she walked quickly in front of Melina toward the ladies restroom.

While in the restroom, Melina repeated the brief conversation and emphasized the feedback aspect. That had her stumped.

Alex being Alex, told her not to worry about it. "If they wanted to let you go, they would have done it already. Your feedback or concerns wouldn't be important."

Melina agreed that Alex had a point and decided not to spend her entire day worried about the meeting with Carrie. When she returned to her desk, she made an appointment to see Carrie at 10:00 a.m. the next day. She reiterated her prayers for help and the presentation of a better situation or opportunity.

Melina almost jumped when she heard the chime from her outlook, confirming that a message was received. Carrie must have been waiting for the invite because she immediately accepted the meeting invitation.

The rest of Melina's day was much like any other. The highlight of her day was the early morning "hush-hush" meetings. All of the frenzy had dissipated and thankfully the hours flew by.

As she began making notes to herself about tasks for the next day, she thought of the prayer that she prayed when she woke up that morning. She had asked God for the strength to get through the day and to show her if she was actually meant to be where she was. She asked the Lord to help her not to complain and to constantly reveal why she should be grateful. She was not grateful for the trial that she felt that she was going through but she should be grateful because she knew that Jesus could deliver her out of any situation; even her crazy job. She recalled reading: *Ephesians 5:20 Giving thanks always for all things unto God and the Father in the name of our Lord Jesus Christ.* With the Lord's help she had made it through the day and was none worse for the wear.

"Praise God!" she said loud enough for her ears only.

Try as she might, Melina found it hard not to think of her meeting with Carrie scheduled for the next day. She didn't like not knowing what she was walking into. She closed her eyes as she leaned back in her chair and silently repeated that all things were going to work out for the good because she knew that she loved the Lord. She had to make sure that she read Romans 8: 28 when she talked to God before going to sleep tonight.

She opened her eyes to find Alex once again standing in front of her with hands on hips that were leaning to the extreme left.

Alex and Melina had been friends since their first day of orientation at Killington. They immediately hit it off. Having similar upbringings and value systems made it easy for them to simply be themselves from the beginning. Alex, a little more on the brazen side, was almost a year older than Melina. Standing at 5'8', she was a statuesque bronze version of what the world called the goddess Venus. Because she had Sioux ancestry, her hair was beautiful. It was the color of shimmering coal, thick and wavy. Her eyes were feline which made people think that she was a little devious but she was anything but. It looked as if she always wore a smile and she tried to never let situations get the better of her. Her smile was contagious. Alex's skin had what some would say a tint of Georgia dirt, courtesy of her lineage and this added to her beauty. Her lips may be considered a little thin for an African American but she was all *sistah*. "Make no mistake!" was her famous tag line. She always said that although she had Native American great grandparents, she was without a doubt 100% African American and her parents made sure that she knew it.

"Why does it seem that you are always standing at my desk?" Melina asked as she reached under her desk to shut off her PC.

"I'm ready to go and wanted to know if you wanted to join me at Zenegals tonight. We can unwind and discuss your strategy for your meeting in the morning with Carrie." Melina considered Alex's proposal as she packed her leather briefcase. She was not dressed to go out. Her suit felt a little confining. Alex on the other hand was dressed in a dove gray pant suit with a matching silk blouse. Melina was too uptight and on edge and really wouldn't be any real company. She didn't really want to go out tonight. She really needed to be on top of her game for tomorrow.

After doing the mental math, Melina decided not to go to Zenegals.

"I don't think that I'll join you at Zenegals. I have too much on my mind," Melina concluded.

"What took you so long to decide?" Alex questioned. "You almost looked like Sheneneh from *Martin* when she had to make a decision or was weighing her options." Alex laughed almost too heartily for Melina's taste. Being compared to Sheneneh was not Melina's idea of funny.

"As a matter of fact, I think that I'll go the gym to work out," Melina decided. She didn't know why she decided she'd make the gym her destination but it sounded good. She would be able to enjoy her music and get her "sweat on." She smiled, cementing her impromptu decision and began walking toward the exit.

Alex grabbed her items and began to walk with Melina. It was a little after 5:00 p.m. and Melina was looking forward to spending the rest of the evening by herself after the gym. It's a good thing that she always kept her workout clothes and sneakers in her trunk. She knew that if she went home, she would not make it back out. She didn't have that much will power.

"Alright, girl, if you decide to come, I'll be there," Alex said as they parted ways in the employee parking lot.

"See ya tomorrow," Melina said. She pressed her car remote twice to open the trunk to retrieve her gym clothes and deposit her briefcase. Starting the car, she adjusted her rearview mirror, applied pressure on the accelerator and drove out of the lot.

Daniel's day had not played out the way he would have liked. Lila had a laundry list of things for him to do. The "to-do" list had him traveling all over Union County and then some.

He was in Hillside, Linden, Roselle and then back home. He couldn't believe all of the running around that she could squeeze into the span of four hours.

"Mom, you sure can put a hurtin' on some shopping," Daniel said, half-joking as he turned into the driveway. She laughed and playfully swatted him on the shoulder.

"I'm glad that you could take me, son. I did get a few good buys today didn't I?" His mother said, a triumphant smile displayed on her face.

He noticed that shopping seemed to bring her joy and he couldn't be angry at anything that brought his mother so much happiness. She looked healthy today. Much better than yesterday, he thought and decided that he wouldn't waste time thinking about what he could have been doing. She was his mother and nothing was more important than seeing that she received what she needed. Much to his embarrassment, she had purchased him underwear and had verbally confirmed his size during checkout without shame. The service lady found it amusing but Daniel was mortified. He was a grown man. He didn't need his mother buying him underwear. To add insult to injury, the sales lady, who was watching him with a gaze that told him that she wasn't worried about commission, presented his mother with male underwear that she stated provided extra crotch comfort. She smiled seductively at Daniel as she explained the garment. He smirked but his mother frowned at the woman. Lila diplomatically thanked her for her assistance with a dismissive tone.

"Little fresh thing," Lila whispered.

"She was just doing her job," Daniel teased. He knew exactly what she was doing and it wasn't her job. At least he hoped it wasn't.

"I know what kind of job, she wanted to perform," Lila said, disgusted with the blatant sexual innuendo.

Daniel laughed as he recalled the turn of events. He turned off the car and opened the car door, but his mother grabbed his arm.

"Thank you, baby," his mother said. "I know that you may have had plans today but just know that I appreciate you taking me around today," Lila said. She kissed the tips of her fingers and placed them on his cheek.

Daniel smiled and exited the car.

He opened the trunk, retrieved the bags and walked to the house. Entering the house using the back door, he walked up the back stairs and noticed that the lights were on.

Baylor greeted them when they entered the family room. He was sitting on the burgundy lazy boy recliner with the pillow from the matching sofa propping up his back.

He looks too comfortable, Daniel thought. He needs to get his behind up and get a job.

The smile that was on his face disappeared and a frown replaced it. The picture of their father that sat on the side table, mirrored Daniel's sentiment.

The framed photograph was turned in Baylor's direction and it seemed to be staring disapprovingly at Baylor.

"Yeah, Daddy, you are right," Daniel whispered to himself, recalling that his father had always disliked a shiftless and lazy man.

He placed the bags on the empty sofa and hit Baylor lightly on his leg signaling that he needed to help get the bags from the car.

As Baylor stood, his face clearly showed his reluctance to get up. He moved slowly to the back door.

"Hurry up. I want to try and get to the gym by 5:30," Daniel yelled after Baylor. Admittedly, he was kind of perturbed this morning when his mother had thrown a wrench into his plans. He decided that even though he may have missed Melina this morning, he still needed to get at least an hour of cardio. He was looking forward to seeing Melina's pretty face but that was a non-issue now.

"Boy, don't you want to get something to eat?" Lila asked.

"No thanks, mom, I'll get something while I'm out," he said. "You just enjoy the rest of your evening. Don't worry about Baylor or me. Why don't you send him to get you something?" Daniel suggested. "Leave the kitchen cold tonight."

"Okay, baby. I think I'll do just that," Lila said admitting to herself that she was a little worn out but satisfied. She enjoyed spending most of the day with her son and shopping just placed the icing on the cake.

Daniel pressed forty dollars into her hand and kissed her cheek. "I'm going to use the bathroom and then I'm going to go," he told his mother. "Are you okay? Do you need anything?" he asked before he turned his back to her.

"No, honey, I'll just put the underwear on your bed," she said letting a little chuckle escape.

"Very funny, mom," he said as he ascended the steps and headed toward the bathroom.

The Son

Nine

*Fulfill ye my joy, that ye be likeminded, having the same
love, being of one accord, of one mind.*
Philippians 2:2

Melina was exiting the group exercise room when she saw him. He was running on the treadmill and looking as fine as he did when she saw him yesterday morning. She didn't want to admit that she felt a rush of warmth when he spoke to her and now she felt that same heat just looking at him.

His legs were hairy and Melina liked that. She could see the muscles in his legs when he ran. "Whew! I certainly don't need to see anymore," she barely whispered and turned away to decide what equipment she would use. She was glad that she happened upon an evening aerobic class but felt that she needed just a little more. The class had kept her mind off of work and she wanted to keep it that way.

The elliptical that primarily worked on the legs and gluteus was available. She didn't want to use the one that required arm movement. After a quick peek in the mirror, she sauntered over to the machine. She perspired quite a bit during class and little beads of sweat were decorating her forehead. Oh well, she thought. I *am* at the gym.

As she passed him, she caught his eye and waved. He smiled. She turned and placed her feet onto the machine. While inputting the time and her weight, she heard a thud. She looked up abruptly, reacting to the sound and saw Daniel holding onto the sides of the treadmill with an awkward smile on his face. She suppressed a smile, knowing that he had been watching her. He had apparently lost his balance and had almost fallen off of the treadmill but held onto the sides to keep from falling entirely off the machine.

She inserted her earphones and began her workout. She hoped that he wouldn't come over and speak with her because she didn't like to be interrupted once she started her workout. She forcefully removed all thoughts of Mr. Manders from her mind and decided to focus on her workout for the next twenty minutes.

Sure enough, during one of her favorite songs, *Soldiers*, by Out of Eden, she noticed him coming her way. Not wanting to show her annoyance, she smiled and wiped her forehead. Placing the song on pause, she stopped pedaling.

"So you have chosen to greet me with your secret weapon," he said smiling back at her. The tingle that she felt when she heard his voice shocked her anew and the slight feeling of intrusion melted away.

Unsure as to what he was referring to, she looked past him. "What secret weapon?"

He absorbed her smile and thought that she was the most beautiful thing that he'd ever seen. Her perspiration seemed to make her look as if she was glowing. Calm down Daniel, he told himself. You can't be falling for her already.

Her eyes didn't meet his and he knew that she was feeling uncomfortable.

"I told you about that smile," he reminded her. "I hope you use that weapon for good."

Her eyes traveled slowly to his. It seemed he held her eyes with his own. She was consumed by his gaze and decided not to say a word.

Daniel, for his part, felt comfortable just looking at her. She was his dream in living color.

"How are you, Mr. Manders?" Melina inquired, finally breaking the silence and turning her attention to the machine she'd been using.

"I'm glad you remembered my name, Miss Lawrence. I'm fine and can say that I'm better than fine now that I'm talking with you."

She couldn't believe that she was blushing. Thankfully, she was dark enough to not let that be physically visible. She looked back at him and lowered the wattage of her smile.

"I'm glad that I could aid in keeping you in good health," she laughed.

"As much as I would like to give you the credit, I would have to give the props to my Lord and Savior Jesus Christ." He lifted his hands as if he was raising the roof.

"You had better," she warned playfully. *"Render therefore unto Caesar the things that are Caesar's and render unto God the things that are God's."*

"I'm glad that you understand." He was pleasantly surprised that she had some understanding of the Word. Only good and perfect gifts like health and lucidity of mind come from God and we ought to be sure that we give God just praise but be careful not to assign the blame for illness or unfortunate circumstances to Him.

"What are you doing after you complete your workout?" Daniel asked. He watched her face freeze for a split second and then open up into a smile once again. He was a little worried about his immediate attraction to her but believed somehow that it was a good thing.

"I had planned on going home to just sit in front of the television, why?" she asked, knowing that he wanted to spend more time with her. His reference to Christ made her a little more comfortable with him but she still had to remember to keep her antenna up just to make sure he wasn't a nut job.

"How about we get together and get some coffee," he suggested.

"I'm sorry, Mr. Manders, I don't drink coffee," she said with a slight grin.

He laughed, cognizant of her attempt at humor. "Well, can we just drink water? I just want to get to know you a little better," he said with unabashed honesty. "Oh, and you can call me Daniel."

"Sure, Daniel," Melina said.

"Is that 'sure' for the water or calling me Daniel?" he asked resembling a child that had just asked for a second piece of chocolate cake.

"Both," Melina giggled. "I should be finished with the elliptical in about fifteen minutes and then if you don't mind, I'll need to shower so give me about thirty minutes."

"Sounds good," Daniel said and feigned relief with an exaggerated exhale. "The shower was a prerequisite."

The Son

Ten

Honor thy father and thy mother; that thy days may be
long upon the land which the Lord God giveth thee.
Exodus 20:12

Driving away from Mighty Plate Diner, one of the diners that New Jersey was famous for, Daniel smiled as he recalled the way that he successfully and almost instinctively allowed his fingers to entwine with Melina's as he walked her to her car. He couldn't help but feel certain that he was meant to meet her. She was lovely in every sense of the word. It was clear that she was intelligent, not to mention a good sparring partner when it came to thought provoking dialogue. Their conversation over a shared generous slice of cheesecake that swam in a strawberry sugary concoction had ranged from their upbringing to their chosen professions and then finally their relationship with Jesus Christ. Their constant and consistent eye contact was electrifying. It was as if neither of them wanted or needed to look away.

Her smiling dark caramel eyes seemed to welcome him. Without reservation he acquainted Melina with his life, ending his narrative at the very moment he met her except for the span of time that he had not shared with anyone.

She listened with sincere interest and had unconsciously moved closer to him as he discussed his feelings about his father's demise.

Signaling that he would be making a right to exit the parkway, he thought of how fortunate he was. He never thought that he would meet a woman that would peak his interest to the point that he would feel the need to see or talk to her again within almost twenty minutes of leaving her. He had it bad and he had only met her yesterday. He cautioned himself to slow down. He knew that he would definitely be calling her after he checked in on his mom and settled in for the night. Melina casually mentioned that she didn't retire until around the 11:00

hour. He checked the dashboard clock and it read 8:58p.m. He could feel the smile widening as he pressed play in his mind and heard her voice. He was glad that he was alone in the car thinking about this gorgeous woman. The way she even said his name was a symphony to his ears.

"Jesus, is this your doing?" he inquired of the Lord. "It has to be, because she is just what I want."

He was a few blocks from his mother's house when he semi-recognized a male figure standing on the corner. Upon closer inspection, he identified the figure as his brother, Major. He wasn't sure if he should acknowledge him and wondered if Major would even acknowledge him. As Daniel slowly drove past Major, who was shrouded in the darkness of the corner, presentiment told him not to stop but continue to the home of his youth. He had not received any divine instruction as to what he should do about his brother. He knew that he had to do something about him. Naimond also weighed heavy on his heart. Although Daniel didn't want to admit it to himself, he knew that he would be the one to bring his brother home. Again, providential guidance as to how that task would be accomplished eluded him, but he was certain that among other things, his brother was one of the reasons God had allowed him to return home.

"Mom, are you home?" Daniel asked as he entered the house. He crossed the threshold that led into the kitchen, expecting to see his mother seated at the table, awaiting his return just as she had done every evening that week. The kitchen was empty. The only light that emitted was courtesy of the fluorescent bulb over the stainless steel sink that glistened pristinely. She took his advice and left the kitchen cold. Good, he thought.

"Daniel, is that you?" Lila questioned. Her voice emanated from the top of the staircase and cascaded down to the living area where Daniel stood after exiting the kitchen.

"Yes Mom, it's me," Daniel responded. He turned to see his mother leaning over the oak banister squinting to confirm that her son had indeed returned home.

Lila couldn't allow old habits to die. Oddly enough, Baylor was home and mentioned earlier that he was in for the night and now that Daniel was home, she could rest easy and even close her eyes and sleep. Unfortunately, she would not allow her body to relax to the point of relenting to slumber unless she knew that her boys, the ones that were staying under her roof, were home and safe.

"That must have been some workout," she added sarcastically, knowing that it was after 9:00 p.m. and he couldn't have been at the gym all of that time.

"Mom," Daniel said, "I stopped to get a bite after working out." He ascended the stairs and took in his mother with his eyes. She had already dressed for bed and he immediately felt bad that he had kept her from sleep. He didn't want her, of all people, to worry about him.

"Mom, please don't worry about me," Daniel implored softly. "I know how to call you if I get into trouble." At that moment, he was convicted that he hadn't done that when he needed her help back in Madison. He rationalized that that was a different situation and she was better off not knowing about it.

"You are my son, and believe it or not, I am tied to you even if you are a grown man," she explained. "I refuse to sleep unless I know that my baby is okay."

"Let's compromise, Mom," he suggested. "If I'm going to be out later than 8:00p.m., I'll call you so that you can get to bed and not worry." He extended his hand in an effort to seal the deal.

"I want to amend this deal," she said, slapping his hand away. "When you do come in late, come into my room and tell me you are home by giving your mom a kiss," she smiled and extended her much smaller hand. Daniel noticed that she still wore her wedding band and it touched him to know that after many years, she still considered herself married to his deceased father.

That is the kind of love that I desire, he thought.

"Deal," Daniel said and gathered his mother into his arms. He lifted her slightly off the floor and she yelped initially and then giggled.

"Boy, put your mother down," she said, still laughing. "You are just as silly as your father." She inspected her robe and tightened her head scarf. "Just like that man." She shook her head and entered her bedroom.

"Good night, Mom," Daniel said. He liked when his mother compared him to his father. He was the best man he'd ever known. He missed him even now.

Lila turned to face her son through the open door and blew him a kiss. That boy always brought her so much joy. She didn't know what she would do if he would leave her again. She seemed to depend upon him knowing that he would do his best not to disappoint her. "Lord, I know that you have plans for him but please don't take him far from me," she prayed. "Use him, but don't take him from me again."

She opened her eyes and for almost a millisecond, she could smell her Obie. She knew that was his way of telling her that she shouldn't ask that of the Lord. In time, Daniel's path would be made clear and he would leave her house. She didn't want to hear what her heart seemed to be telling her and tried to silence what she knew was true.

Melina's arrival home was not as buoyant. As she traveled the side streets, she held Daniel's visage in her mind's eye. Although he was definitely all man, he was gentle and warm. Those qualities, above all, were the most endearing about Mr. Manders. She simply enjoyed and relished getting lost in his eyes. During their endless conversation, his words seemed to smoothly and effortlessly glide out of his mouth which made him even more seductive without his knowledge. His lips released each word and even each syllable, as if he had kissed each one. Okay, she thought to herself, you are taking this a bit far.

She laughed aloud at the visual of him kissing each word, especially her name. His command of the English language was an unmistakable turn on and she had to look away from him once as she visualized those same lips covering hers in vivid color. The confidence that he exuded was not dipped in arrogance, but amazingly enough, made him seem humble and honest. Melina couldn't explain the feeling that stirred in her chest when Daniel talked about his father and how much he loved him and missed him. She was attracted to him in a way that she could not reason. It was as though he was unknowingly drawing her to him.

"Like a moth to a flame," Melina said aloud. "I just don't want to get burnt." Although she knew that she should have been frightened, she was defiantly all the more intrigued by this light-eyed Adonis.

She would certainly dream of Daniel and awake with him on her mind.

As she entered her townhouse, she smiled. Her prayers were answered. She hadn't thought about her meeting with Carrie thanks to Daniel. She placed her keys on the hook in the kitchen and absent mindedly pressed the button on her answering machine. The robotic voice announced that she had two new messages. Almost immediately, the unmistakable voice of her sister Neici flooded the atmosphere.

"Hey, Mel, it's me. Sorry that I had to put you on blast yesterday but you know how Mommy uses me to do her investigative work. Anyway, I just wanted to let you know that Mom is having a crisis and didn't want Dad to call you. She is not in the hospital but she is in great pain. Give her a call simply to have prayer with her, okay. You may want to try and come home this weekend." Neici paused and exhaled. "I know work is kicking your behind but maybe a weekend home will do some good. Where are you anyway, it's almost 9:00 p.m.?" Another pause, "Well, I'll talk to you later sis. Call me if you get a chance. Bye."

Melina pressed the stop button and immediately called her sister back, knowing that she had just left the message.

"Hey, Neici," Melina said, greeting her sister with some trepidation. "How is Mommy?"

"Mel, what's up girl? I assume you received my message," Neici quipped. "Mommy is doing okay. She won't go to Cooper's Hospital so Daddy is just keeping her home. She is taking some of the pain medicine. A lot of good that does," she said almost angrily.

"I know. Nothing seems to help. She should just go to the hospital so that they can give her the injection," Melina stated with a little annoyance. "That would decrease the pain a little."

"You know Mom. Besides, she has already decreed that this crisis will not last long because she has to be at the church on Saturday for a Women's Breakfast," Neici informed with a voice that sounded like their mother. "Why don't you come?"

"I don't know if I can. I may drive down after work on Friday just to check on Mom. Are you going to be around?"

"Yeah, I should be here. We can go to the mall afterward," Neici said with obvious thoughts of spending money on her mind. Friday was payday and she needed a couple of new outfits. She had just lost twenty pounds and her clothes were beginning to resemble bags of material hanging on her diminishing frame. She wanted to see her sister's face when she saw her. Melina had been very supportive and thankfully didn't ask how the reduction plan was going every time she talked to her. Neici hadn't seen her sister in almost two months. This was going to knock her socks off.

"Alright, that sounds like a plan," Melina confirmed. "I'll leave from work so I should get to Mommy's around 6:30."

"Good. I just spoke with Mommy and she could tell, I don't know how – that I called you. She wanted me to tell you that she was going to try and get some sleep.

Call her in the morning before you go to work okay?"
Neici recommended.

"Alright, I'll do that." Melina really wanted to talk to her Mom but understood she needed her rest. She'd set her alarm to wake her an hour earlier than usual so that she would have time to pray with her Mom. "I'll see you soon, sis."

"Good night and don't worry. You know Mom believes that Jesus will take care of her," Neici reminded.

"I know and I believe in divine healing as well but she is my Mommy and I hate to hear that she is in pain. That sickle cell anemia is something," Melina exhaled. "Sweet dreams, sis." Placing the phone back in the cradle for charging, Melina thought of her mother and how she always said, *"Life and death are in the power of the tongue."*

She knew that her Mom would get better because of her unwavering faith in the Lord to make it so. Walking to her bedroom, Melina verbally aligned herself in agreement with her Mom, speaking the word of God and believing that by the time she arrived at her Mom's house, she would be doing a lot better.

M. Ann Ricks

Eleven

*No man can serve two masters; for either he will hate the
one and love the other; or else he will hold onto one and
despise the other. Ye cannot serve God and Mammon.*
Matthew 6:24

Major saw Daniel drive by and purposefully
ducked back into the shadows. The last thing he wanted
was his goodie two shoes brother to see him. It hadn't
always been like this and Major knew it. Lighting his
Newport and then discarding it, Major nodded to his
cohorts informing them that he was calling it a night. His
main lady was due home and he wanted to be home when
she arrived at the apartment. Truth be told, he missed
Charla. He had even cleaned up the apartment so that she
could relax and enjoy the night. Charla was one of those
women that reminded you of your mother, he thought, as
he jumped into his dark blue dodge charger and turned the
ignition. His mother. Why did she treat him like a step-
child? He had tried everything to make her proud of him.
He knew that she loved him but... But what? She did
love him. He was the one who couldn't... no, *wouldn't* get
it together.

If he was being honest with himself, he would
admit that his mother had tried to support him in
everything that he did. If he didn't see an immediate
return or experience instantaneous success, he would give
up. He was the same with his women. For some reason,
Charla seemed to stick with him. Major knew that she
was what they called a "good woman" but he continued to
have dalliances with other women. Major liked the
attention that he received from his one-niters. They
seemed to hype and pump him up. He was sure that his
seemingly exorbitant lifestyle was a lure and of course his
rugged good looks didn't hurt. Major wanted someone to
dote on him.

Charla knew he had her heart but she was not
going to spoil or baby him. He was her man, no matter

how many women said otherwise but she had begun tiring of wondering if she was really the one for him. Before she had accepted Christ a month ago, she had committed her version of payback but now that was over. She worked hard and was hoping that he would get on the good foot and get his life together.

Charla, growing up in Newark, NJ, didn't have an easy life. Much of her education was in Hillside, a town so close to Newark that she was able to use a Hillside address to attend elementary school. She simply used a friend's address that lived in the neighboring town so that she wouldn't have to contend with the rough and unsupervised schools provided by the Newark School system. Her Lyon's Avenue environment wasn't that bad but her mother didn't want her falling in with the wrong crowd. She soon found out that Hillside High School wasn't any better than what Newark could offer so her mother, being a resourceful person, applied for high school scholarships for Charla.

Her mother was a woman that believed in the importance of education and more importantly, the right kind of education. She had called those things that were not, as those they were and Charla won a scholarship to attend a private prep school in Unionville, an upper middle class town thirty minutes away by bus. Going to a school with snotty, privileged white girls had been the largest part of her education. The racial slurs and constant condescending at the hands of her teachers, unfortunately solidified in her mind that she didn't want to continue her education at any university. Her mother told her that the whole world was not like Peanrgy Prep but Charla wouldn't hear of it. Although she continued to do well in high school and graduated with honors, her aspirations did not include college. After a couple of career mishaps, she finally landed a job with the Airlines and fortunately, the company had a hub out of Newark International. She liked her job and had been able to move up in the company. As a senior flight attendant, she now had seniority and could basically choose her flights.

Major walked into the apartment and to his surprise, Charla was sitting in the living room. She wore a worried but resolute demeanor and he immediately questioned whether or not he had completely cleaned up any evidence of the nameless woman that had been there the night before.

"Hey, baby," Major said tentatively as he walked over to Charla and kissed her on the cheek.

"Hi, Major," Charla replied. Her voice broke and he could tell upon closer inspection that her eyes were brimming with tears.

"What's wrong?" he asked, feeling an unwelcome tug in chest.

"Baby, as much I love you, you have to go," she said. Charla turned to look at him. Her hair, liquid black, blanketed her shoulders. Major thought she look like an angel. The large brown eyes with naturally long lashes searched him. Her chocolate skin was flawless and her lips were eternally pouted. They looked soft and inviting. He found himself wanting to lean into her and kiss her.

"Major, I have made a commitment to Jesus Christ and I can't live with you anymore."

"What?" Major asked, incredulous. He did not raise his voice but the surprise in his voice, caused her to jump.

"I am sorry, sweetie, but I can't live like this anymore. I need to think about my soul and how Christ would want me to live. I have been thinking about this for some time and its wrong for me to let you live here and not be my husband." She stopped speaking and straightened her back to sit erect. "It's wrong."

Major stood and walked into the small kitchen. He opened the refrigerator and grabbed a beer. He said nothing. He was surprised that he understood. She told him that she had renewed her relationship with Christ and that she wanted to live holy.

"So, what... You gonna throw me out into the street?" he asked, noticing a little base in his voice.

The Son

"No, baby, I have been trying to tell you for weeks and I thought that you understood," she said. Tears began to fall from her eyes and he realized that this was very difficult for her because he knew that she truly loved him. "Baby, I have to choose God.'"

She stood up and joined him in the kitchen. She placed her hand on his taut back. "Can't you stay with your mom until you find someplace to live? I mean, this doesn't mean that we have to end our relationship. We just can't do things the way we used to."

Turning to look at her, he wanted to scream and say, "It's over!" After all, he had other women but he silently nodded, and moved away from her.

Charla was worried but she couldn't let anything, even her love for Major, stop her from having a true relationship with her Lord and Savior Jesus Christ.

If Major wanted to end this, well..., she thought.

"Why don't you come to church with me on Sunday?" There was a strength in her request that he had not heard before.

He continued to stare at the woman who had just told him to hit the bricks and his mind told him to tell her to go to hell but he found himself saying, "Charla, you have just kicked me out of your house and now you invite me to church?"

Her eyes searched his for an answer. She silently prayed that God would intervene. She used to believe that her heart was set on this man but now she wasn't so sure. He was beautiful to her and she knew that he was as smart as they came. When they had conversations about her career moves and what she should do, he always provided her with sound advice. His business acumen, although not exercised, was that of Donald Trump. He had to be destined for something. He just needed to focus.

"Come with me, babe," she said and smiled, showing the deep dimples that had initially caught his eye a little more than six months ago.

"I'll meet you there," he said. "Pastor Cuffe is going to have a heart attack when I walk in there and my mom is going to have a fit when I show up at her place."

"You can stay here tonight, but you have to move out in the morning," she reminded. "Major," she almost sang his name.

"Yeah," Major said, thinking about how he would explain this to his mom.

"Thank you," Charla said. She kissed him softly on the lips.

"You are not welcome," he said, with a smirk.

Charla excused herself to take a hot bubble bath. The flight from Heathrow was a long one and the lay-over in Los Angeles had been longer than initially communicated because of the weather. She was so happy when they touched down in Newark that her smiling goodbyes and "bubb-byes" were the most genuine ever. She was anxious to get home and talk to Major. Pouring the Bath and Body's Sheer Freesia bubble bath into the running water, she smiled at the way Major pouted when she told him that he had to move out. Although she was going to miss him, she really needed to begin to work out her soul salvation like the bible said in Philippians 2:12-13. *Wherefore my beloved, as ye have always obeyed, not as in my presence only but now much more in my absence, work out your own salvation with fear and trembling. For it is God which worketh in you both to will and to do of His good pleasure.*

Charla knew that she had to stand on her own two feet and make the right decisions. The decision she had just made was difficult but she knew that God was with her. She had to reflect the light that beamed from a new source. Jesus Christ. She couldn't proclaim the gospel of Christ living with a man that was not her husband. She just couldn't.

Shedding her robe, she slid into the inviting water, allowing the bubbles to envelope her. She leaned back, and placed her head on the pillow.

The Son

"Thank you, Jesus. It wasn't as hard as I thought it was going to be," she said aloud appreciating how good her God truly was. Closing her eyes, she began to let her body relax.

Twelve

*For godly sorrow produces repentance leading to
salvation, not to be regretted; but the sorrow of the world
produces death.*
2 Corinthians 7:10

Major decided to leave and take a quick trip to the
liquor store. He felt that another beer was in order. He
didn't have a clue as to why he was so understanding.
Every time he wanted to blow up at Charla, he couldn't.
Not one nasty or mean comment made it past his lips. In
the far recesses of his mind, he knew that she was doing
what she had to do and couldn't actually be angry at her.
After all, he was not the ideal boyfriend. The funny thing
was, she always wanted him and he'd always come back
to her. Well, he really never left. He doubted if he could
find any woman better than Charla. That thought alone
made him wonder. How much longer was she going to
put up with him? What was he searching for? The other
women were recreation, plain and simple.

He sighed and thought about how he and his elder
brother Naimond used to talk about their women.
Naimond wasn't really a ladies man but Major had always
found it easy talking to Naimond about his many
girlfriends. Naimond didn't condone Major's ways but he
did find them humorous and that was all of the
encouragement Major needed. Naimond hadn't had too
many girlfriends but there was one – Chantilly. They'd
met in high school. Naimond was a junior and Tilly, (her
nickname), was a sophomore. They met the first week of
school and became inseparable. Naimond spent most of
his time at her house. She lived in the Westminster
section of the city. Its inhabitants were considered
affluent. It was clear that they were in love.

Major, being the flirt that he was, tried to put the
moves on her during their second year, Naimond had been
a senior and was busy with working immediately after
school. Major saw that promise of financial security that

Chantilly offered and wanted her for himself. He shook his head, thinking of how stupid he was back then. She was a minor, how much money could she really have given him. Did he want Tilly because of the money or because she was monopolizing all of Naimond's time? He admitted to himself that he had been jealous of the relationship. He didn't have anyone in his life but then again, he told himself that he didn't want anyone. He knew that it was wrong but pursued Chantilly anyway. He couldn't explain why he felt that he should have Tilly.

Daniel was involved in sports and didn't spend time at home and Baylor was in Junior high school. If Naimond wasn't working or spending time with Tilly, he was with Major and Major didn't like being number three. Because they were only a year and a few months apart, they had similar friends and some of same interests, including Tilly.

When Tilly told Naimond that his brother had been calling her and trying to "put the moves" on her, Naimond refused to believe her. She was hurt but continued to date Naimond hoping that he would one day find out for himself. She had no intention of taking Major up on his offers.

Naimond decided not to go to college but Tilly had already been accepted to a university. Major decided to accompany Naimond and Tilly's family to help her move in, using the excuse that they may need some extra muscles. They had all but completed the move when Naimond and her father went to the car to get the last of the items while her mother used the restroom. Major used the opportunity to get closer to Tilly.

"What do you want with Nai?" he'd asked Tilly. He was walking toward her with a look that was sickening.

"For one thing, Major, he is not you," she said and moved out of his path. She had never liked Major. He was known to be a male whore around school and would scandalize his conquests to no end. "Why do you continue to make these unwelcome advances? You know

I don't even like you and even more important than that, I LOVE Naimond!" She screamed the last words.

"Why does everybody love Nai? He don't look better than me," he laughed arrogantly.

"You, You You, Major! Let it go and get over it. I don't want to have anything to do with you," Tilly said with whispered vehemence. Her eyes darted to the door, clearly hoping that someone would enter.

He rushed her and pushed her up against the standard issue dormitory oak bureau. Her eyes looked into his and she shivered. Major was strong and held her under him as she wriggled to achieve freedom.

The fear that he saw in her eyes scared him. Realizing that he had gone dangerously too far, he immediately released her and at that moment Naimond entered the room. Naimond stared at his brother and then he looked at Tilly. Major saw the fear in her eyes melt into relief. He walked to where Tilly stood and embraced her but didn't take his eyes off Major.

What is wrong with my brother? Naimond had probably thought.

Major discarded the empty beer can into the trash receptacle as he released the memory. He realized that he and his brother had never been the same since. Needless to say, Tilly and Naimond's relationship ended during the Christmas break following the incident. Tilly couldn't get past Naimond not believing her in the first place. Major had caused the breakup. Not many years after that, their father died and Naimond abruptly left home. He had caused more pain to his family than anyone even realized. "I'm sorry Nai," he whispered into the night. The darkness did not offer a pardon. Naimond's dark brown eyes became visible with the help of Major's memories. The way his older brother's eyes filled with moisture the night their father died was a memory that he had not been able to forget.

"Naimond," Major said, "you didn't have to leave." Major's voice cracked on the last syllable. "I wish you would come back to us," he pleaded to no one. "I'll own up to it, I promise."

Major knew that he needed to be the man that he always said that he was. Could he be that man to Charla and to his family? "Don't I need to get myself together first?" he asked audibly.

Thirteen

*A merciful man doeth good to his own soul but he that is
cruel troubleth his own flesh.*
Proverbs 11:17

Exercise class was really invigorating and Melina enjoyed the use of spiritual house music to really workout. The song, *Church Lady,* really sent her into workout overdrive. She really liked step class. The mixture of music and choreography kept the class flowing and before she knew it, the class was over. She wanted more but didn't want to be the only one. As she surveyed the room, everyone seemed as if their oxygen supply had been cut off.

Melina turned to her friend Cassandra and said, "Tell Marlie that we should do the routine one more time."

"Girl, no. These people will be waiting for me outside if I make us go through it again," she said to Melina. "These people ain't playin'. Look at them." Melina followed Cassandra's eyes to the mousy haired white woman in the front right corner of the room. The woman was holding her stomach with one hand and wiping her forehead with the other. She looked even more pasty than usual. She noticed the ladies looking at her and smiled weakly. Cassandra's attention returned to Melina and silently communicated, "What did I tell you?"

Melina allowed a chuckle to escape and nodded her agreement. Cassandra and Melina exited the exercise room and ran right into Daniel and someone that looked like his twin with braids.

"Hey, beautiful," Daniel said in greeting. His eyes took in all of Melina. She must have been really working out, he thought. Her sports bra was saturated. He quickly averted his eyes from the area of temptation.

"Hi yourself," Melina said. She exited his embrace and smiled when she thought of how much of a gentleman he was. His kiss was lingering on her cheek when she remembered that Cassandra was standing next to her.

Daniel, still looking at Melina, introduced his younger brother Baylor and Melina did the same with Cassandra in similar fashion.

Baylor and Cassandra looked at each other and laughed. The lovebirds seemed totally unaware of anyone else. Melina and Daniel had talked almost every night since their semi-date. The first weekend was rough for Daniel because Melina went home to visit her mother and wound up staying until Sunday night. Melina's mother's health had improved and she'd just returned after going home once again for a quick visit. She called him and told him that she would be at the fitness center and hoped that she would see him. That was all she had to say. She also told him that she was bringing a friend home with her so they may not get to spend too much time together. He hadn't realized how much he missed her smile. After only three weeks and two days, he was falling for this woman. Daniel knew it but Melina needed more convincing. He hadn't even kissed this woman yet. They held hands and hugged but that was the extent of their physical contact. He wanted to kiss her lips but didn't want to tempt himself. Kissing leads to everything else, he thought. He didn't want to contend with that just yet.

Melina and Cassandra finally communicated that they needed to hit the showers. They both excused themselves and walked toward the locker rooms. Daniel's gaze followed Melina until she disappeared from sight.

"Man, you are awfully rude," Baylor commented. The statement brought Daniel back to earth.

"I'm sorry Baylor but I haven't seen or talked to her since Thursday night."

"She is cute," Baylor agreed. "But newsflash brother, it's only Saturday."

"Alright, point taken," Daniel relented.

"Are you finished?" Baylor asked. He wasn't into the whole "fitness thing" like his older brother. He wanted to stay fit but didn't visit the gym or even workout. He didn't see the need.

"Yeah, I'm about done. I just want to wait for Melina. She didn't tell me what service she was going to tomorrow and I wanted to spend the afternoon with her after church." During one of their late night conversations, when they talked about their church, he was happy to find out that they attended the same church. He'd thought that it was a sign that God had already blessed their friendship. He didn't believe in coincidences.

"You have been spending an awful lot of time at the church lately," Baylor verbally observed. "What is up with that?"

Daniel wanted to share his good news with Baylor but he would find out soon enough.

"Pastor Cuffe is just helping me with solidifying my job situation."

"He is helping you find a job?" Baylor asked, confused by Daniel's answer.

"In a way," Daniel answered evasively.

"Walk with me on the treadmill until Melina and her friend are done and then we can go."

Baylor, although ready to go, acquiesced and set the machine to ten minutes and began to walk on an incline.

"Hi again," Melina said to both men. They were about twenty minutes into what should have been a ten minute walk. Her eyes were covered by the beak of her baseball cap.

"Are you going to eight or eleven o'clock service?" Daniel inquired.

Melina turned her attention to Cassandra. Cassandra shrugged her shoulders.

"I guess we can go to eleven o'clock service. Why?" Melina responded.

"No reason. I just wanted to take you out to lunch or an early dinner afterward," Daniel explained.

"Oh, that sounds nice," Melina said reluctantly. She didn't want to leave Cassandra to her own devices while she was with Daniel. After all, she was visiting to spend time with her.

"Good. I'll see you after church," Daniel confirmed. He was oblivious to Melina's apprehension and was looking forward to spending time with her.

"I'll ride with Alex and Cassandra. Can you take me home afterward?"

"It would be my pleasure," Daniel said and bowed gallantly.

Melina giggled, Baylor rolled his eyes and Cassandra, although intrigued by Melina's new friend, simply waved and walked toward the exit doors. She didn't know if she liked this man. He seemed too good to be true. There was something about him.

Cassandra didn't think that her friend was a good judge of character. She was entirely too sweet. She, on the other hand could always tell a phony when she saw one. She didn't think that Daniel was a phony exactly, but the way his eyes shifted toward his brother, as if he needed his brother's approval or something didn't sit well. He has something to hide, she thought. Men weren't to be trusted.

Cassandra liked visiting with Melina. Although she wasn't happy about Melina's mom's illness, she was pleasantly surprised that Melina had come to Willingboro last night. Melina always called when she was in town and they always found time to get to the mall for a quick shopping spree. Neici always came along. She was fun and always good for a laugh. Zenia looked fine and of course Melina had given the credit to the Lord for her mother's recovery. "To God be the glory," Cassandra mimicked. She wouldn't dare say that aloud in Melina's presence but she was so tired of hearing about Melina's success. A month ago, she was complaining about her job. Now, seemingly overnight Melina was on cloud nine. She had met a new man and received a promotion at work – a promotion that she didn't know that she was even being considered for. Her mother was doing one hundred percent better as well. Was there anything that Melina didn't have?

Cassandra on the other hand, didn't think that she had the favor of the Lord. After graduating from college, her career choices were limited, or so she thought. Cassandra married her college boyfriend and decided to not work. Johnson opened his own business. She decided to help him get his business off the ground and not pursue a career of her own. The company expanded and was doing quite well and now she no longer felt needed. Johnson tried to convince her that she was still an integral part of the company, but to no avail. She, on the other hand, due to his traveling schedule, began to feel neglected. She even went so far as to accuse him of being unfaithful. Johnson had no intention of straying; he loved his wife but was tiring of her insecurities. If it wasn't her complaining about not being needed at It's Done! Construction, she was accusing him of cheating. He simply thought that she needed a diversion.

Johnson did find himself spending extra but unnecessary time at the office so that he wouldn't have to hear the nonsense.

When Melina suggested that she visit with her for the weekend, Johnson agreed almost too quickly, which he was sure raised some eyebrows but he didn't care. Cassandra needed a new environment. He hoped that being around a positive person like Melina would help. After all she was Cassandra's best friend. Johnson loved his wife and wanted nothing but to make her happy. Getting her to spend sometime away from home would do her some good he hoped.

Melina looked over at her friend while driving and asked, "Well, what do you think?" She was anxious to receive her friend's opinion of her new man.

"He seems nice enough," Cassandra said nonchalantly.

"Is that all?" Melina responded.

"Well, we didn't get a chance to really talk," Cassandra huffed. Why was she so excited about this man? Cassandra thought dryly. He's just a man.

Too elated to notice Cassandra's negative vibe, Melina nodded. "You have a point. Maybe we'll get a better chance to talk when he brings me back from lunch tomorrow. Is it okay if I bring you back late Sunday evening?"

"That should be fine. You are some friend, leaving me for a tryst with some man."

Beginning to feel a little guilty, Melina asked, "Are you really upset about me going out for lunch with Daniel?"

"Yes and no but I'll get over it," Cassandra said. "Go and have a nice time, just don't be gone too long. Besides, it will allow me to have some Cassandra time." A forced smile found its place on Cassandra's face.

"You sure?" Melina asked.

"Yes, I am. Just don't get too excited, too fast," Cassandra warned. "Don't go too far with this man. You know they only want one thing."

Melina laughed. "You know that is not me. He is fine but he is not that fine," she said. "Even still, I'm not going that route, only my husband will be able to dig for my buried treasure."

Cassandra couldn't help but laugh. Melina had her priorities straight and would do her best to abstain. She knew Melina pretty well. Although she thought she was a little too naïve, she knew she'd make the right choice. She loved her friend and really did want the best for her.

Fourteen

*Being confident of this very thing, that he which
hath begun a good work in you will perform it until the
day of Jesus Christ.*
Philippians 1:6

Pastor Cuffe seemed more jubilant than usual. He was smiling, singing and taking part in every aspect of the service. It was as if he had taken a Jesus energy pill. He wouldn't sit down. Mattie, his wife, although proud of being able to put it on him last night, didn't know that turning him out like she did, would have resulted in this behavior. Feeling the heat rush to her face, she giggled. It had probably turned beet red in record time. She placed her handkerchief up as a cloth veil. She wished that he'd just sit down but when he was like this, there was no stopping him. He wasn't as young as he used to be. Sometimes he just didn't realize it.

"Praise the Lord everybody!" Pastor Cuffe shouted. "The choir is certainly singing this morning!"

The congregation responded enthusiastically as the choir exited the choir loft still clapping and singing *Encourage Yourself* recorded by Donald Lawrence.

"Speak a word over your own life," Pastor Cuffe said. The organist hit the appropriate chord on cue. "You know what the Lord said about you and what you can accomplish through him." Cuffe slammed his hand down on the podium. He looked out into the audience and began to sing the song. "I'm encouraged, I'm encouraged. I'm encouraged." Cuffe knew that he could sing. He purposely hit a few vocal runs going up and down the scale. The church stood to their feet and that was all she wrote. The famous shouting chord was played and church was jumpin'. The choir sang at full force as Cuffe led the song in a reprise. Mattie smirked. She hoped that no one noticed her but she couldn't suppress it. She had heard it said before and wholeheartedly agreed; there was nothing like a minister who could sing. After almost thirty years of being a pastor's wife, when the spirit moved like this, there was nothing like it.

Because she was raised in a Catholic religion, Mattie was used to a silent and more reserved type of service. This type of outward display of praise, in her initial words; "over the top praise" was something to behold. As time progressed, she admittedly began to enjoy the new type of service and even started to enthusiastically participate. It was a wonderful feeling being able to praise the Lord as loud as she wanted to. Early in Elias' ministry, she heard one of the deaconess mention that she was not going to let any rocks cry out for her. Mattie hadn't understood what that meant and asked Elias about it.

"Well, baby, the word of God states that if He doesn't get the praise that is due him, the rocks will start praising him," he explained good naturedly.

Mattie was unfamiliar with most of the bible because most what she was taught was what the priest said during Sunday mass. Rarely did they get a chance to participate in a bible study or actually be taught the bible in the literal sense. She found the explanation provided by Elias interesting and stole away one afternoon to find it in the bible.

She found her answer in the New Testament book of Luke 19:40. Jesus was entering Jerusalem and there was a multitude of people rejoicing and praising Jesus as he entered into the city. The bible said that there were Pharisees among the throng of people and they said to Jesus that he should rebuke the people praising him. Jesus answered that if the people were to hold their tongues and not praise the Lord and hold their peace, the rocks would immediately cry out. Mattie realized that this was the moment that God was establishing His eternal kingdom and that it was cause for great celebration. Mattie thought about what the scripture was saying. She concluded that as Christians we should always open our mouths to praise God because we have been afforded the opportunity to be his heirs and are part of that eternal kingdom. We were required to verbally praise God and not be silent. God was going to receive the praise that was due to Him because of who He is, even if the rocks would have to cry out in praise.

Mattie also thought about the way she was taught to pray. She was taught to close her eyes and to speak to God without using her voice but she also received revelation during one of Elias sermons that the bible does not teach us to keep our mouths closed when praying either. According to Mark 11:23; y*e shall say to the mountain, be thou removed, and be thou cast into the sea, it shall be done.* Jesus doesn't say think about the mountain being removed but He says to open your mouth and say it. From then on Mattie would open her mouth whenever she was praising God or seeking his instruction through prayer. She learned that God tells us to use our voices to communicate with Him. She would now talk to God wherever she was.

Returning her attention to the service, Mattie noticed that calm had settled over the congregation. There were a few lone Hallelujahs but for the most part, it had become somewhat quiet.

"Now that's what I'm talkin' about church," Cuffe said and he nodded his head and looked out into the congregation. He smiled proudly at the congregation that the Lord had blessed him with.

Melina, Cassandra and Alex entered the sanctuary just before church caught on fire. Melina and Alex jumped right into praising God. Cassandra, a little reserved, sat down immediately. She decided that during their drive back to Willingboro that evening, she would find out what was bothering her. Cassandra had been on the moody side all weekend. Whenever Johnson was mentioned, Cassandra wanted to change the subject. Something was up.

Melina scanned the congregation looking for Daniel. Her eyes finally locked on him. He was sitting near the front, in the fourth row, next to an older woman that had to be his mother. She recalled seeing her at the earlier services. She was smiling and patting him on the arm as she listened to the shouts of praise that were exploding like firecrackers around the church. She whispered something in his ear and he laughed. His smile was gorgeous. At that moment, he looked up at her in the balcony. He winked at her and she mouthed. "Hi."

She thought that she heard Cassandra suck her teeth but decided not to acknowledge it.

"Is that him?" Alex queried, nudging Melina with a snicker in her voice.

"Yup," Melina said. Her smile remained as she sat down.

"Yummy," Alex whispered.

"Sssh," Melina admonished, stifling a laugh.

"Church, isn't it good to let the Lord have His way?" Pastor Cuffe said as he took his bible in hand and opened it.

The church responded affirmatively with "Yes Lords" and "Amens".

"Well, that is going to be the subject of my sermon this morning. 'Let Him have His Way'". Cuffe walked around to the front of the podium. "I know that we are all guilty of trying to do things our own way and not allowing God to have His way our lives. Oh, yes we may sing the songs that say that we are going to trust and believe and so many times we utter the words, 'thy will be done' but do we really mean it?" Cuffe paused. "I don't think that we really do."

The church was quiet. There wasn't an "Amen" to be heard. "I didn't think that I was going to get any participation but that's okay."

The church had become as quiet as a morgue. It was a stark contrast to only fifteen minutes ago. Cuffe chuckled as he thought about how fickle the children of God could be.

He was once there and had to allow God to have His way with him. He decided to share his story with his congregation. He had not shared it with anyone except his immediate family and two close friends. He decided that he would start with examples from the bible and let the Spirit take it from there.

"Beloved, let's turn to the book of Esther." Cuffe said.

The Son

Fifteen
As for me, here I am, in your hand; do with me as seems
good and proper to you.
Jeremiah 26:14

Major entered the sanctuary after having a knock down, drag out fight with himself. Although he promised Charla that he would join her at church, he had tried to change his mind. After he had moved his items into his old room at his mother's house and endured the SS interrogation by his mother, he had become angry at Charla and defiantly decided that he would show her. He would not join her for service and that would definitely send a message. Some message. Here he was, dressed in a suit, clean shaven except for his goatee, smelling of his favorite cologne. At least the latter was of his own volition. Truthfully, he'd chosen Perry Ellis just to tempt Charla. She loved that scent, especially on him.

Charla smiled as Major made his way to the seat she had saved for him. She thanked God and turned her attention to Pastor Cuffe.

"We all know the story of Esther. She was chosen by the King of Persia to be Queen. As her story progresses, Haman, an enemy of the Jews that held a high position in the kingdom, was planning to do harm to the chosen people of God. Because of Haman's hatred of the Jews, he had maliciously and skillfully tricked the king into signing a decree that would allow the murder of innocent Jews, even the women and children. Esther had not revealed to the king that she was Jewish and neither had her uncle Mordecai who was a scribe. As the story goes, she was the only hope for the Jews because she had access to the king but only when summoned. If she went to the king without him calling her, it could mean death."

Cuffe faced the congregation and smiled. The expressions on the faces of the congregations seemed to say 'Are you going somewhere with this?'

Cuffe decided that he had better get to the meat of the story. "Well, Esther didn't act quickly to seek an audience with the King because she was worried about herself. She was concerned of course about Mordecai because he had told her not to reveal her true self. Mordecai, after seeking God and sitting in sackcloth and ashes, finally sent word to Esther that it was really up to her. Her people needed her and she had to get to the king. Esther sent word back to Mordecai that she would do it. She said, "If I perish, I perish." She realized that she had to trust in the God of Abraham and Isaac.

Would we have done the same? Would we have trusted God to have his way with our lives? Allowing God to have his own way is committing ourselves to what God wants and trusting Him for the outcome. God chooses to work through those willing to act for him."

Mattie, knowing her own testimony and how she had to essentially allow the Lord to have his own way, stood to her feet and shouted, "Yes, Lord. Yes to your will."

"You know the rest of the story. Esther was able to save her people from mass murder and Haman received his fatal reward."

Cuffe acknowledged his wife. "Praise him Sister Mattie." The joy he felt overcame him and he closed his bible and began to communicate what the Lord had placed on his heart to share.

"I'm not sure if you all know the story about my coming to the ministry but if you will indulge me this morning, I am going to forego the other examples that I had ready."

Mattie had regained her composure and she smiled at her man, the smile radiated the love and dedication that she felt toward her man of God.

When I met Madeline, I was a junior in college; I thought that I had it all together. I was going to a well known university on a partial athletic scholarship. The rest of my money came from grants that had been awarded to me because of my academic prowess. Because the college was in New England and ninety percent Caucasian, I had become popular among the minority population on campus without trying. I have to admit that I was having the time of my life." The congregation laughed. "Don't get me wrong, I exhibited home training but I was having my share of fun. I was brought up in the church and I knew that God had something planned for me so I refrained from activity that would cause someone to falter. Whether we want to believe it or not, we Christians are always being watched by someone who is on the fence. We have to be living epistles and I knew that I still had to be an example. I was however avoiding the Lord's calling as long as I could.

During my senior year, I met an enchanting dark-haired beauty. There was a connection immediately but I had to "pump my brakes" as Will Smith would say, you people didn't think I knew that phrase did ya," Pastor Cuffe said as he chuckled. "Anyway, because this dark-haired beauty was of European descent, my real feelings for her would not bode well with my family or friends. I saw no harm in she and I becoming friends so that is what happened. As we became closer friends, I knew that I had begun falling for her. She was understanding, sweet and said that she was a Christian. I felt that was all that I needed. Well, I found out after meeting her parents that she was Irish Catholic." The congregation gasped.

"Yes, I know. I knew that we were unevenly yoked and that I had to stop the relationship but I didn't and we eventually married. Fast forward ten years and three children later. I had tried every occupation that my degree prepared me for and I was not fulfilled. One Saturday, I visited my barber, the one that I had been going to since I was a child. He knew me when I was a leader in the church of my youth and constantly said that I was called to preach the word... Old Brother Mapson." Cuffe paused and thought of that dear man. God had called him home years ago. He missed that man who spoke the promise of God over his life. "At that time,"

Cuffe continued, "I didn't think I could be what God wanted me to be because of all the discord that it would cause in my life. I could not and stubbornly would not acknowledge or answer the call to the ministry. My wife was a devout catholic and would probably leave me and take my children. I couldn't have that. Well, you know what God has for ya, God has for ya."

Pastor Cuffe, walked over to the other side of the sanctuary and continued, "I began feeling unusually tired and stressed and experienced blinding headaches. When visiting with my physician he told me that I had high blood pressure and I knew that it wasn't entirely from my diet but it was from mentally running from the calling of God. I had been experiencing dreams of my demise that were unrelenting. Well, I told my wife and she didn't believe me. She was totally against me becoming a minister and she threatened to leave me. I couldn't continue with the pressure and relented to the Lord. Well, she made good on her promise and left me." Pastor Cuffe touched his chest with an open palm as he remembered the overwhelming sadness he felt as he watched his children drive away that afternoon.

"But oh, thanks be to Jesus, who is the author and the finisher of our faith. Because she came back twenty one days later with a testimony of her own. My oldest son, Matthew had been crying seven nights straight. Nothing could console him. The next week, his brother behaved exactly the same. The last week my baby girl, Marissa, cried until she fell asleep in her mother's arms as well. Mattie didn't know what to do. They all said that they missed their Daddy. You see, Mattie didn't believe that we needed to know Christ for ourselves, she didn't believe that Christ could actually talk to you. She believed that good deeds could get you into heaven. Yes, she believed in Jesus Christ but she failed to realize that we have to have a relationship with him for ourselves. We have to live for him so that the Spirit of God can dwell in us. Traditions can't get us into heaven. She was really thrown for a loop when I told her about speaking 'in tongues'. The thought of her not repenting to a mere man but to Jesus and Him only was sacrilegious to her. Oh, but Jesus!!! What He will do for you when you let him have His own way with you. He'll take you to a place that you would have never imagined." Cuffe had picked up steam and began to walk into the middle aisle of the sanctuary and continued. "The kids would only sleep if they talked to me. On the 21st day, Hallelujah! Mattie called me and asked me to come over to my mother in-law's house. I almost didn't go but I did. I loved Mattie and I had been praying to the Lord to restore my family. The Lord said to go and be loving." Cuffe stopped and looked at Deacon Johnson, "Be loving? This woman had taken my children and left me all because I wanted to serve the Lord." Deacon Johnson high-fived Pastor Cuffe. "I went and prayed that the Lord would guard my tongue and allow only what He would have me to say, escape my lips. When I arrived, my son ran to me with tears in his eyes. He said, 'you came Daddy, you came. I'm so glad that you have not forgotten about us. Don't ever leave us again.' I looked into Mattie's eyes and she was crying.

She was pointing in my direction and said, 'You are He'. She then said directly to me. 'I will stand by you.'" Cuffe began to clap his hand while actually jumping up and down.

"Mattie later told me that she saw someone that was transparent walking with me as I strode toward the house. She said that she had never prayed to actually receive an answer but the night before my visit, she sincerely asked God to tell her what to do. She told Him that she would be abandoning everything that she believed in. Her family would no longer consider her family. Her community would cast their eyes downward and not acknowledge her if she would stay with me and worship the way I worshipped. The answer that she received was too real for her to ignore."

Cuffe walked over to Mattie and stood next to her. "This woman saw a man walking with me toward her. Who Mattie saw was representative of the answer that she needed. She knew that if Jesus was walking with me, he'd certainly walk with her. She said that she was afraid at first but then felt completely at peace and secure. She repeated it again. 'You are He?'" and the man nodded."

Mattie too began to jump up and down. "Let him have his own way and you'll be blessed beyond measure. "Look at me!!" she shouted. "He has done what he said he would do. He is faithful."

Cuffe began to close his story. "I had to follow the Lord and commit myself to Him. He had to have His own way with me and my life. My wife left me, but I still had to let Him have his own way. I thought that I'd lose my family but I had to let Him...," Cuffe let the congregation finish the sentence. On cue, the audience, shouted, "Have his way."

"I ran and ran, thinking that I could be someone without Him. I wouldn't take Him at His word but I realized that His word will never return void. Because I trusted in Him, He revealed Himself to my wife. She is now the most on-fire woman for God that I have ever known. Trust in Him and let Him have his way and He will come through for you. At the very moment she ran into my arms, the words of Paul in 2 Corinthians 2:14 became my testimony. *Thanks be unto God, who always causeth us to triumph in Christ.*"

"When you don't know what to do... let Christ have His own way. When you have done all that you could do, let Christ have His own way. Have the courage to stand on the promises of God. Look at Joseph, he was about to marry a woman who turned up pregnant and he hadn't touched her. Think about Abraham. God asked him to sacrifice his son, the son that God had promised him. He let God have His own way. The bible is full of people who had to let God have His own way. You have to be steadfast and unmovable. He will bring you through and you will triumph. Lean not unto thine own understanding. Let Him have His way and I guarantee that He will bring you out smelling sweeter than when you came in.

The Son

The organ had followed Pastor Cuffe chord by chord and the church was once again on fire.

"Amen Pastor," Lila Manders shouted as she stood to her feet.

Daniel felt something stir in his chest. He was beginning to feel unusually warm and beads of sweat were forming on his forehead. The word "now" was being chanted in his brain and heart. It was becoming louder and louder. He shook his head and looked up at Pastor Cuffe.

Pastor Cuffe, feeling the unction of the Lord, walked over to where Daniel was sitting and stood at the end of the row. The word "now" was at full blast. Pastor Cuffe heard the word "now" as well and recognized it as the Holy Spirit. It was clear that he, Daniel and the Holy Spirit were on the same wavelength. Lila felt her son began to shift in his seat and then slowly rise to his feet. She didn't have the slightest idea as to what was going on.

Major wondered what was going on. He saw his brother standing and it looked like he was making his way to where Pastor Cuffe was standing. Baylor conveniently decided to take this Sunday off. At least that's how he'd put it. Did Baylor know what was about to commence? Why was he always out of the loop? Nobody told him anything. He felt Charla's eyes on him. He turned to her and shrugged his shoulders.

Melina, Cassandra and Alex all wore expressions of confusion on their faces as well.

"What is he doing? Does he sing?" Alex asked.

"Don't tell me Mr. Wonderful can blow too?" Cassandra said.

Melina grimaced and turned to Cassandra. "What is your deal with Daniel?" she whispered, trying to control her growing frustration with her friend. She had tried to overlook Cassandra's comments but this was not the time to show her behind. She was concerned about what was about to transpire. Bewilderment fused with concern began to overwhelm her. Her intense glaring at Cassandra had resulted in the desired effect and Cassandra lowered her eyes and looked away. Her departing look was apologetic but Melina didn't think it was genuine.

"Come forward Brother Manders. Your obedience is certainly a sign of wisdom," Cuffe said. His arms were extended as Daniel made his way to the aisle.

"Here am I Lord, send me!" Daniel said. He stretched his arms wide and smiled. He was happy. Jubilant was the best way to describe the feeling he was experiencing. Making the public announcement had freed him of having to keep secrets from his family. He hugged Pastor Cuffe. Tears of joy began to flow down his cheeks. While embracing Cuffe, his eyes traveled to his mother. She too was silently shedding tears.

Lila's tears were those of pride. She always knew that her son, Daniel, the one that never gave her an ounce of trouble or reason to worry, was destined to be something the Lord could truly use. She clapped her hands and then raised them to the heavens, "Thank you, Lord!"

"This young man has decided to let the Lord have His way. He has decided to answer the call to the ministry and has accepted a position here under my tutelage at He Is Risen Christian Center. He will be attending seminary and receiving instruction and direction from me and the leaders of this church." Cuffe's face was damp. He threw his arms around Daniel again feeling the joy of the Lord.

Mattie was the first to congratulate Daniel. She warmly embraced him with the love of Christ. She looked into his eyes and nodded. "He is with you too," she whispered into Daniel's ear as she released him.

The deacon board, although a little taken aback by Cuffe's announcement, stood and in single file, shook hands with Daniel. Some murmured an indistinguishable welcome to the ministry but others simply smiled. Cuffe could tell that they were not happy with his impromptu decision to have Daniel join the ministerial staff but he believed that it was ultimately his decision. Daniel had been visiting with him almost every day. They prayed and became engrossed in deep and thought provoking bible discussions that really opened up the Word to each of them. Cuffe enjoyed their debates and he learned something every time they talked. He believed that Daniel had the heart of God; very similar to David.

As Daniel continued to receive congratulatory hugs from the leaders of the church, Melina sat in complete and utter shock. *A minister?* Could she really date a minister? She didn't think that she was first lady stock. He never let on that he was headed in this direction. She had to admit that he did talk about God and how awesome the word of God was many times during their conversations. He could quote the bible better than any man she knew and that included Pastor Cuffe. She didn't think that she was up to this. She simply sat in her seat looking out onto the congregational activity in the lower level.

"Did you know about this?" Alex asked. Alex's voice revealed a little nervousness. It wavered and Melina could tell that she was worried about her.

Melina opened her eyes. Refusing to face her friend, she said, "No, I had no idea." She added nothing else to her explanation.

Melina looked down at Daniel. He must have felt her eyes because he returned her gaze. It was penetrating but strangely enough, it appeared as if he was wordlessly requesting her approval. She knew that he would follow the path that the Lord had placed him on whether she approved or not but his petition was just like him, considerate and undemanding. Placing her palms gingerly on her lap, she summoned all of the faith that she knew that she had and gave him her best smile and nodded affirmatively. Turning her head slowly, now looking directly at both of her friends, she confidently stated, "I have to let the Lord have His way."

Sixteen

*But if we hope for that we see not, then do we with
patience and wait for it?*
Romans 8:25

What a service!" Lila exclaimed as she entered the house. She had no idea that God would chose Daniel for the ministry.

"That's alright, Jesus," she said, smiling with every muscle of her face. She removed her sweater while walking into the kitchen. She felt like cooking a feast. No one could talk her out of it. Daniel looked crestfallen when she announced that dinner would be at her house in celebration of his entrance into the ministry.

The ministry, Lila thought. She was still in what she called "seventh heaven."

"Obie, you would have been so proud to see him surrender to the Lord," Lila almost sang to her dead husband.

Her heart was so full of joy and pride. She felt a tear find its way out of her eye and rest silently on her cheek. "I miss you so, honey." Her heart began to ache for her Obie, the love of her life.

The sound of someone descending the stairs allowed her to refocus on the task at hand.

"How was church mom?" Baylor asked.

To her surprise, he was dressed. She hadn't noticed when entering the house but the entire place was spotless. The kitchen was sparkling.
She smiled at her youngest son.

"It was wonderful. God had His way," she chuckled realizing the pun.

"I'm sorry that I didn't go with you but I promise to try and go with you next…"

"No need to make promises that you may not be able to keep," she said, cutting short Baylor's statement. "The kitchen looks great. Thanks for cleaning."

The Son

Lila turned in the direction of the front door when she heard it open. Daniel, Melina, Cassandra & Alex entered. Lila walked to the door to welcome her guests.

"Come on in," she said, extending her hand toward the living room. She kissed her son while visually taking in the woman that held his hand and said, "She is pretty, Daniel."

Daniel returned the kiss and said, "Mom, she is *beautiful*."

Smiling at her son to acknowledge the comment, she felt a pang in her chest. Not a physical pang but one that signaled something. She wasn't sure what it meant but she knew that she didn't like the way he called her beautiful. She didn't want any long-legged hussy derailing her son's life. He was to be a minister, not a husband just yet.

"Daniel, bring the groceries into the kitchen so I can get started," Lila directed. "Baylor, ask the guests if they would like anything to drink."

Lila's eyes settled on Melina and considered her. She seemed nice enough and she was happy that Danny had found a church going girl but decided that her son wasn't ready to settle down. Actually, *she* wasn't ready for him to settle down. Lila turned to leave the room and the door opened again. In strutted Major, looking quite handsome in his black Fubu suit. It was single breasted which was supposed to be the style. Her second eldest son smiled mischievously, as he entered.

Cassandra boldly assessed the brawny and braided specimen.

Alex saw the lingering stare and nudged Cassandra.

"You are married, girl," Alex reminded Cassandra.

They both smiled.

"He does have a nice build, though," Cassandra whispered and secretly high-fived Alex.

"Hi, Mom," Major said. "There's someone that I'd like you to meet."

An angel faced, chocolate doll, appeared from behind Major's frame. Her eyes were large cocoa moons that illuminated her face. As she turned her attention to Lila, her mouth expanded into a gracious smile.

Baylor found that he was drawn to this woman. He watched the exchange between his mother, Major and his guest. He had to meet her.

After ensuring that all of Daniel's guest's were satisfied with their beverages, he made his way to the three, still standing and now laughing in the front entrance way.

"Hey bro, don't tell me that you made it to church this morning," Baylor chided.

Major didn't appreciate the jab. Lila found it funny and smiled but quickly suppressed it.

"Well, my lady, Charla, invited me to join her and I decided that I would grant her wish," Major said, emphasizing the words, my lady. He planted an innocent kiss on Charla's cheek. Charla smiled but her eyes lingered on Baylor.

Daniel walked past the three and headed in Melina's direction.

"Hey there," Daniel said. He took her right hand and brought it to his lips. "You okay with everything?" He asked. Genuine concern was evident in his eyes as he continued to hold her with them.

"I'm fine and am very happy for you." She loved the way that their eyes seemed to lock. It was if their souls were magnets. Once attached it was difficult to separate them.

The concern diminished but he followed her eyes as she looked past him. He turned around and noticed that his mother was looking at the two of them. His mother's look was one that he could not construe.

As Lila walked toward them, Daniel began to feel a little uncomfortable. She was protective of him when it came to white women but Melina was as brown as they came.

"You two seem cozy," his mother observed.

The Son

Laughing, Daniel tried to determine why this comment unnerved him. He released Melina's hand.

"Mom, do you need any help in the kitchen? What's on the menu?" He realized that he sounded a little rattled and decided to allow his mother to respond to at least one of his questions.

Lila stared in Melina's direction but was interrupted by her son's inquiry.

"What did you say, baby?" Lila asked.

"What are you gonna cook?" Daniel asked while smiling at Melina.

Lila wondered how long they had been seeing each other. She knew that he was talking on the phone to someone late at night almost every night for the last month. Where had he met her? Who was her family?

"Mom?" Daniel asked. "Are you okay?"

Refocusing her attention on her Danny, she answered. "I'm fine son. Oh, and I'm cooking your favorite; veal parmesan with pasta. We'll have a fresh salad and I have a chocolate cake straight from the bakery that opened its doors just for me."

She embellished the truth a little. She was grateful to her friend, Mr. Palmeiri for letting her in the store. The bakery was only open until one o'clock on Sunday.

It was twenty after the hour when Lila pulled up. Dom saw her and mouthed 'closed' . She exited the car and walked up to the door and gave him her best smile. Thankfully, he relented and opened the door.

"That sounds great, Mom. Thank you," Daniel said. He loved his mother's cooking. Anything that she made was excellent but veal parmesan was his favorite. He should have guessed that she was going to make veal. After all, it was on the food list.

"I'm making it the way you like it, sweetie." She purred, all the while smiling at Melina.

"Mom," Baylor interrupted, "let me help you in the kitchen."

"Baylor, you don't have to help. Melina here can help me." She continued to look at Melina but her smile was gone.

"Sure, Mrs. Manders. I'd love to help," Melina agreed. Lila could tell that Melina was beginning to feel uncomfortable but to the girl's credit, she didn't make it obvious.

"I can help too," Daniel said. He wasn't sure if Melina and his mother in the kitchen alone was a good idea.

"Nonsense. The dinner is for you," Lila reprimanded, almost playfully. Melina and I will be fine. It'll give us a chance to get to know each other." The smile returned. "By the look of things, she seems pretty important to you. Am I right?" Lila didn't want to know the answer but the questions just slipped out.

"Yes, mom she has become quite important to me," Daniel said with certainty as he placed his arm around Melina's waist.

He smiled as if he was holding Miss America, Lila, thought. Daniel was right, she was an attractive girl. Thankfully, she wasn't one of those frail looking girls that looked like they needed a good home cooked meal. Lila remembered that she used to have a nice shape like Melina but those days were over. The fact remained that her son was not going to get married anytime soon and now that he had joined the ministerial staff at He Is Risen, he would not be leaving town either. This child posed no threat. God knew that she needed her Danny with her and He wouldn't allow any pretty young thang to take him away.

"Well, Miss Melina, let's make Rev. Manders his dinner," she said to Melina.

Melina hesitantly followed Mrs. Manders.

Alex, catching Melina's eye, realized that she had better join the ladies departing for the kitchen. She didn't like the vibe and didn't want Melina to have deal with what might be an uncomfortable situation.

"Hey ladies," Alex said. "I'm not too bad in the kitchen, I'd like to help." Relief washed over Melina's countenance and a half smile emerged.

"The more the merrier," Melina said.

"Is that okay, Mrs. Manders?" Alex asked.

"Sure, sweetheart. Let's get to it," Lila said and headed to the kitchen to start the dinner.

Lila was drying her hands with a paper towel after washing them when the phone rang.

"Hello?"

There was silence but she could hear someone breathing.

"Hello?" Lila stated again with a hint of annoyance. She heard someone clear their throat on the other end. "Hello, for the last time." Lila was about to hang up the phone.

She glanced in the direction of Melina and Alex as they sliced the tomatoes and red onions for the salad. They returned Lila's look with a puzzled expression of their own.

"Goodbye, whoever you are," Lila said and exhaled. Who would play on her phone on a Sunday? She thought.

"Mom, wait," the voice pleaded.

"Who is this?" Her voice began to tremble. She knew who it was. She knew her child.

"It's me Mom," he said. He was grateful that she hadn't hung up. His mother was not one to play around.

"Naimond?" Her voice was a choked whisper. He was alive. She had never believed that he was dead but …

"Yeah, it's me, Mom," Naimond said releasing a small chuckle. His heart was flying. He was talking to his mother. He had missed her terribly.

"Baby, are you okay?"

"Yes, I'm fine," he said, clearing his throat again, a nervous habit that he hadn't conquered. He continued, "I'm doing great out here and I wanted to call you because

I have been thinking about you and wanted to be sure that you were okay. Are you okay Mom?"

Lila had begun crying and Melina helped her to a chair.

"Naimond, I'm fine but would be better if I could see you."

"Would that make you feel better, Mom?" Naimond asked.

"Yes, baby. That would do my heart a world of good." Lila couldn't believe that she was speaking to her eldest son. "Come and see about your Mom."

"Mom," Naimond paused, "I'll try and make some arrangements at work. I'll call you next week to talk more. Please don't tell the guys that I may be coming home until I'm actually there. Okay."

"Sure, Nai,"

"Promise me, Mom."

"I promise." She could barely see. Her eyes were filled with liquid and she was sure that her face was soaked as well.

"I'll talk to you soon," Naimond said, closing the call.

"Yes. Continue to take care of yourself," Lila said, almost laughing, unable to control her joy.

"Bye."

"Good Bye."

Lila placed the phone on the table. She began thanking the Lord for allowing her son to contact her. He sounded well and so grown-up. He was actually fine and was going to try to come home.

"Boys!" Lila shouted. "Your brother Naimond was just on the phone." She placed her hands across her heart, closed her eyes and spoke very softly as if she was sharing a secret. "Obie, he called me. He is fine."

Baylor, Daniel and Major rushed into the kitchen. "What's wrong?" Major asked.

All three seemed to notice that their mother had been crying but wasn't visibly hurt.

"I said that your brother was just on the phone." She was smiling and was certain that she was showing all of her teeth.

"Thank you Jesus!" Daniel exclaimed.

"That's great news!" Baylor said and hugged his mother.

Major was silent and didn't show any obvious signs of elation. This was not lost on Daniel and Melina. They made eye contact. Daniel wondered what was going to be revealed in the weeks to come. He felt that something was about to erupt within the Manders family but didn't know what and didn't have a good feeling about it.

Would he be ready to deal with it? This is what he had been praying for. God had answered his prayers once again. Deciding not to worry about what was to come, he silently recited; *I can do all things through Christ who strengthens me.*

Major exited the kitchen. "I didn't mean that he had to resurface so soon," he said aloud into the air as if speaking with God.

Daniel, standing in the hall, heard the comment. Confused, he quickly stepped back and re-entered the kitchen with the others.

Major leaned back in his chair and tried to conceal the sound of his burp.

"I heard that," Charla said, contorting her face in feigned disgust.

He smirked playfully and then touched her hand. Other than the news that Naimond had called, he was having a wonderful day with her. He wondered how long it had been since they shared a silly little secret like that. He thought that he was being feminine but what the hell. These are the type of things that they would laugh about when they were alone together.

Charla smiled at Major for a moment. She wished that it could always be this way. He'd kept his word and attended church with her today and he finally introduced her to his mother after six months of being together. She exhaled and thought, "With God, all things are possible." She was afraid to consult God about Major. She didn't want to know if he was the one for her. Deciding not to think about it, she turned to Mrs. Manders, "May I help you clear the table?"

Lila turned her attention to Charla, "Thank you dear. I would appreciate that."

"Mom, the meal was the best that I can remember," Major interjected.

"To Mom," Daniel said and raised his glass of lemonade.

"To Mom," they all said in unison. Melina felt uncomfortable calling anyone Mom except her own mother but made an exception in this case.

There he goes again, Major thought, throwing invisible daggers at Daniel with his eyes. Major was tired of Daniel always taking the spotlight. He had just told his mother that the dinner was great and Daniel had to go and do one better and toast the woman just to make him look bad.

They all sipped their beverages and took their seats once again.

"Mrs. Manders, you have to give me your recipe. This was veal with a touch of soul," Melina stated.

Everyone laughed.

"My dear, I'm taking the recipe to my grave. On second thought, how could I do that to my Danny?" Lila stood and walked over to her son. "Daniel the recipe is yours. Only you and your wife, should you ever decide to marry, *years* from now, I hope, will have the Manders veal parmesan secret."

Melina smiled but Lila knew that she had touched a nerve. She hoped the message was received.

The verbal jab caused Cassandra's and Alex's radar to sound and they knew they had better get up to help in the kitchen to get out of the line of fire. They began to help clear the table. Alex lightly tapped Melina on the shoulder and nodded in the direction of the kitchen. Melina stood, excused herself and walked into the kitchen to help with the clean up effort. She knew it was time for her to go.

"Oh Danny boy, the pipes, the pipes are calling......" Baylor began to sing.

"Cut it out Baylor, "Daniel said, sounding embarrassed. "Mom, I asked you not to call me that in public."

"I'm sorry, baby. It slipped." His mother looked contrite. "It will not happen again. Promise."

Lila winked at Baylor and they chuckled just loud enough for Daniel to hear them.

In an effort the change the subject, Daniel inquired. "What did Naimond have to say?"

The room suddenly became silent. All looked in the direction of Mrs. Manders. They had all tip toed around the subject during dinner, not wanting to upset her anymore than she had already been when she initially received the call.

The expectation of doom was apparent on everyone's face. Much to their surprise, Lila smiled broadly and calmly stated, "That, my son the minister," she stated, admitting to herself that she loved saying that, "is between Naimond and me."

Each of her sons simply stared at her. No one had a follow-up question. They knew that when their mother closed the subject, the subject was closed and not up for further discussion unless she wanted to discuss it. Alex, Cassandra, Charla and Melina listening from the kitchen, laughed. Mrs. Manders wasn't budging. All concluded however, that Naimond was planning a return trip but made Mrs. Manders promise not to share the news. Why else would she say the word "promise?"

Seventeen

There is no fear in love; but perfect love casteth out fear
because fear hath torment. He that feareth is not made
perfect in love.
1 John 4: 18

"Well it's nice to see you," Lila said, not turning to acknowledge her son's presence. She was ironing a blouse because she'd decided to go bible study. It was about time she reconnected with her friends at church and delved back into the word of God. She also thought she needed to be seen more at the church, especially now that her son was being groomed for the ministry. Taking her blouse off the ironing board and turning it to iron one of the sleeves, she rolled her eyes. She was a little miffed at Daniel. He hadn't been home very much. It had been a month since his announcement at church. He'd thrown himself into his studies with Pastor Cuffe and enrolled in the seminary that was thankfully just thirty minutes away in New York. If he wasn't at the church or at school, he was with Melina. The latter had thrown her into a toddler temper tantrum one evening last week. Fortunately, he had not been there to witness it. No one had been. Recalling her little fit, she felt a little ashamed. "That tart is monopolizing Danny's time," she had raved. She didn't like that at all.

Daniel, ignorant of his mother's feelings, walked into her bedroom and kissed her on her cheek.

"What are you talking about, Mom?" he asked. "Where are you off to tonight?"

"Son, you have been so involved in your studies and other people, I'm surprised that you noticed that I was even here. You are just in and out, like you are living in a hotel."

Lila opened her mouth to tell him what was really eating at her but she closed it and decided not to. He was a young man, she reasoned, and needed the attentions of a young lady. She didn't think that he could be very serious about that girl because he was always at school and church. He had already stated that becoming a minister was his first priority.

"Mom, I'm sorry, you know that I'm doing so much now. I have school, my responsibilities at the church ..." He let the sentence trail off and sat down at the foot of the lavender and mauve comforter. She finally turned and sat next to her son. She placed her dark maple hands on his and stared purposefully into his eyes.

"I can truly understand your obligations and commitments but remember you want to eventually preach and you won't be able to do that if you continue to spread yourself so thin. I think that you need to prioritize your time.

This inference was not lost on Daniel. He knew that his mom felt he spent too much time with Melina. He believed that she was worried Melina would cause him to get sidetracked.

Lila knew in her heart that her son would be a minister. She just didn't want to verbally admit her fear of Melina taking him from her.

Daniel didn't want to argue with his mother. It would be pointless. Daniel exhaled and smiled at his mother.

"Mom, believe me, I'm not spreading myself too thin. If you are referring to Melina, she's my biggest supporter."

Lila certainly didn't like Melina being cited as his biggest supporter. *She* was his biggest supporter. She was the one who had always supported him. She was *his mother*. She let the comment slide because she didn't want to rock the boat and cause him to feel the need to leave the house. She wanted him to stay where he was.

"I'm glad that you have found someone, baby. I am." She saw that Daniel wasn't sold on her comment and she continued, "Just know that I'm here for you too and have always been." Daniel leaned over and kissed his mother on her cheek.

"Thanks, Mom. I've always known that you are here to support me and I am counting on that. I need your support because the choices that I will make may not always be my own. I will not be leaning on my own understanding but will be trusting in the Lord. You have to understand that above all else, okay?"

He could tell that his mother didn't fully understand that he was referring to his growing relationship with Melina. He had been praying about their life together and had been getting positive responses from God. He enjoyed Melina's company and they not only had fun together but she was the kind of woman he had been in search of. They seemed to connect on every level. He knew it was too soon to think about marriage but he felt more and more certain that she was the one.

"I understand, son. Just be careful okay," his mother said. She turned and continued to iron. She decided on a long auburn and black print skirt. "Now, if you would be so kind to excuse me, I have to get dressed for bible study. There are stuffed shells and a salad in the fridge if you are hungry."

Daniel was glad to hear that she cooked, he was starved. He wanted to get over to Melina's house tonight but didn't think that he had the energy. School and his sessions with Pastor Cuffe were kicking his behind. He was learning so much that he dared not complain.

The conversation that he had with Pastor Cuffe earlier today caused him to become a little tentative about his role in his family. Pastor Cuffe said that he needed to be the example his family needed to see. Elias realized that Daniel's brothers were somewhat errant and because Daniel was the one that had been called to the ministry, he may feel responsible for bringing his brothers to Christ.

"I don't know what to do about them," Daniel confessed.

"The Lord will make it clear as to what you should do," Elias told him. "You should be in constant prayer about that. The Lord will make it clear as to what you should do," Elias repeated very seriously but smiled to ease Daniel's fears. "God is using you to reconnect your family."

"I had a feeling that was coming next," Daniel said and sat down in the blue suede chair that had become his favorite.

"Don't sound so down about it, son," Elias said. "It is not going to be easy but with Jesus, all things are possible. I know you believe that." Elias stood and walked over to Daniel. "Don't you dare doubt what God can do. If he can change the heart of Paul, a persecutor of Christians, you can certainly make a difference in your brothers' lives."

"You are right," Daniel agreed.

Elias clapped Daniel's back. "Son," Elias said in what sounded like a grave tone, "a loved one is going to enter your life again, and it will be a trial because of what you will learn but remember what God said in Isaiah 41: 10. *Fear not, for I am with thee, be not dismayed for I am your GOD and I will strengthen you. Yes, I will help thee; I will uphold you with the right hand of my righteousness.* You may also have to make a life decision regarding a loved one." Elias returned to the large chair behind his desk. "Don't let anyone or anything stop you from doing what God says to do."

Daniel shook his head. He was always in awe of the Holy Spirit. He knew God had placed it on Elias' heart to tell Daniel to follow the Apostle Peter's example and gird up the loins of his mind to get ready for whatever comes. Daniel had to place all of his trust in God.

Almost immediately, Daniel realized that the person reentering his life was his brother, Naimond.

Wow, he thought.

Daniel feared that Pastor Cuffe could hear his heartbeat because it sounded like a university drum line.

His brow furrowed with uncertainty because he hadn't any idea as to what the big life decision would be or who it would involve. For as long as he could remember, he felt that he was the one that had to make everything right. He would always try to be the peacemaker when his brothers would argue about nonsensical things. He had practically been the referee when Naimond and Major had come to blows over a girl that Naimond had been dating. He felt it was his responsibility to help his mother and even his father understand the reasons why his brothers would make stupid decisions that landed them in trouble.

Daniel didn't know why he'd felt that he had to ensure that his family stayed a cohesive unit but he knew that it was something that he had to do. He had to admit that he had tired of being the one that seemed to have the level head and the wherewithal to ultimately make the right move at the appropriate time. He used this rationale when he decided to stay in Wisconsin. Living on the other side of the country allowed him the mental rest and space he needed. Realizing now that his family was falling apart around him, his feelings of guilt were augmented. Shame had also been a resident in his psyche during his last months in Wisconsin. He had apparently not been successful in eluding the sense of duty that he felt regarding his family.

He recalled his mother asking, "So when are you going to come home to your family, we need you?" Lila had become accustomed to him being an anchor for the family after his father died. Naimond leaving without a word didn't help matters.

Naimond, why did you leave and what was in that letter? Daniel thought. The letter that was left seemed to be jumping into his mind on a frequent basis lately. Daniel wondered why that was the case all of a sudden.

Daniel's eyes refocused on Pastor Cuffe's and noticed that his lips were moving but he hadn't heard much of what he'd been saying. He pulled himself out of his mental conversation and finally heard the words that were being released. He knew they were undeniably true.

"You are the person that God has chosen. You have been brought home so that your family and those connected to your family can be found in the Book of Life."

"Daniel, don't let anything deter you from the path that you have chosen," Lila continued.

Daniel looked at his Mom as he returned to their conversation, the memory of his conversation with Elias slowly dissipating.

"Thanks, Mom," Daniel said as he walked out into the hallway. "Have a good time at bible study. I'm glad that you are getting out."

"I will," Lila said. "Please do me a favor and help tidy up Naimond's old room. Just straighten it out. He called again."

Daniel was happy to hear the news and smiled as he walked over and hugged his mother.

"He will stay here if he decides to visit. He knows that I won't it have it any other way."

Her happiness was evident as she informed Daniel that she would have all of her sons in the house for at least a week. "I'm trying to talk him into staying longer but I don't think that its possible," she sighed. "Oh well, he may be coming home and that is most important." She looked at Daniel. "Okay now, get going and get something to eat. I'll see you when I get back."

Eighteen
How fair is your love, my sister, my spouse!
How much better than wine is your love
and the scent of your perfumes than all spices!
Song of Solomon 4:10

Daniel devoured what was left of the food and decided that he wouldn't visit Melina. It was getting harder and harder for him to leave her embrace. Sometimes they would just sit and talk about what was going on in their lives. She said that she couldn't believe that she was enjoying her new job. The additional money had come right on time and she certainly felt more appreciated. Dina, her old boss, had been transferred to another department and she was happy that she didn't have to see her everyday especially after what went down.

Daniel plopped down in the living room and laid down on the comfortable sofa. He told himself that he was going to get up and call Melina just to let her know that he wasn't stopping by. He knew that they were both exhausted. She too, could get some extra sleep. They would hook up toward the end of the week. Daniel closed his eyes and thought about Melina and how providential it was that he had met her when he did.

Last night she had fallen asleep with her head on his chest. She looked so precious, he didn't want to wake her. He'd paid her a visit right after his meeting with the He Is Risen staff. They placed him on the payroll as a Student Minister as well as the Assistant Youth Pastor. He was excited that he had a job that was paying money. After she made a quick dinner, she suggested that he join her on her couch to relax. As they settled into a comfortable cuddle, he began to gently caress her bare arm. She sighed softly which encouraged the intensity of the touch.

"Comfortable?" he asked, beginning to feel relaxed and just a little warm.

The Son

He looked down and saw that she had drifted off to sleep. Her breathing was even and it sounded as if she was purring. Daniel laughed as he gently moved to position them to lie together on the couch. He lay behind her on his side and his arms went around her waist. They seemed to fit like a puzzle. She stirred just a little and opened her eyes. Closing her eyes again, she smiled and snuggled closer to him. She brought his arm to her face and placed her cheek on his hand.

As she moved her hips, oblivious of the effect the movement was having on him, he removed his hand from her cheek, gently brushed away a strand of hair that had made its way out of her ponytail and onto her neck. He slowly kissed her exposed and inviting neck. Her lips formed a smile and a tiny but perceptible giggle escaped but Melina didn't open her eyes. They laid there for a few moments and then she turned to face him, their bodies touching and eyes locked. At that moment, Daniel began to feel a pull that caused his heart to beat faster. He looked away. He let his eyes settle on a photograph of Melina's mother and father. They looked disapprovingly at him. At least that's what he thought. Melina sensed Daniel's apprehension. After a moment, Daniel turned his attention back to Melina, shaking off the feeling of guilt. He had done nothing wrong. He began to focus on Melina's lips. They were a plum colored hue. Probably her lipstick from earlier today, he thought. He found her eyes and leaned closer to her.

"May I taste you, Melina?" he whispered almost prayerfully. He didn't hear her response but he read the lips that he viewed as fruit. The fruit gave its consent and he softly but purposefully covered her mouth with his. She tasted like his favorite fruit; a ripe, juicy peach. The kiss was like nothing he had ever experienced. He'd kissed a number of women before but for some reason, this kiss released him. It released him from the need to do anything else. He was just happy, no, elated while simply tasting his woman. They searched each other's mouths like they were savoring a meal. Each lip, from one end to the other was sampled. They enjoyed taking pleasure in the taste and the feeling that accompanied the newness of their lips merging together. A moan escaped Melina and Daniel slowly and very reluctantly ended the kiss. He looked at her and Melina's mouth enticed him again. Her eyes lowered and she bit her bottom lip.

"Don't do that, baby," he entreated, his voice, deeper and huskier than usual revealed the heat of their exchange.

"Do what?" she asked, still not looking at him.

"Don't bite the lips that just brought me so much joy," he said and slyly smiled.

"You are crazy," Melina responded as her lower lip was released.

"I think that I'd better go," Daniel announced. Disappointment became evident on Melina's face.

"I don't want to go, baby, but I think that it may be best." Daniel stood up and readied himself to leave.

"I understand but I don't want this to become a pattern." Melina took a step back. "I enjoyed kissing you and it's not wrong. What would be wrong is if we don't understand that we can't make love."

She shook her head, not sure if she was being clear. "Just because we kiss and hold each other does not mean that we have to make love. You don't have to run from me." She touched his chest with her index finger to make her point.

"Believe me, you don't have to worry about me running from you. As good as you taste..." He took her finger and kissed it.

She smiled.

Daniel continued, "We know how difficult it may be to abstain but because we are on the same page and continue to look to God for strength and not get ourselves into compromising situations, we'll be okay."

Melina nodded and smiled coyly. "I won't be a hindrance. I only want to be a helpmate."

She quickly placed her hand to her mouth, not realizing that she had said that aloud. "I mean I just want to help you." She could have kicked herself. It was too early to talk about marriage but she had been having daydreams about seeing him at the end of a path in a tuxedo smiling lovingly at her as she approached. She remembered that she walked slowly as rose petals became her path.

"I know what you meant," he chuckled. He couldn't help it. He was glad that they were in sync. He too had been thinking about making her his wife.

"Alright, Daniel, you had better go, if you are going," Melina said beginning to feign a demeanor of disappointment.

"You are not upset, are you?" he asked tenderly as he closed the gap between them and placed her face in his hands. He held her face...beautiful.

The kiss that served as their goodbye was again, soft and sweet. He held onto her lips with his until she started to giggle like a school girl.

"They are so good," he sighed.

"Get home safe," Melina said, beaming. He made her feel so special. His compliments were not the run of mill, "baby, you look so good" but ones that were relevant to her. He really spent time thinking about her because it was evident in what he said when they talked.

"Dream of me, baby," he said standing on the other side of her door.

"That's a given," she agreed.

"Pray for me?" he requested.

"Always," she confirmed

"Goodnight," he concluded.

"It certainly was," she countered and closed the door. Melina smiled and headed in the direction of her bedroom to keep her promises.

Daniel hadn't realized that he had fallen asleep until her heard his mother enter the room and call his name.

"Hey, Danny, did Naimond call?" Lila asked.

"I'm not sure. I fell asleep right in this spot as soon as you walked out of the door," he admitted.

"There are two messages on the machine. Check it for me okay? I'm going to get out of these clothes."

"Sure," Daniel said as he stretched and stood. He yawned and realized that he had not called Melina. He missed seeing her face but knew that he needed to get to bed. There was no point in putting off the inevitable. Sleep.

"Bible study was good," Lila added as she ascended the stairs.

"I'm glad you enjoyed it," Daniel said walking toward the phone in the hall.

He pressed the button on the answering machine and leaned against the wall, still a little groggy. He hadn't heard Major enter the house but jumped when he felt the boyhood pluck on the back of the head courtesy of his older brother.

He turned to see Major stifling a laugh. Daniel motioned for him to be quiet by placing his index finger over his own lips.

"Mom, its Naimond. I just wanted to let you know that I have been able to get some time off and plan to arrive in town early next week."

Major and Daniel exchanged expressions of genuine surprise but the source of the surprise was not identical.

"Okay, I guess that you're not there so I'll call you Sunday night to give you my flight information. I can't wait to see you, Mom. Bye."

The sound of Naimond's phone clicking to end the call was the last sound they heard. Daniel quickly pressed the stop button before the next message was played.

"So... Naimond *has* been planning to come home," Daniel said to no one in particular.

"Sounds like it, Sherlock," Major said with sarcasm. "Why do you think he has been calling Mom?" He moved into the kitchen, flipped the light switch and opened the fridge. "I wonder why he has chosen to talk to only her." He closed the fridge after retrieving a bottle of apple juice, turned off the light and returned to the hall to find that Daniel had retreated to the living room.

"Daniel," Major said. "Where did you go?"

"I'm just sitting down. Is that okay with you?" Daniel asked with a laugh. He really didn't want to have a conversation with Major. They always turned into fights or disagreements. He wanted to mend fences but he wasn't up to sparring with him tonight. He'd been successful so far but Major had only been living back at home for a month. He knew that Major was just biding his time.

"I have to admit that this is a shock. You know, Naimond coming home or even contacting us after all of these years." Major sat back in the mushroom colored plush chair. He placed his hands behind his head and asked nonchalantly, "Do you think that he'll tell us why he left the way he did after Daddy's funeral?" He quickly eyed his brother to gage his reaction to the question posed.

Major was getting the feeling that Daniel didn't want to discuss their brother. He didn't like being ignored and could feel himself become a little annoyed by Daniel's disinterest. He sat up and leaned toward Daniel. He knew exactly what to say.

"Aren't you worried that Naimond will still be angry with you for making him leave home?"

Major almost jumped when Daniel abruptly stood. He'd succeeded and smiled inwardly when he saw Daniel's eyes darken.

"Why do you continue to believe that I had something to do with Nai's leaving?" Daniel stood and walked toward the stairs. "I'm not going to go through this with you again."

"Why do you always get so worked up?" Major asked, proud of his handy work.

Daniel, standing on the bottom stair turned and glared at his brother. The stare was penetrating and seemed to last an unusually long time. Major was expecting Daniel to say something but no words were uttered. Daniel began to lean in Major's direction. Major stepped back anticipating some sort of retaliation. Seeing that, Daniel shook his head as if he pitied his brother and slowly ascended the stairs.

The Son

Nineteen

But evil men and imposters will grow worse and worse,
deceiving and being deceived.
2 Timothy 3:13

"I guess he's stuck at the church. He is usually here by now," Melina said to Cassandra. She was wondering where Daniel was. When she talked to him earlier, he said that he'd call when he was on his way but she hadn't heard from him and it was almost 9:00 p.m.

"Girl, you know how men can be. He may be caught up with some church woman trying to get him to lay hands on her." Cassandra laughed at her own silly joke.

"I'm not worried about that," Melina said. She snickered just a little.

"Alright, be blind if you want to," Cassandra warned.

"How is Johnson?" Melina asked, desperately wanting to change the subject.

"He's good. He had a dinner meeting, or so he says." Cassandra sighed.

"You know he loves you, Cass," Melina said trying to reassure her friend. "That business is doing well because of the both of you."

"I know. It's just that I sometimes feel so neglected," she confided.

"Well, you better get off the phone, take a nice hot bath and get ready to greet your man with some 'legal lovin' when he gets home." Now, Melina laughed at her own silly joke.

"Legal Lovin?" Cassandra asked.

"Yeah, you two are married, so it's legal," Melina laughed again. "It is okay for you to turn that man out. He is your husband and the marriage bed is not defiled."

"You are right, girl, and I'm about due for some acrobatics," Cassandra agreed.

"Don't hurt nobody!" Melina said.

"You have started something now," Cassandra chimed. "I think I will take your advice and get myself ready for my husband." She extended her pronunciation of the word husband.

"Alright, I'll let you go do that."

Melina was happy that her friend now sounded excited about romancing her husband. She didn't like it when Cassandra was sour and sullen. She was one of her oldest and dearest friends. She had a husband who loved her and they had a good life together. She just had to let go and trust. Cassandra knew Jesus as her Savior and Melina didn't like to hear her being so negative.

"I'll call you before the end of the week," Cassandra said.

Melina could hear running water in the background and smiled. "Okay, like I said, don't hurt nothin'. Love ya."

"He'll heal if I do. Love you too. Bye"

As Melina exited her bedroom, she clicked on the television in the living room to pass the time. She wanted to climb into the bed but fought to stay up just in case Daniel called. He said he'd call when he was on his way...

There wasn't anything on the network channels so Melina turned to the History channel. She could always find something good on that channel or the Discovery Times Channel. She popped some popcorn and watched "Mysteries of the Bible." Melina enjoyed watching this type of programming. They were focusing on Sodom and Gomorrah; the story of God destroying the two cities because of unnatural sexual behavior. God sure didn't play, she thought. Melina wondered how Lot and his family lived in the midst of such craziness. She pulled out her bible to try and find the story in Genesis. She found it and began to read the story while half-listening to the television's version. What surprised her was that the people in the city were so bold with their sin. They had the nerve to go to Lot's house and demand that Lot tell the two angels that came to warn Lot and his family, who resembled men, to come out so that they might "know" them. "Know", in the biblical sense meant sexual intercourse. She could never understand why people were so easy to overlook and condone homosexuality or any sin for that matter. The bible is clear. Sin, in any form without repentance, separates man from God. Melina was reminded of what the eighth chapter of Romans stated. *Because the mind of the flesh, with its carnal thoughts and purposes, is hostile to God, for it does not submit itself to God's Law; indeed it cannot. So then those who are living the life of the flesh, catering to the appetites and impulses of their carnal nature, cannot please or satisfy God, or be acceptable to Him. If anyone does not possess the Spirit of Christ, he is none of His. He does not belong to Christ and is not truly a child of God.*

Realizing that she was not perfect and had stumbled in her life, she tried not to judge. She'd come to understand that God hated the sin and not the sinner. She realized that all were born sinners and just had to make the decision to accept Christ and sin no more. That is why she was so thankful to Jesus. The bible, in that same chapter, also reminded her that; *There is therefore now no condemnation to them which are in Christ Jesus, who walk not after the flesh, but after the Spirit. For the law of the Spirit of life in Christ Jesus hath made me free from the law of sin and death. For what the law could not do, in that it was weak through the flesh, God, sending his own Son in the likeness of sinful flesh, and for sin, condemned sin in the flesh.*

She put her bible on the coffee table and placed the decorative pillow under her head. Why couldn't she ever finish the entire episode without the dozing off? This was going to be a good one, she thought to herself.

Her eyelids began to get heavier and she surrendered to the fatigue from the day. "Daniel," she said, allowing her eyes to close, "I hope I hear the phone when you call."

The sanctuary was filled with people. All of them wore smiles while some were crying through their smiles.

She was walking toward something, no someone. She could see Daniel. He was standing at the end of the rose covered path. She was less than three feet from him when all of a sudden, she felt herself tumbling. Her face was parallel to the petals and her dress had been ripped. She could see that her hair had come undone and the beautiful tiara that she had worn was now was a few inches away from where her head landed. She reached for it and as soon as she was able to grasp it, a baby blue satin sling back shoe stepped on her expertly manicured nails. She tried to remove her hand but the person that controlled the shoe added pressure. Melina winced and looked up to see who was causing her so much pain. When her eyes traveled north, she couldn't believe that she was looking into the face of Lila Manders. Mrs. Manders' demeanor was one of artificial concern.

"Dear, are you okay?" Lila stood back but made no effort to assist Melina in rising to her feet. "It seems that I have caused you to fall." She smiled openly as if pleased. Her countenance then hardened. "You don't want to tumble with me," Lila hissed. Her eyes became slits.

Melina couldn't understand why this woman was saying this to her. What could she have possibly done to her to make her so violent?

"My son is not for you. He is not for you," Lila seethed.

Melina woke with a start and immediately sat up. The nightmare was unsettling. She'd been receiving negative vibes from Mrs. Manders but this was something different. Thankful that it had been only a dream, she reached for the ringing phone.

"Hello," Melina said almost whispering.

"Hey baby," Daniel said. "Are you sleeping?"

"I was. Are you coming?" She asked.

"No. I fell asleep myself. It's too late now," he stated. "I just called to say good night."

He was so sweet, Melina thought. "Please get some rest. I know that you have been running in too many directions lately," she said. She was disappointed but knew that he was probably tired. School and his new position at the church were blessings but he was running himself ragged. She decided not to communicate her concerns.

"I know," Daniel said, grateful that she understood.

"Okay, baby, I'll talk to you tomorrow," Melina said. The uneasiness she felt about the dream she'd had, re-entered her psyche.

"Sweet dreams, baby," Daniel said.

"You too, good night," Melina said and kissed the air believing that the kiss would find its way to his lips.

Walking to the door to ensure that it was locked before turning in, she again thought of the dream that unsettled her. "Sweet dreams my behind," Melina said and chuckled aloud as she padded to the bathroom. She brushed her teeth and jumped into bed hopeful that she would not dream of Mrs. Manders again.

The weekend came and went so quickly that Lila didn't even realize that she had cooked the entire time. She'd prepared all of Naimond's favorites. She loved cooking for all her sons. Only Naimond and Daniel seemed to appreciate the time and love she placed in every dish. She still couldn't believe that Daniel would be back shortly with her eldest son. He'd called as promised and gave her the flight information. Daniel seemed to take the lead and helped prepare the house for his arrival. He told her to stay at the house while he went to get him from the airport only a couple of hours ago.

Lila was nervous and she didn't know why. Naimond was her son. She wanted to just hold him for as long as he would allow. As she walked into the living room to inspect the room, her eyes traveled up the stairs and thought of the letter that Naimond wrote on the day he left. Her heart ripped into two anew. She exhaled and rested in the fact that her son was coming home, finally.

She sat down, beginning to feel a little light-headed. Her heart was beating faster than usual. She couldn't get too excited. If she did, she would certainly send herself into cardiac arrest. As much as she wanted to be with her Obie, she wasn't ready yet.

"Oh, Obie. I wish you could be here," she told herself. "I wonder how or if our boy has changed much." She knew that Obie couldn't hear her but she spoke aloud in the empty room as if he could.

She heard the door open. She jumped to her feet and removed the apron by quickly lifting it over her head. She checked herself in the hall mirror and smoothed her dress.

"Mom?"

Lila recognized the voice and let out a disappointing sigh.

"Major, I'm in the kitchen," Lila said and opened the fridge to retrieve a pitcher of ice water. Her throat was dry with anticipation. She needed something to drink and knew water would satisfy her better than anything else.

"Hey Mom," Major said with a nervous smile. Lila didn't read the smile as nervous but she did notice his strange body language. Major was looking around the room as if he expected someone to jump out of the closet.

What is eating him? Lila thought.

"Is he here yet?" Major asked and chuckled. The mirth was manufactured.

"No. Daniel hasn't gotten back yet," Lila said. "They should be here any minute." She smiled and could feel the air on her teeth. She was happy and there wasn't any reason why she shouldn't show the world. Her eldest son was coming home.

"Oh," Major said without emotion. "Are you going to ask him to explain why he left?" Major began to lean against the wall in an effort to seem nonchalant. "I mean, you do still have the letter that he left, right?"

"Yes, I do have the letter and I'm sure that the reason for him leaving will be revealed during his visit but I'm not going to ask him to tell us. He will probably tell us but not because any of us forced him to."

"Uhmm, yeah," Major said. "I see that you've cooked enough food to feed an army."

"Yes, Lord. You know how much I love to cook for you boys," she said and stood. She walked over to the oven and opened it.

"Major, grab an oven mitt and take the peach cobbler out of the oven," Lila instructed.

"Sure, Mom," Major said. "Daniel is going to love you for life. You know how much he loves peach cobbler. Especially the way you make it."

Major placed the dessert down and began to think of Charla. She could cook just as well as Mom, he thought. He hadn't seen her since last week. She limited their actual time together to once or twice a week. His appetite for other women had not diminished and he secretly blamed her for that. He believed that if she hadn't told him to leave, he wouldn't want other women. It wasn't his fault. She told him to move out.

"Major, you okay?" his mother asked. "You are standing there like you stepped into the twilight zone."

"Yeah, Mom," Major responded, a little embarrassed that Charla took over his thoughts. "What did you do with that letter?"

"What letter child?" his mother responded seeming to only half listen to her son.

"You know, the one that Nai left," Major said, becoming a little impatient. He dare not let that show. His mother would be all over him like slave owners on Nat Turner.

"Why?" Lila queried. She didn't want to go there with Major. She'd heard his initial inquiry but feigned ignorance. It hadn't worked.

"I was wondering if I could see it," Major admitted. He had never seen the letter that Naimond wrote to his mother the morning he left all those years ago.

"There isn't any reason for you to see it," his mother declared.

Major recognized this tone and decided not to ask anything additional about the letter, Naimond's departure or even arrival. He shoved his hands into his khaki pants pockets.

"You are keeping your hair nice," his mother complimented.

He smiled his thanks. Major had to get used to his dramatic hair cut. He cut off all of his hair almost a week ago. He'd cut his hair so short, he looked bald. He smiled as he recalled the look on Charla's face when she saw him.

"When are you going to bring that pretty girl back over here?" Lila asked. She liked the girl as soon as she'd met her. She was just the type of woman that could set Major right.

"Who, Charla?" Major knew who his mother was talking about.

"Yes. That's her. I'm glad she put you out. I could tell that she has some sense." She turned toward the window because she heard a car turn into the drive way. Her heart began to flutter. Lila sat to gather herself and then quickly stood.

"He's here," Lila said. Her voice was unsteady. The nervousness had given way to joy and she felt her eyes begin to fill with liquid.

Major, on the other hand seemed to become jittery like a death row inmate finishing his last meal. Lila noticed his mood change and thought it was odd.

"Well, mom, he is the one who left, no one forced him to." He realized that he sounded resentful and decided that he had better be quiet.

"Are you sure about that, Major?" Lila asked as she stared almost angrily at Major's back. He had already started toward the front door. Major heard the question posed by his mother and it almost stopped his heart. He almost stopped to turn and look at his mother but thought better of it and kept walking.

Lila heard the keys enter the lock and recognized the click signaling its disengagement. The large heavy redwood door opened toward Major and Lila. Daniel walked into the house smiling like a child with a secret. His lone dimple was more prominent than ever. Lila thought it was so fitting that her Danny, the minister, would bring her eldest son home. She was convinced now more than ever that Daniel was special; her special one.

Daniel was carrying a small suitcase and a larger tote bag under his arm. Once stepping over the threshold, Daniel moved to the left and a tall, milk chocolate, extremely muscular man with a bald head emerged. The man had expressive, smiling eyes that resembled the color of pure black oil. He was certainly a Manders man. Without a doubt, he resembled Obadiah more than all of the Manders men.

The guest smiled and opened his arms.

"Naimond, you are here."

Twenty

*But let those that put their trust in thee rejoice; let them
ever shout for joy, because thou defendest them; let them
also that love thy name be joyful in thee.*
Psalms 5:11

"Yes, Mom, I'm here," Naimond responded as he
continued to smile at his mother. He placed the large
shopping bags on the glistening hard wood floors,
courtesy of Daniel, and began to walk toward her. He
placed his large arms around her and hugged her gingerly
at first. He felt his mother shudder as she released a sigh
and then a muffled sob. His squeeze tightened as he
allowed himself to relax and give her the embrace that he
wanted to give her for what seemed like a hundred years.
Eyes becoming moist, Naimond inhaled her familiar
lavender scent and lifted her so high that her feet dangled
in the air. Lila began to laugh through her tears.

"If you don't put your mother down...," she said
with apparent joy in her voice.

Naimond gently set her down and stood back to
examine the woman that he had not seen for far too long.
Her eyes looked tired and there was more gray in her hair
than he remembered. Her temples were all gray but
overall her hair was still blue black. The sheen was still
there as well. He hoped that it meant that she was healthy.
She always said if your hair didn't shine it was either dirty
or your body was sending a message that things weren't
working the way they should. She had thinned a little but
not too much. She probably wasn't eating as much as she
did when Dad was alive, he thought. It didn't look bad on
her, he reasoned. His gaze traveled back to her eyes and
stayed there to complete his assessment.

She still didn't have very many wrinkles; just a
few tiny ones around her eyes. Her skin was supple and
flawless. There was something in her eyes that he
couldn't place, however. Was she really alright? He
wondered silently.

"Mom, you look great!" he said, concluding his inspection. "Don't go trying to get supermodel-skinny on me, okay?" He laughed at his little joke.

Daniel and his mother joined in.

"I'm the one who would be gaining weight if I hadn't joined the fitness center immediately after moving back. She has been feeding me like crazy," Daniel added, laughing and guiding his mother and Naimond to the kitchen.

"When you first moved back you could have made that claim, but lately, since you have been in school and working at the church, you haven't been home long enough to have a bowl of Cheerios," Lila corrected.

"Yeah, Mom, Daniel told me about his calling," Naimond said. "Good for him."

"Good for all of us," Daniel said.

"Good for whom?" Major said finally joining the reunion. He'd escaped to the bathroom as soon as the door opened and Daniel stepped in. Initially, Lila found it odd that Major couldn't wait to use the bathroom. She was so occupied with Naimond and his arrival, she didn't give it a second thought, until now.

"Major, how are you?" Naimond asked.

A feeling similar to an incision without anesthesia traveled across Naimond's shoulders as he walked over from his mother and hugged his younger brother. He could feel Major's body tense.

Yeah, you need to be scared man, Naimond thought.

Although he missed his brother, the memory of the night of their father's death was one he couldn't erase from his mind. The years wouldn't allow him to release the lingering hurt that remained. Naimond continued to tell himself that no matter what, they were blood but all had not been forgiven.

Major did not welcome the hug. The embrace was one-sided but it didn't seem to bother Naimond. He smiled and stood back.

To Naimond, Major looked exactly the same, except for the close cropped hair cut.

"You are looking good man," Naimond acknowledged. "You look like you have some cheddar." He rubbed his thumb and middle finger together for visual aid.

I wonder what kind of hell you're raising around here, Naimond thought to himself.

"Nah man, I'm doin' okay though. You are the one that is looking good."

"Thanks man," Naimond said. "There is someone missing," Naimond verbally realized, looking around. Choosing not to spend anymore time on his wayward brother, Naimond asked, "Where is Baylor?"

Baylor sat at the bar with a cold beer in his hand. He was nervous about seeing her. She was the most beautiful woman that he had ever seen and he couldn't stop thinking about her. He was finally able to get her telephone number and after a few days, he called her to meet him here. She seemed unsure on the phone but thankfully decided to meet him anyway. He needed to see her again but had to do it on the QT.

"Baylor?" she said.

He turned around to see the chocolate cherub standing behind him. Her smile was mesmerizing and her eyes sparkled. The violet colored eye shadow accentuated her luminous eyes. Her lips looked as though they were teasing him when they said his name. They too, had a similar shade of purple. She was gorgeous.

"Hi, Charla, thanks for meeting me," Baylor said, motioning to her to take a seat.

"Sure, Baylor. What can I do for you?" Charla asked.

"Well, I need help and I was told that you are the person that could help me," Baylor answered as he began to put his plan into action.

"I know that you went to Peangry and heard that you were a wiz in French. I need to pass the French elective that I never should have signed up for, in order to finally get my degree. I know that it's weird that it has taken me so long to make the decision to graduate, three years as a matter of fact, but I don't know diddly about French and I need you to tutor me."

"Baylor," Charla smiled in response. "I can certainly tutor you."

Her smile was like a warm caress.

"You will?" Baylor said with a modicum of overt relief. He casually placed his hand atop of hers.

"Sure. You know what? I had no idea that you and I were only three years apart. Your brother makes you seem so young when he mentions you. We probably know some of the same people."

"I bet we do," Baylor said with a smile. "I was teasing him about you, you know."

"Oh yeah? What were you saying?" she asked, giggling.

"Oh, I just said that he was robbing the cradle and said that you were too young for him. After all, he is," Baylor admitted.

When the laughter from his not-so funny joke faded, he asked, "When is my first tutoring lesson and how much is this going to cost me?"

"Please, Baylor, don't insult me. I wouldn't charge you money. Food, however, is another mode of payment altogether," she smiled and continued. "How about you meet me at the airport, day after tomorrow? We can go get something to eat and map out our schedule."

"Sounds good, Charla," Baylor agreed. "Should I meet you out in front of A terminal? I know that is your airline's major hub."

"Okay. My flight gets in around 6:30 p.m. Is that too late for dinner?"

"No, that's fine. Oh and if you can keep a secret, keep this one. I want to surprise everyone when I graduate in January."

He placed his hands on his bottle of beer and continued, feeling the need to explain. "I know that it is a little late. After all, mid-terms are only two weeks away but I know that you can help me."

"It's no problem. I'm not seeing too much of Major since he moved out. This will be our little secret." She extended her mocha colored hand to Baylor and he gladly accepted it. They shook hands and she winked at him conspiratorially.

Why did she do that? He thought. He felt like someone was rubbing fire on his chest. They both laughed.

Charla liked Baylor's smile. She also liked the way he spoke. His voice wasn't deep and penetrating but it was husky and oddly clear and crisp. There was an air of gentility in the way that he made his words into his own unique language. She always wanted a man that could make her tingle with his words. She wet her lips with the tip of her tongue, a physical warning that she was becoming nervous.

"Why am I nervous all of a sudden?" She whispered to herself.

"Lord, I don't need any temptation right now," she pleaded in a whisper only she could hear. "Paul was certainly right about the flesh," she mumbled.

She turned to look at Baylor and he was smiling at her. His lone dimple was evident. Somehow, she thought, it looked so much better on him.

Melina hadn't seen Daniel all week. The dream that was plaguing her was beginning to get under her skin. She knew that she had nothing to worry about but felt that Mrs. Manders was making inroads and was keeping Daniel away.

"You have to trust God," she told herself aloud. "You have to rebuke and resist the enemy and he has no choice but to flee." She lifted her head and faced herself in the vanity mirror. She resigned herself to the fact that she wouldn't let any insecurity or spirit of jealousy destroy what she had with Daniel. She had to trust him too.

She removed her sweat dampened clothes and threw them into the wicker clothes hamper. Turning on the water, she recalled the conversation she had with her good friend. She called Alex and they met at the fitness center for a quick stress relieving workout.

Alex, being a true friend, sensed the anxiety in Melina's voice.

"I'll meet you there in forty-five minutes. It's time that elliptical machine and I became acquainted." Alex laughed and Melina couldn't help but chuckle. Melina knew that Alex always avoided that machine. They wound up having a good discussion and a drenching workout to boot. It was just what they both needed.

Melina shared her feelings with Alex and although her friend agreed that there were some vibes that certainly weren't positive, the understated jabs and crazy dreams shouldn't dictate her relationship. Melina was dating Daniel not his mother.

"Make no mistake, Melina, if you are this stressed now…" Melina didn't need Alex to finish the statement.

"I just want to enjoy being with Daniel and not have to worry about what his mother is saying about me to him."

"If you don't think that Daniel can be a man when it comes to you and your relationship then you don't need to be with him."

That was just like Alex. Straight, no chaser.

"He loves the Lord and he seems to consult Him on everything. I'm certain that he prayed about you even before he asked you out on your first date," Melina's confidant stated.

Alex could see Melina relaxing as her words provided solace. "I even remember him telling his mother that you were very special to him."

Melina couldn't help but smile. She was so elated by his declaration, she wanted to kiss him right then and there but his mother was hovering with an unmistakable demeanor of censure.

"Girl, talk about someone who was pleasantly surprised," Melina said.

"I know. You were beaming. He might as well have said that he wanted to marry you right there. I can see that he cares about you and it's only been ... what, a few months, right?

"Alex, it feels so right with him. Sometimes when I think about how deeply I feel for him, I become blissfully happy but then, almost immediately I allow his mother to invade my thoughts and I just get anxious." Melina shrugged her shoulders.

She checked the display and it showed that they had been on the machine for almost forty-minutes. "If that isn't the worst of it, his brother Major has been a constant problem. To top it all off, his older brother, the one who has not been seen or heard of for years is returning home after being missing in action for I don't know how long." Melina raised her arms in exasperation.

Alex, once again hearing the frenzy in her friend's voice stopped her machine and turned toward Melina. She placed her hand on Melina's and said, *"Be anxious for nothing, but in everything by prayer and supplication, with thanksgiving, let your requests be made known to God; and the peace of God, which surpasses all understanding, will guard your hearts and minds through Christ Jesus."* Alex continued, *"Whatsoever, things are true, whatsoever things are honest, whatsoever things are pure whatsoever things are lovely whatsoever things are of good report, if there be any virtue and if there be any praise, think on these things."* Alex smiled. "All of those things, based upon what you told me, were characteristics of your relationship with Daniel. It's true, lovely, pure and honest and most of all virtuous. Think on all of the good things and pray to God with thanksgiving. God will continue to hear your prayers and he will direct you. Just trust Him."

Melina was so grateful to have a friend like Alex. The word was so clear on what she should do. She had to hold on and believe that God knew what He is doing.

The Son

The shower was refreshing. She had a clearer perspective and was feeling a lot better about her relationship with Daniel. The feeling that something was coming, a storm or a faith fight of some sort could not be eluded, but she decided not to think about it and focus her attention on Jesus as she knelt by her bed. She closed her eyes as she thanked God again for Daniel and all of the people in her life. She prayed for Mrs. Manders and asked God to open up her heart so that she could be happy for her son. As she concluded her prayer, she heard a scripture whisper into her heart that caused her to open her eyes. The scripture was Jeremiah 29:11. *For I know the thoughts that I think toward you, saith the Lord, thoughts of peace and not evil, to give you an expected end.*

"Thank you, Lord," Melina almost shouted. She was so encouraged that she raised her hands and began to bless the Lord. "I hear you Lord and I thank you Jesus. I will lean on you, Lord." She was so happy that she stood and walked around the room and continued to bless the Lord until she heard the phone ring.

"Hello?" Melina said, almost jubilant.

"Hey, Baby." It was *her* Daniel.

"What's up, baby?" she said laughing.

"I just wanted to say good night and let you know that I began to hear your name over and over in my head and in my heart," he said, not exactly knowing why he shared that last part with her.

"You were on my mind too," she said, about to burst. "I was just praying about you and for you."

"Is that right?" Daniel said. He was a little taken aback by her revelation. He was used to hearing that she was praying *for* him but not *about* him. "Is everything okay?"

"Yes, everything is as it should be." Melina was using her power of creation. Although she was previously feeling unsure about Daniel and the issues that she explained to Alex, she was determined to speak to her circumstances and use her faith.

"I'm glad to hear that," Daniel breathed. He didn't want her to feel neglected. He realized that he needed her and wanted her to be a constant in his life but thought that it was too soon to tell her.

"I have to tell you all about my brother's homecoming. Can I see you tomorrow?" he inquired. "I was hoping that we could get together after work. Is seven okay?"

"Sure. Just give me a buzz when you are on your way."

"Let's go out for dinner okay?"

"Your wish is my command," Melina said and giggled. She was still high from her conversation with the Lord.

"I like that," Daniel said.

"Then I'll see you tomorrow," Melina said.

"Melina, I love you," Daniel said and meant it.

There was a dead silence and Daniel was beginning to regret that he shared his heart with her, but he just could not keep the words from flight.

"Melina, did you hear me?" Daniel asked. "You have my heart."

"Daniel, I was just thanking God. I feel the same way. My heart *is* yours." Tears were falling from Melina's eyes like a quiet waterfall. His words were the manifestation of her belief that she would find love. "I can't wait to see you," she finally said. She wanted to tell him that she loved him in person. She wanted to look into his eyes and truly give her heart to him.

"I'll say goodnight now but can I tell you again?" Daniel asked, he couldn't help smiling and was thankful that she couldn't see him grinning like a schoolboy.

"Say it as much as you want to," Melina laughed.

"I love you, Melina."

"Good night, baby."

The Son

Twenty One

*A wise son maketh a glad father but a foolish son is the
heaviness of his mother.*
Proverbs 10:1

Lila woke up with a feeling that she had not
known for sometime. She smiled as she walked through
her home and hummed as she cracked the eggs and
prepared the dough for her homemade biscuits. The
aroma of sausage was in the air as she returned from
retrieving the paper from the front steps. When passing
the staircase, she heard the shower. One of her sons was
in the shower. All four of her boys were in the house.
"Lord, I can't believe that all of my sons are here," she
said aloud. She ascended the stairs and walked toward
Naimond's old room. The memory of his leaving lay
siege to her heart and almost caused her to stop walking.
She remembered that she sat in his room for an entire day
grieving for the son that had left her right after she buried
her husband, his father.

She thought of the turn of events and still had
questions. She never understood why Major and Naimond
never called to explain why they hadn't needed her to
come to the police station when the charges that were
supposedly levied against Naimond were dropped. She
found the whole situation unsettling. Naimond was over
twenty-one but she and Obadiah should have been a little
more involved in something like that. She would have
thought that Naimond would have called his parents but
he and Major seemed to handle it.

She never saw anything in the newspaper and
Major said that there wasn't any paper work that required
their review. She found it hard to believe that drug
charges caused Obie's heart attack. She didn't know why
people said that and still wanted to know who started that
rumor in the first place. Something like that wouldn't
have, shouldn't have, run Naimond away. Obie had a bad
heart and that was all there was to it.

143

She remembered sitting in Naimond's room brooding in and out of sanity, reading the note that he left with confusion. Obadiah couldn't speak when he was being taken to the hospital that fateful night but he kept looking at Lila as if he was trying to communicate something to her. He kept looking and then shifting his gaze to Naimond. She thought he was trying to tell her that Naimond, being the oldest, should ride with her in the ambulance. His mouth opened and remained that way. He was trying to say something but he couldn't.

"What was he trying to say?" She asked aloud without even realizing it. Lila shook her head releasing the memory and knocked on Naimond's door.

"Naimond, are you up?" Lila asked. "I've let you sleep in the last two days but today we are getting up and going to church." She was on cloud nine because Naimond had stayed longer than expected. He was able to finagle another week and had told them about it just last night.

"Mom," Naimond called from behind her. Lila almost jumped. "I have been up for hours thinking of Daddy." He kissed her on the cheek.

"Good morning, son. I was just thinking about your father too," Lila said. That was weird, she thought. "Let's go down and get some breakfast," Lila suggested and led him to the stairs.

"Is Daniel, Baylor or Major going to join us?" Naimond asked.

"Daniel is already at church. You can go ahead and knock on Baylor's door. Major, didn't come in last night."

She was going to have to talk to Major. She didn't like him acting like a whore while living under her roof.

Naimond didn't like the way Major was using his mother either. Major was always a user and a liar, Naimond thought. On the other hand, Naimond was glad that he was getting a chance to spend time with his mother, Daniel and Baylor and he knew that his showdown with Major was coming. He had to let Major know how he felt. Major was wrong and what he did affected the entire family. The pain Naimond felt was never-ending. It was like a curse that needed to be removed. Only by revealing the truth, would the family be able to heal and move forward. *He* needed to move forward. Naimond observed that Major had successfully kept his distance during the past week but he couldn't avoid him forever.

"I'll meet you downstairs in a minute. I'm sure Baylor is hungry. He always liked breakfast," Naimond recalled.

"Okay, I'll just put the biscuits in. They should be done in no time. Do you still like cheese in your grits?"

"You remembered?" Naimond asked grinning.

"Yup," she said over her shoulder.

Naimond knocked on his baby brother's door and stood back. He remembered Baylor's morning issues and didn't want to be close to the door when he opened it.

"What?" Baylor slurred.

"Get up and come downstairs. Mom cooked and she wants you to join us," Naimond announced but couldn't help laughing at Baylor's annoyed response.

"Cheese grits?" Baylor asked as he opened the door.

Naimond stepped back but to his amazement, Baylor's dragon breath was a non- issue.

"What are you smiling about?" Baylor asked.

Naimond looked at his brother. Baylor was a man. He still couldn't believe it. They had an opportunity to spend some time together and had even enjoyed a really good conversation about his future. Naimond noticed an air of maturity that his baby brother now seemed to possess. This was a recent change according to their mother who said that Baylor had been floundering for the last two or three years.

Lila and Naimond were out and about almost every day since his arrival. Daniel was kind enough to let him tag along to the church a couple of times. He was really enjoying his time with each member of his family.

"Nothing, man," Naimond said refocusing his attention to the task at hand. "Are you eating?"

"You know that," Baylor said. "I know you're going to church with Mom."

"Yes, I was *told* that I was going with her. Some things never change."

"I hear that. I'm going too. My French tutor invited me," Baylor said, unable to keep the smile from spreading across his face.

"Is that right?" Naimond asked. "Does she go to He Is Risen?"

"Yes, she does," Baylor said. "She is one together sista."

"Are you grown men coming down her to eat or do I have to get a switch and come after you?" Lila yelled from the bottom of the stairs.

Naimond walked to the top of the stairs. Lila was staring in his direction with one hand on her hip and the other waving a dish towel.

"We are coming, mom," Naimond said laughing. It felt good being home. Even the threats of bodily harm were a welcomed reminder that he had not ceased to be a part of the family. He'd questioned his place in the family for many years but right now he felt that he was where he was meant to be.

Lila walked out of church as proud as a peacock that spread it's uniquely colored feathers for all to see. She was with her sons, save Major. One of her sons was in the pulpit, leading the services and the other two sat on either side of her throughout service.

Even Major's pretty friend sat with them. Lila noticed that Baylor was a little more attentive to Charla than she thought that he should have been. It was nice that she'd befriended him to give him French lessons.

Baylor knows he can't keep a secret, she thought, smiling.

The Son

Anything to get him out of school was okay with Lila. Nothing could ruin her mood.

That *Melina* girl, didn't sit with us, she huffed inwardly. She sat with her friend Alex, the nice girl, in the balcony. Lila could see Daniel looking at Melina throughout service. They were out pretty late last night. Daniel kept his promise and crept into her room and kissed her on the cheek to let her know that he was home safe. Lila didn't have a good feeling about that girl. He was falling for her and she knew it. Naimond had even mentioned that Daniel talked about Melina quite a lot for someone he just met.

"Hello, Mrs. Manders."

Lila turned and was surprised to see Melina. She was wearing a deep indigo wrap dress that accentuated her figure. The neck line was questionable. A little low but not unseemly, she guessed. Lila grudgingly tried to give the girl the benefit of the doubt.

"Well hello, dear," Lila said and smiled at Melina. "Did you enjoy service? I noticed that Daniel was giving the balcony a great deal of his attention."

Melina continued to smile but said nothing. She may try to stab me but she won't draw any blood, Melina thought, resolving that she would exercise one of the fruits of the spirit; **Temperance**.

"I did enjoy service, Mrs. Manders, thank you," Melina responded and nudged Alex.

Alex, feeling her cue, greeted Daniel's mother. "I hear that your eldest son is visiting from Oregon. I'm sure you are enjoying all of your men being around you," Alex said.

Lila smiled warmly at Alex which resulted in Melina being more confused than insulted. What have I done to this woman? She asked herself. She seems to like everyone else.

"Yes, my eldest son, Naimond, is home. He'll be with us for a few more days," Lila said. She turned to tap Naimond on the shoulder and motioned for him to come and meet Alex and Melina.

"Naimond, this is Alex and Melina. Melina is Daniel's friend. You know, the one that you said he was talking your ear off about." Lila snickered just loud enough for Melina to hear her.

Naimond immediately picked up on the vibe and didn't like it. He smiled courteously at Melina. "It is very nice to put such a pretty name to an even more pretty face," he said a little too gallantly. Lila huffed and shifted from one foot to the other.

Naimond's eyes seemed to widen just a bit when he looked in Alex's direction. He was immediately captivated by her beauty. Melina was just decent compared to this woman, he thought. Man!

Without speaking, he extended his hand. After staring at her and holding her hand for what seemed to be five minutes, he finally said, "Alex, is it?"

Alex, just as taken with Naimond, opened her mouth and said, almost barely, "Yes."

"It is nice to meet you," Naimond said and continued to hold onto her hand.

Alex unconsciously moved closer to Naimond while he used his other hand to cover hers.

"Well, now that all of the introductions are done," Lila said, with a smirk. "Why don't we catch up to Baylor? I don't know where he has gotten off to."

Naimond, slowly coming out of the trance that Alex had unwittingly placed him under, returned to the conversation.

"I think that he went to walk Charla to her car," Naimond said. He could tell that his baby brother liked the woman. Baylor hadn't mentioned anything to him but he could tell.

"I'll go and find Daniel," Melina said and winked at Alex.

Alex, in rare form, subtly shook her head "no."

"Don't leave me alone with this man. Make no mistake, he is fine beyond words and I'm at a loss," Alex whispered.

"All the more reason for me to go. You'll be fine. You are two gorgeous people," Melina whispered back.

"Melina, I am sure that your mother instructed you that it was rude to whisper," Lila said, displeasure lacing her comment.

"You are quite right and forgive me Mrs. Manders but the words being exchanged were for Alex's ears only." Melina smiled. She was convinced that Mrs. Manders was angry because she didn't know what was being said and worried that it was about her.

"Excuse me, Mrs. Manders, I'm going find that gorgeous preacher man of mine," Melina said.

Take that Mrs. Manders, she thought as she reentered the church.

Alex looked at Naimond and shrugged. Naimond smiled and realized that his mother had met her match. He remembered how she had always felt about Daniel. His mother had another woman to contend with and she wasn't taking it very well.

Twenty Two

The living, the living man, he shall praise You, as I do this day; The father shall make known Your truth to the children.
Isaiah 38:19

"No, I'm going to ask him," Baylor said. He's been here over a week and we haven't even talked about it. It's been nice to have him back but I want to know. I think he owes us an explanation."

Major grabbed Baylor's arm violently and pulled him back onto the burgundy sofa. Baylor looked at Major as if he had lost his mind.

"Man, let go."

"It's not the right time. Even Mom said that we shouldn't ask him but just be happy that he's visiting with us after all these years."

"Yeah, I don't even know him," Baylor retorted.

"What is the big deal?" Major asked, almost pleading. He realized that he was losing this fight and would have to face the music soon enough but wanted to put it off as long as possible.

The test of wills started when the two were enjoying a beer while their mother, Daniel and Naimond were out. Daniel was with Melina and Naimond and their mother were out visiting family. Baylor would have been with Charla but she had to cancel because she had to cover a flight for one of her co-workers.

"You know I heard that Charla is tutoring you," Major said. He looked at his brother and tried to read his face.

Attempting the same, Baylor was unable to read his brother's expression but because the truth was out, he responded, "Yeah, she is a great teacher."

"That, she is," Major said sardonically.

Baylor knew what Major was trying to imply and didn't like it. "You should have treated her right when you had the chance. It won't be long before some worthy brother will snatch her up." Baylor hoped that he would be that worthy brother.

"I'm not worried. She loves me. Always has. Always will," Major responded, although not too confidently.

"Don't be too sure," Baylor said.

"What are you trying to say, man?" Major asked, his patience with the young and inexperienced brother waning.

"I'm not saying anything. It's just that I enjoy her company and I believe that she feels the same. She has opened my mind to other aspects of life. Her faith in God is wonderful and I hope to be able to get closer to her God by getting closer to her."

"You don't have to get closer to her to know God, man," Major said.

"Oh, but I do my brother," Baylor said. "She can certainly help me to see the man that I can be by allowing the Lord to lead me. I was so wrapped up in how I thought I should act and the more and more I think about it, I'm reminded of Daddy and the kind of man that he was. He was a man of God and I sure do miss him."

Major looked away. His eyes settled on the picture of their father. Obadiah Manders was smiling at the person taking the photograph. Major didn't want to talk about his father and stood up to leave.

"Whatever, man," Major said.

"Don't you remember how Daddy used to talk to us about God and how important it was to know Jesus?" Baylor smiled as he recalled the days that he would sit with his father in the kitchen. His father would test him on the stories in the Old Testament and the lessons in the New Testament.

"What is the fruit of the Spirit, Baylor?" Obadiah would ask.

Baylor would quickly turn to Galatians 5:22 and read. *"But the fruit of the spirit is love, joy, peace, longsuffering, gentleness, goodness and faith, meekness and temperance."*

"Why are those characteristics called the fruit of the Spirit?" His father would inquire, just to make sure that Baylor was not just repeating back what was in the bible.

"If the Spirit of God is truly resting in you and has taken up residence in your life, these characteristics will be evident in you and people will see it. We can recognize a tree because of the fruit it bears; we should be able to recognize a saint of God because of the fruit he or she bears."

"Good job, son, you are learning. You are doing almost as well as Daniel." Obadiah smiled.

"One last question, the bible mentions one thing that we must have or it is impossible to please God. What is it?"

Baylor knew this one. "Without faith it is impossible to please God."

"Go 'head boy." You are on a roll." Obadiah rose to hug his son. "I'm proud of you son. Never let anyone keep you from having faith in God. Believe and you will receive."

Baylor smiled at the memory and looked at Major.

"Daddy was a man of God and I failed him by not being the kind of man he taught me to be. I mean, he worked hard but still found time to love us and show us what love was. He wasn't a quitter like me and look at how he just loved on Mom. You could tell that he loved her the way Christ loves the church." Baylor liked the way the bible explained how a man should love his wife. He and Charla talked about relationships and how God expected them to behave in and outside marriage.

"I'm not living right and I'm not the son that he was so proud of back then." Baylor paced the floor and then turned back to look at Major. "Neither are you, Major," Baylor said sadly. His voice was one of guilt and he lowered his head in shame.

"I wish that I had gotten a chance to say good bye to him," Baylor said as he stood and looked at himself in the mirror. He knew that Daniel and Naimond looked like their father the most but he looked like his dad too. He stared at himself and wondered aloud, "What caused Daddy's heart attack again?"

Major noticed that Baylor's voice was barely a whisper. "There were a number of rumors," Major mumbled. No one really knows what did it."

"Please, Major, you know the truth, please tell me," Baylor implored. "Maybe that will help me understand why Naimond left too. It all happened so quickly. I never understood why."

"Really, Baylor, let's not make a big deal out of it. He's home and he is once again a part of our family. Isn't that what is important?" Major reasoned.

"I'm going to ask him as soon as he walks in the door," Baylor said loudly with finality.

The door opened and Naimond and their mother walked in laughing but their eyes were reddened, as if they had been crying.

"Hi," Baylor greeted. He stopped short when he noticed their bloodshot eyes. "What happened?"

"Nothing, we were just visiting your father's grave and got a little emotional," Lila said, dabbing her eyes with a handkerchief.

"Well, we were talking about Dad too." Baylor looked at Major.

Major shook his head but Baylor, ignoring his older brother, thrust out his chest and pulled his shoulders back. "Naimond, why did you leave?"

The question was out there now, Baylor thought. It seemed that he just *had* to know a few moments ago but now he wasn't so sure.

"Naimond, man you don't have to tell us about it. It was so many years ago and..." Major began.

"I'm not surprised that you want to keep the secret Major," Naimond said. His voice was low. The words sliced the air and all eyes darted in Major's direction.

Major said nothing.

Naimond turned his attention to Baylor and continued. "No, I think that I should tell you." He released Lila's hand and took a seat on the matching burgundy love seat.

The front door swung open and Daniel walked in smiling. He stopped when he saw that he had obviously interrupted something. Everyone's facial expressions were grave. "What's going on?" he asked.

The tension in the room was almost stifling. No one seemed to be moving. This isn't normal, Daniel thought and slowly entered the room.

"Naimond was about to tell us why he left all those years ago," Baylor said.

"He doesn't have to," Major said trying to prolong the inevitable.

"I see no reason not to share the story now. We are all grown men and women aren't we Major?" Naimond's eyes remained glued on Major and a knowing smirk teased his full lips. The look, although a smirk, seemed tinged with sadness as he nodded at each one in the room. "I think we can all handle it."

Major laughed nervously.

Naimond looked at him angrily. "Major you know why I left. Why haven't *you* told anyone?

All eyes once again shifted to Major.

"You knew why he left and blamed me all of these years?" Daniel shouted. "How could you?" Daniel's hands began to shake. He placed them in his pants pockets. It took everything in him not to pummel his brother.

How could Major let the family believe that it was something that he said when all the while he knew that it was his doing? Daniel's blood was boiling. He was hurt and angry. All the years of lies… Daniel stopped short when he remembered the words Pastor Cuffe said and tried to suppress his anger. He would not let the devil cause him to sin.

The Son

Major shrugged and stood as if he was going to make an exit.

"Oh no, Major, you are going to stay right here," Lila said and pushed him down. Her heart was beating fast. She didn't want to get over excited but she wanted to finally know everything.

Twenty Three
And ye shall know the truth and
the truth shall make you free.
John 8:32

Naimond looked down at the carpet, as if waiting for a cue and then began.

"Dad was in the den reading the bible. I think he was studying the bible and Major came rushing into the room. Major had been up in the attic and found some sort of notebook that Dad would write in from time to time. I guess he just needed to put his thoughts down on paper. Major and Dad had an argument a couple of days earlier about a decision Major made regarding some money. Dad obviously told him not to do something but Major had gone and disregarded Dad and needed money quick. Major told Dad if he didn't at least lend him the money, he was going to tell me the truth. Dad laughed and said that no son of his was going to bribe him. Dad didn't believe that Major knew anything. Major revealed a page from Dad's notebook and began reading it."

Naimond stopped telling the story, reached into his pocket and unfolded a piece of yellowed paper. He began to read:

"I am so glad that I married my Lila but I think that we should tell Naimond about Opal. Every time I bring up the subject with Lila, she begins to cry. I know that she is his mother now but he has to know his real mother. Lila says that there isn't any point because Opal died during childbirth but I feel I owe it to the boy. As soon as I placed the baby in her arms, she fell in love with him. Lila told me that she had always loved me but could never think of us being a "we" because of the baby that Opal carried. I told her that Opal would have never been my wife because she loved someone else. She never loved me and I guess that I always knew that. I love Lila but I want to do right by Naimond. The boy looks just like me.

The Son

I see a little of Opal in him but not enough to matter. I still don't feel right about not telling him. I have to talk to Lila some more about this but someday I have to tell Naimond...

I hope the Lord forgives me for not telling that boy that his mother was Opal Matthews, a good woman that died bringing him into this world."

Naimond folded the paper and slowly placed it back into his pocket. He continued looking at the carpet. He didn't want to look at anyone. The anger, hurt and confusion resurfaced and he wanted to reach out and strangle Major. After so many years, he had not rid himself of the burden.

Lila's face was frozen, her expression unreadable. She lifted her head and let a lone tear flow down her cheek. The tear seemed to follow the same pattern of the tears that were shed less than an hour ago when visiting Obadiah's grave site. She suddenly became angry as she realized that Major tried to use this information to bribe Obadiah into giving him money to settle a deal gone bad.

"How could you do that to your own father Major? Don't you have any shame? What is wrong with you?" Lila asked, her voice raising an octave after each pained inquiry.

As Lila asked each question, she was making her way across the room to Major. Her eyes were overflowing with hurt, confusion and immense disappointment. Admittedly, Major had done a lot of horrible things in his short life but this topped them all. The anger she felt became more evident in her voice. "Are you some kind of demon?"

"Mom, I can..."

Major almost fell out of the seat because of the power of the blow.

Baylor, Naimond and Daniel quickly stood. Daniel grabbed his mother's hand and held it gently before she could take another punch at him. She was shaking violently. This nonsensical situation had caused the absence of her eldest son? Years of lost time...

She fought to get another opportunity to levy another punch. How could a son of hers be so low?

"I can't understand you. What is wrong with you?" she screamed.

Daniel sat his mother down and Baylor helped Major to his chair. Naimond just stood there. After a few minutes, Naimond said, "Mom, I can understand why you didn't tell me because you are *really* my Mom but I shouldn't have found out the way I did. I don't blame you and I don't blame Dad either." He turned back to look at Major. "I blamed you and for many years I even hated you."

Naimond paused and let his hand graze his bald head.

"What does the bribe have to do with you leaving? Did Major eventually tell you the truth?" Baylor asked.

"No, he didn't get a chance to. I was standing in the door when it was all going down. I ran in and grabbed the note out of Major's hand and began to scream at Dad. I called him a liar and a fraud and asked how he could he call himself a man of God if he could lie so easily to his son all of these years." Naimond stopped and looked at his mother.

"That's when Daddy started to breath funny. His eyes rolled back into his head as he clutched his chest. He fell to floor as if he were a freshly cut tree and I had yelled timber." Naimond's eyes brimmed with water. He knew that if he blinked the dam would break and all of the pain from that night would once again overwhelm him. He didn't care anymore. He blinked and began to sob through the rest of the story.

"I called the ambulance and called Mom at work. They said that Mom had already left so I just waited for the ambulance. Dad was still breathing and his eyes were open but he couldn't talk."

Naimond walked over to his mother and sat beside her. Looking into her eyes, he could see that she too was reliving it all over again.

"Major ran outside to see where the ambulance was and I stayed with Dad. Scared and ashamed, I told him that it didn't matter and that I loved him for taking care of me. I kept saying that over and over and then you walked in, Mom." Naimond stopped and squeezed his mother's hand. "The ambulance arrived and took him to the hospital only to be told a few hours later that he had died."

Naimond sobbed loudly and Baylor joined him on the couch and placed his arms around him. "I put up a good front for the funeral but I couldn't stay. I felt that Daddy was gone because of me. If it weren't for me Dad would not be in the casket. He had to lie all those years and it was because of who I was. To make matters worse, I caused him to have a heart attack because of my hateful words. My vile words judged and killed my father."

"Baby," his mother said, lifting his head to look at her. "You didn't kill your father. He had a bad heart. It wasn't your fault."

"Mom, if you could have seen the way he looked at me when I was holding him and waiting for the ambulance," Naimond explained. "His eyes held so much love for me even after what I said to him." He dropped his head again. "I couldn't stay and face my family knowing that I was the one who caused so much sorrow."

"Who made up the drug story?" Daniel asked.

"I told Major to tell you guys anything that he wanted. I didn't care because I believed that I'd never come back," Naimond said. He wiped his tears and looked at Daniel and smiled.

"If it weren't for Daniel's letters, I would have never called."

"Daniel, you knew how to reach Naimond and never told us?" Lila said, clearly astonished.

"Not for a long while. When I did contact Naimond, he asked me not to tell you and I promised that

I wouldn't if he promised that he would think about coming home. I'd been praying about what I should do and when I returned to Jersey, God placed it on my heart to just call him and talk to him. God said that you were ready and you were brother." Daniel smiled warmly at his brother.

"Yes. You are my family and I can't run from who I am because *I am* you," Naimond said. A weary smile began to form.

"Major," Lila said, "You are wrong. I can't believe any son of mine would do something so deceitful," Lila spat with a voice that stung Major more than lashes from a whipping.

"You know what!?" Major asked, rising to his feet. "I am a man," he said, punching his chest. "I'm tired of being the one everyone is ashamed of. Daniel is the good one, Baylor is the baby and Naimond was the lost lamb that now, Praise God, is home." Major looped his hands in the air in an over the top mimic of praise.

"I have never received any praise or attention from anyone. I'm always the one that needs everyone's pity because no one thinks I can get it together. I'm sick to death of all of you. You don't have to tell me that I don't belong because I don't ever think that I did." Major's eyes were cold and his body language was hard and self righteous. He allowed his gaze to linger on Naimond. Daniel, looking past the act, almost saw regret in Major's countenance.

"I can't and won't stand here and be judged by any of you!" Major stomped out of the room and left the house slamming the door behind him.

The Son

Twenty Four

Seeing ye have purified your souls in obeying the truth
through the Spirit unto unfeigned love of the brethren, see
that ye love one another with a pure heart fervently:
1 Peter1:22

"The whole story is out now," Daniel said to
Melina. They'd been searching for Major for the last two
hours. Major had not come home in three days and Lila
was worried. They'd already been to Charla's house but
she said she hadn't seen him in almost a month. His other
friends said much of the same. No one seemed to have
seen Major.

This was not good. Daniel understood his
mother's reason for worry but Major would show up. He
prayed the last couple of nights for Major specifically
before going to bed. He hadn't been going to bed until the
wee hours of the morning because he, Naimond and
Baylor had been up talking, waiting and hoping for Major
to return. The good news was that Naimond seemed to be
at peace and Baylor finally understood everything.
Naimond was visibly upset when Major didn't take
responsibility for his part in the whole chaotic situation
that unfolded. Daniel had a better understanding of the
turn of events as well. He still couldn't believe that this
was all Major's doing. Understandably, he couldn't blame
Major entirely, his mom and dad should have told
Naimond the truth and Naimond shouldn't have let the
fact that their mother, not really being his birth mother
keep him away for as long as he did. Daniel understood
how Naimond could feel guilty and somehow responsible
for the death of their father but that was simply not fact.

Daniel silently thanked God that their mother was
still alive. Their mother passing away prior to all of this
being put to rest would have been a tragedy for all
involved. Daniel did not verbally communicate his
thoughts to Melina when replaying the whole story but his
mother's reaction to the reason why Naimond left home

did not seem to surprise her as much as he thought it would have. He once again thought of the letter that was left by Naimond all those years ago. He just wished he knew what it said.

"Are you going to go up to South Orange to see if Major is there?" Melina asked. "What was his name?"

"Anthony is his name and he lives in East Orange on a street off of Springfield Ave.," Daniel informed. "I don't even know his last name. "He is one of Major's running buddies," Daniel sighed. "Major doesn't seem to be with anyone else we've been told about so this guy is our last stop."

Baylor tried to give them as many people as he could and so far they'd come up empty.

"I hope we find him soon. My mother is really upset about this. She is angry and hurt but Major is still her son. I told you she punched him like she was Mike Tyson."

It wasn't funny, but Daniel chuckled just a little recalling how Major didn't see the blow coming that knocked him completely off the couch. He didn't think his mother had that much strength.

"Yeah, you told me." Melina felt sorry for Major but from what she heard, he'd had it coming. "I just hope that your mother doesn't become too ill over this. She didn't look good when I stopped by to pick you up."

Melina had taken the afternoon off from work to help with the search. Even Alex offered to help. She and Naimond would use Daniel's car. Once confirming the address, they pulled into a parking space in front of Anthony's house.

"Do you want me to go in with you?" Melina asked. She didn't want to go but she felt that she needed to be with him.

"No, I'll be okay. I see Major's car. He is here." Daniel wasn't sure what he was going to say to his brother but he prayed as he held Melina's hand. He prayed that

God would protect him as he went inside the strange looking house. He hoped that he would be able convince Major to come home with him just to let their mother see that he was okay.

"God, we thank you for the victory in the turn of events that we are facing now. We know that what the devil meant for evil, you have changed it to make it good. We know that this will all work out because we truly love you Jesus. Lord, we ask that you intercede so that we can bring Major home to mom. Please steady her health so that she can look upon her son and be at peace. We thank you again for the truth and we bless your name. Protect us in the name of Jesus. Amen." Melina kissed Daniel on the cheek.

Daniel exited the car and headed toward the door of the brick house. It looked unkempt. The front lawn was weed ridden and the grass was too high. Melina saw a short Hispanic man, wearing a sleeveless undershirt and black jeans answer the door. He greeted Daniel with dark glasses and a grimace. He and Daniel exchanged a few words. After a few moments, Major appeared.

Major began shaking his head and stepped back into the house. Daniel reached for him and Major pushed the hand away. Melina began to pray aloud, thanking God that Major decided to get in the car to come back to the house. She thanked God for interceding and believed that she had the power to change the outcome through Jesus Christ.

She turned her back to the house and just waited. She wanted to turn around and look at them but she told herself that she wouldn't. She sat in the car thinking about of how wonderful her new job was turning out to be. She began to praise God for that as well. She believed that when the praises go up to God, the blessing came down. Carrie Knowland, her boss, had already heard great feedback about her.

Carrie had also mentioned that she wanted her to hire someone that could be her right hand but work directly under her. It seemed that she was going to be needed to perform other duties. She was not going to be as close to the employees as she was now. The person that Melina would choose would essentially be the person that would oversee day to day operations and would free Melina to be involved in the strategizing aspect of HR. This new position was sure to come with a hefty raise. She hadn't even told Daniel, Neici or her mom about it yet. She was very excited.

"Thank you Jesus!" she said aloud, enjoying her private praise time.

"Oh, no. Do I have to hear this all of the way home?" the irritated voice said.

Melina smiled and said it again. "Thank you, Lord."

"Awww man," Major said as he entered the car.

Daniel opened the driver's side door and kissed Melina. "I saw you and felt your prayers. Thanks." He looked into the back seat." This guy was giving me a rough time but the prayers of the righteous availeth much."

"Yeah, yeah, whatever," Major said.

"I certainly didn't mean for you to have to spend your evening scouring the streets of Essex and Union county. This is not how I want to spend time with you," Naimond said as Alex turned into the Manders driveway.

"I'm glad that I could help," Alex said and smiled.

"I know that this is a crazy question and may not make sense to you but I'd like to take you out for a nice dinner," Naimond said.

"Why is that a crazy question?" Alex asked.

"Well, I'm leaving at the end of the week but don't want to do so until I get to know you a little better," Naimond explained.

"Oh, I see," Alex responded. She was sad to hear that he was leaving and wanted to spend time with him as well.

Naimond walked around to open Alex's door. She took his extended hand and exited the car. She stood.

Her face was inches from his. Her heels evened the playing field so she wasn't too much shorter than him. After all, she was 5'8' barefoot.

"May I call it a date?" Naimond asked.

"What else would it be?" Alex countered.

They walked into the house and found Melina, Daniel and Baylor sitting in the kitchen.

"Where's Major?" Naimond asked.

"He's with Mom," Daniel said. His eyes lifted to signal that they were on the 2nd floor.

"How is he?" Alex asked

"He is ashamed of himself but doesn't want to act like it," Baylor said. "I can't believe he caused all of this mess."

"That is just like Major," Naimond said as he shook his head, still not understanding his little brother.

Alex and Melina just shrugged their shoulders.

"We'd better get going," Melina said. "I think that you guys need to spend some time as a family."

Alex nodded, looking in Naimond's direction. "Call me. Here is my number." Alex scribbled her home number on the back of her business card.

"I will and thanks for today," Naimond stated quietly.

"I wanted to help but you are welcome," Alex whispered.

Melina stood and pulled Daniel to his feet playfully. She kissed him on the cheek softly and whispered that she'd talk to him later. They smiled into each others eyes. He mouthed. 'I love you'. She returned the sentiment in the same manner.

Daniel walked the women to the door and made sure that they were in their cars safely. He then watched them as they both drove away.

He promised Melina that there wouldn't be any drama tonight and he would try hard to keep his promise. Major was a tough one and knew what buttons to push. He hoped that Major would not remember the buttons and more importantly that his "talk" with their mom had made a difference.

The Son

Twenty Five

He shall receive the blessings from the Lord and
righteousness from the God of his salvation.
Psalms 24:5

Baylor was feeling very triumphant after passing his French final exam. Charla had been a great help and he'd not only learned French but was learning more and more about God everyday. After a three year delay, he would finally be able to graduate from college. Their tutoring sessions during the last months had helped him immensely. He'd miraculously passed his mid-terms with flying colors.

Spending time with a woman like Charla was just what he felt he needed. He wanted to be Charla's man, her one and only but he worried that she still harbored feelings for Major. He couldn't and wouldn't step to her unless he was sure that she was over him.

Walking up to her apartment, he looked down at the beautiful bouquet of roses. They were yellow, pink and red. He didn't want to get all red roses and have her burst his bubble.

"Hey, Baylor. I didn't think that we had a session today," she said as she opened the door to greet him. As a matter of fact, she was pretty sure that they had concluded their lessons. Charla stepped to the side and allowed Baylor entrance into her apartment.

As he entered, he saw Major sitting on the sofa. He looked very comfortable and this made Baylor very uncomfortable.

"What's up, man?" Major said to his brother. His brother wore a smile but it wasn't one of the smug ones that he was used to seeing.

"It's all good," Baylor said and turned to Charla. "These are for you."

Charla's face lit up. She loved flowers and even more, she loved receiving roses. She smiled unabashedly and kissed Baylor full on the lips.

"Oh..... Baylor, I'm sorry." I shouldn't have done that, she thought to herself. She had wanted to do that for a while but kept her cool. Now, she just knew that her cover was blown.

"I'm not offended by any means," Baylor returned. He couldn't help grinning.

She turned and headed toward the small kitchen to find a vase for her flowers.

"Well look..., let me get going," Major said. He stood and grabbed his jean jacket, walked toward the door and stood next to Baylor.

"I'm not mad at you, man," Major whispered "You are what she needs. I used to be what she wanted but no more."

"Man, I..."

"No explanations necessary, man. I knew it was over when she put me out. It took a while for me to get the point but better late than never, right?" Major said with a chuckle.

Baylor couldn't get over how subdued Major was. It was just weird seeing him like this. This is not my brother, Baylor thought to himself.

"She is a good woman, Major," Baylor said in an effort to explain his interest in Charla. "Beautiful inside and out."

"You don't have to tell me... I missed the boat," Major said almost too calm. "Do you want to do the same thing?" he warned.

"Hey what are you guys talking about?" Charla asked as she walked back into the living area with the roses beautifully arranged in a glass vase.

"I'm just heading out," Major said. He walked over to Charla. "I'm sure that I'll see you two around." He winked at her, letting her know that all was okay.

They had talked about Baylor. Charla had been honest with him and told him how much she liked his younger brother. She said that she felt uneasy about doing anything about it because she used to be involved with him.

Major was not as stupid as some may have thought. He knew that he wasn't what Charla really wanted or needed and Baylor could be. At least he could keep close tabs on how she was being treated because his brother would be the one dating her. He wanted nothing but the best for her. He would always have much love for his Charla. Truth be told, she was just too good for him.

Charla winked back and Major let himself out. "Take it light."

"Mom, I'm back!" Daniel shouted as he entered the house with Chinese take-out. He told his mother not to cook and he would take care of dinner. She said that she wanted Chinese, so Chinese it was. She seemed a little more fatigued than usual and said that she was feeling a little dizzy. Although, a little worried, Daniel prayed that his mother would soon come out of it. She had been almost monk-like since Naimond left town. The end of his visit with the family was good and it seemed as if all the fences had been mended but something still seemed out of whack. The best part was when all four brothers went out to dinner and bowled a few games at Bowltastic in Hillside, the Friday before Naimond left.

Major, the competitive one, had to show off his bowling expertise by bowling all strikes the first game. Thankfully, he had finally taken responsibility for his part in what went down the day that their father died. He admitted to all of them, even their Mom, that he was wrong. He asked for Naimond's forgiveness and confessed that he had been hoping that Naimond would come home so he could at least own up to what he'd done. He'd admitted that he just didn't expect it to happen so quickly. He wasn't ready and didn't want his family to hate him. The timing was not what he expected but he told his brothers that he had always been a selfish person and needed to put an end to it but just didn't know how.

Major knew that he needed direction because it was something he sorely lacked. His father had made the same statement and so had a number of other people. He realized that those people were not demeaning him but trying to help. He needed help but didn't know how to ask without sounding like some sort of whimp.

"I just need you guys to help me become a better man. I know that I have to be one. I know now that I had a good example in Dad," Major finally confessed.

"Be careful of what you ask for," Naimond said and clinked beer bottles with Major. Naimond realized that his brother needed help and although he still felt pangs of hurt when he thought of the years that he lost with his Mom and family, he resolved to make an attempt to forgive his younger brother.

Daniel just enjoyed the night with his brothers. Baylor, although wanting a beer, decided not to indulge. He really didn't see any harm but didn't think that he should drink that night.

Naimond admitted that he shouldn't have stayed out of contact for so long but he thought that if the family knew the real truth, they'd hate him.

"Naimond?" Daniel asked. "Do you think that Mom knew why you left?" Daniel had to ask the question.

"I'm not sure if she knew the real reason but I know that she found out that I knew that I wasn't her son," Naimond said after gulping down the last of his beer. "The letter I left inferred that I knew that she wasn't my biological mother."

"What did your letter say, man?" Daniel asked.

Major and Baylor leaned in to hear Naimond's response.

"Man, I'm not going to tell you that. That letter was for Mom and for Mom only. If you want to know, then you ask her," Naimond said.

Although enjoying his time with his brothers, Naimond needed to get home because his small newspaper, *Portland's Journal,* needed him back. He was the editor-in-chief of the growing African-American weekly paper. He'd achieved his goal of becoming a reporter and now he was the editor-in-chief of his own publication. He told his brothers how much he loved it and how he didn't think that it would have happened if he would have stayed in Jersey.

"I guess everything does happen for a reason," he confirmed.

Melina and Alex joined them around nine o'clock for the third game and much to everyone's surprise, Alex was an outstanding bowler. Major couldn't stomach the competition and was bowling gutter balls by the end of the game.

"She was just lucky. After all it was my third game," Major said, making excuses.

"Whatever you want to tell yourself is fine with me," Alex said, extending her thumb to the left and her index finger north, making an "L" for loser.

Everyone laughed, even Major. When the laughter died down Baylor leaned in and asked.

"So Daniel, what made you decide to do it man? Weren't you scared? Being a minister is a big deal," Baylor said. He was curious because wanted to make a commitment to the Lord but was afraid that he would have to change his whole life.

"I mean telling the world that you are a Christian and really want to live for Christ... Wasn't it hard to change some things in your life?"

"Baylor, although I had accepted Christ when I was in high school, I hadn't made the decision to live for Christ until my last years of college and even up until recently I wasn't totally committed. Initially, I was scared but then I began to read the bible to help me. Baylor man, you have nothing to fear."

Daniel knew that Baylor was delaying accepting Christ because he realized that he would have to change.

"Let God change whatever needs to be changed. The only thing you have to do is accept and believe in Him."

Baylor, looking a little embarrassed said, "Man, you know that I sang in the choir at church and was involved in a lot of the youth church activities."

"Yeah, but did you ever accept him as your personal Savior?" Daniel asked.

"No… I didn't think… I used to study with Dad all the time," Baylor stammered, trying to dodge the question.

"But did you accept Jesus? Were you born again?"

"Daniel, man, I guess that I never really accepted Jesus but I do know how."

"Do you want to?" Melina asked, feeling her heart leap. She was excited for Baylor.

"I think… Yes."

"Right now?" Major asked, eyes rolling. He was trying to do better but this was really not the place, he reasoned inwardly.

"Sorry if that is going to ruin your good time Major, but, yes, now. Daniel, I see how God is using you and I want him to use me too. I know that God is real. I believe in his son Jesus. "

"That is all I need to hear," Daniel concluded as he pulled out his pocket bible. "Romans 10: 9 says, *That if thou shalt confess with thy mouth the Lord Jesus and shalt believe in thine heart that God hath raised him from the dead, thou shalt be saved.*"

"I believe that Jesus Christ is the son of the Living God and that He died on the cross for my sins. I believe that He was resurrected and now sits on the right hand of the Father in heaven . I know that Jesus Christ is the only way to God." Baylor said the words with conviction. Daniel, Melina and Alex whooped and hollered.

"Praise God!

"Thank You Jesus!"

"One more for the kingdom!!"

The Son

Naimond, although happy for Baylor, didn't join in on the celebration. Major, thinking that this was all too much, started walking away when Baylor was talking.

"Baylor we are proud of you!" Alex said.

"Yes we are!" Daniel said as he pulled his brother to his feet and hugged him. "Don't worry about what you need to change. When you accept Christ, the Holy Spirit will convict you and guide you. When you need wisdom ask God. Remember Psalms 37: 23 *The steps of a good man are ordered by the Lord and he delighteth in thy way.* Trust that God will direct you."

"Daniel, don't forget to give him Psalms 32:8 *I will instruct thee and teach thee in thy way which thou shalt go, I will guide thee with mine eye,"* Melina said excitedly.

"That's a good one, love," Daniel said, smiling proudly at her.

The remaining group held hands right in the middle of the bowling alley and Daniel started to pray.

"Father God, we just want to thank you for simply revealing yourself to Baylor. Your word is so true. Flesh and blood could not have revealed your Son to him but only you could do it through the Holy Spirit. We thank you for Baylor and trust and believe that he will do great things in your name. We thank you again for our brother Baylor and we thank you for making it happen. In Jesus name..."

They all said, "Amen"

Daniel couldn't help but laugh aloud remembering the way people were looking at them when they left the bowling alley.

Naimond left around noon the next day. The visit had been a good one and Naimond went so far as to say that he was glad that he came home although apprehensive initially. He was intrigued by the scene in the bowling alley and would seek God but wouldn't make any promises. He was satisfied that he was reconnected with his family but there was still some additional healing that needed to take place.

From what Melina told Daniel, Naimond and Alex had spent the better part of the remaining night talking and solidifying their friendship. Alex seemed to really like Naimond and he apparently felt the same. Naimond declined an offer to the airport because Alex offered to drive him. Naimond smiled broadly when he said that he wanted some alone time with his new friend. The family's goodbyes were done at the house. Mom cried a little and he and Major parted on what seemed good terms. Baylor was also sad to see him go but promised that he'd go out to Oregon to visit in the spring. Daniel was really going to miss his brother. Although he hadn't returned his correspondence in the years past, Naimond said that he'd really read the letters. His elder brother admitted that they provided the opportunity for him to get to know Daniel.

The nagging feeling that something was incomplete was a constant for days after Naimond's departure. Daniel realized that Naimond, although a good guy had not accepted Christ although he did say that he would "seek" Him out.

Wasn't he supposed to reconnect his family? Wasn't it his assignment to bring his family to Jesus? He had certainly played a role in reconnecting the family. They were all together again. They could contact one another whenever they needed but he didn't feel like he'd been successful. He observed that Major was coming to grips with who he was and who he needed to be. That in itself showed signs of maturity.

Better late than never, Daniel thought.

Baylor was now saved and a man of God and Naimond was back in their lives again. Still, Daniel felt that the task was far from over.

Daniel, being reminded that he was hungry after hearing his stomach growl, placed the Chinese food for his mother on a plate and grabbed some utensils from the drawer. "What are you thinking about so hard that it's causing you to frown?" his mother asked.

Daniel hadn't heard her descend the stairs. He turned to greet her. She was wearing a white and blue flowered print house coat and her favorite blue terry cloth slippers. Her hair was in rollers covered with a powder blue scarf. Her smile was genuine.

"I was just thinking about our family," Daniel said.

"Well Baylor is certainly something these days. That boy sure is in love with a pretty chocolate girl. It's too bad Major couldn't get his act together," Lila smiled.

She was glad that her baby boy had found someone to love him. She could tell that Charla Norris would be good for her son. She didn't know why she didn't feel uneasy about the fact that Charla had dated another one of her sons but it simply didn't bother her. That boy was on fire to find a job. You can't tell her that the change wasn't due to the Lord and that good girl.

"Praise the Lord," she said aloud.

"Yes, indeed. He is worthy," Daniel agreed. He too was thinking about the changes in his baby brother. God is good.

Twenty Six

*Not withstanding, the Lord stood with me and
strengthened me; that by me the preaching might be fully
known and that all of the Gentiles might hear: and I was
delivered out of the mouth of the lion.*
2 Timothy 4:17

Daniel stood once hearing his name called. He
had been praying as Pastor Cuffe introduced him to the
congregation as the speaker of the hour. Admittedly, he
was a little nervous about speaking in front of the
congregation for the first time.

This was his trial sermon. It was the Christmas
Eve service and he felt honored that Elias granted him the
opportunity to speak during this service. Christmas was
always his favorite holiday and he wanted to truly be used
of God on this holy holiday; the celebration of Christ's
birth.

As he stood appraising the congregation, Daniel's
mind traveled for a brief moment to when he was kneeling
in the holding cell in Wisconsin. He had been running
from his appointment. God had been patient up until that
point or so it seemed. He had done things the way he
wanted and lived the way he wanted. He knew the Lord
Jesus was his Savior but he was not committed to living
for Him. He didn't think that he had to make it a true life
decision. He foolishly thought that God would be okay
with that. That, he now realized, was simply not true.
When he thought of what could have happened to him...

He was grateful to the Lord for delivering him
from certain ruin. What would he have done without
Jesus? He smiled knowing that God had predestined him
to be here at this moment and decided to begin.

"Let the redeemed of the Lord say so!" Daniel
shouted to his audience.

He was bowled over by the "Amens" and "Praise
Gods" that he received in response. He smiled as he
surveyed the sanctuary.

"Many thanks to Pastor Elias for allowing me the opportunity to deliver a word on behalf of the Lord on today, Christmas Eve. I'm so grateful to him for his kindness and patience. I'm more than honored to be taught by that wonderful man of God. Let us all Praise God for our Pastor, Elias Cuffe and his lovely wife."

The church stood and applause seemed to shake the church.

"Amen, Amen," Daniel said and opened his bible. "Thanks to the entire He Is Risen church family. *My* church family."

As Daniel clapped, his eyes traveled to the fourth row on the right side of the sanctuary. All of his brothers, save Naimond were in attendance. Charla, Alex and Melina were sitting there as well. His mother was sitting on the end of the row near the center aisle with her festive red silk outfit and red wide brimmed hat. Her smile exhibited joy and pride. Daniel winked at Melina. She was a vision of beauty. The coral suit that she wore illuminated her skin. He had never seen her in a hat before. She wore the mushroom styled light beige crown with a coral stripe dancing around its circumference with style. She kissed two fingers and blew on them. He felt the kiss land like a feather on his lips. He couldn't wait to join her and her family for dinner tonight. There was so much to talk about.

After audibly praying for the assistance of the Holy Spirit, he opened his eyes, already feeling strengthened and exhaled.

"What would we do without Jesus?" Daniel asked. "Think about it church? While you are thinking about it, turn with me to Romans 3:23-25. According to the bible and in this particular instance, the author Paul tells us that all have sinned and come short of the glory of God. We have been justified by Jesus by His grace through the redemption that is Christ Jesus. Because of the blood that He shed; His death and resurrection, we are redeemed and now all of our sins are past and forgiven by faith." Daniel stopped and watched the audience. He saw nods and decided to move on. "We were doomed to death. Do you understand that?" He again saw nods of understanding.

"Teach, Rev. Manders," Sister Cuffe said, smiling proudly at her adopted son.

Daniel continued. "Romans 5:8-9 states that because God loved us so much that while we were sinners, Christ died for us. We have been saved from the wrath that we were right on schedule to experience. We also enjoy God the Father through our Lord and Savior Jesus Christ because we have been atoned through Him!"

"Alright now!" he heard someone say.

"That's right. That is a 'Thank You, Jesus' moment right there," Daniel said smiling. "Does anyone realize that we were headed for all kinds of mess if it weren't for Jesus!? He saved us from all of the hell that awaited us because we had no direct access to God. He is the one way to God. He says that no man can get to the Father except through him. He is the only way."

"He is the only way Reverend," Deacon Charles said.

"Because of Christ we have been reconciled to God. Does everyone now know why Jesus is so important?"

Daniel didn't feel as though he was getting enough interaction from the congregation.

"Say amen if you understand," he requested fervently.

"AMEN!" was the congregation's response.

Daniel laughed. "That's what I'm talking about. I knew that I wasn't here by myself."

"Amen, Reverend," he heard Elias say from behind him.

"Okay. How many of us think about how important Jesus is on a daily basis?" Daniel inquired of the congregation.

A sprinkle of hands went up. Some nodded.

"How many think of the importance of Jesus during the holidays. You all say, 'Jesus is the reason for the season'."

Many laughed and said, "Preach, Rev."

Every hand in the church was up.

Satisfied that he made his point, Daniel said, "We just read and saw what a big role Christ played in our freedom from death right? So why do we only celebrate Him on Christmas? He is a gift from God to us. The wages of sin is death but the gift of God is eternal life through Jesus Christ our Lord. Christ made life, everlasting life, possible because He died for us. He didn't have to be born to endure the death that was not fit for a dog but He did it for us. We weren't worthy but He, Jesus, took the lashes, and the punches and the kicks for us. You all saw the movie, *Passion of Christ.* I'm sure that it was ten times worse than what we saw. He did all of that for me and you. How dare you not recognize His importance in your life everyday that you draw breath!"

The church was clapping and some were standing on their feet in agreement with Daniel. Daniel felt the spirit of God working in him.

"Yes, He is the reason for the Christmas season but more importantly, He is the reason for you being able to walk in abundance, He is the reason for you to be able to call those things that be not as though they are!" Daniel could feel perspiration on his brow. He wiped the moisture from his temple and continued. "Do you not understand that His name, Jesus, is the name that is above all other names? Jesus, our Savior Jesus, is sitting at the right hand of the Father making intercession for us. He is our go-to guy."

Daniel stopped to engage his audience. "Ephesians tells us that we are no longer strangers and foreigners but fellow citizens with the saints and the household of God. Oh , thank you Jesus!"

"Thank you, Jesus!" someone shouted.

"Thank you, Lord," another said in thanksgiving.

"Because of Jesus, my Savior, I can boldly go to my Lord and make my requests known and know that I will receive an answer! He said if you ask it in my name, Jesus, and believe, you will receive it. I can exercise my faith because I know that Jesus has paid the ultimate price to make me a part of the family. I am a son! Call me righteous since Jesus changed my nature!"

"Preach, Preacher," Deacon Jackson said as he stood to his feet.

"Let me get to the part of this that I like and really had to come to understand. So many times we think that we have to endure all of the things that the devil tries to place in our way, like sickness, poverty, depression..."

Daniel watched the congregation. He turned to his mother and she was rocking in her seat like the old saints used to do when they were getting a true word from God.

"The bible tells us that God has placed Jesus' name above everything. All we have to do is believe on him. His name is above, sickness, because by His stripes we are healed. His name is above poverty, because, Jesus came to give us life and life more abundantly. Hallelujah! You don't believe me? Let's go to it in the word and then I'll close," Daniel promised. "Turn to Luke, the 12th chapter, verses 22 through 30. Jesus is telling his disciples that they should not worry about their life, what they will eat or drink or be of a doubtful mind. God knows that we need all of these things to survive. His word tells us that we should seek the kingdom of God first and all other things like: cars, homes, and beautiful clothing, will be added. It is our Heavenly Father's good pleasure to give us all of those things. Church, I can remember the old saints saying almost daily that they had never seen the righteous forsaken or their seed, meaning their children, begging bread. Because of Jesus, we can have all of what we want and need. Simply obey Him and look to Him. Recognize His importance in our lives and give Him the praise and honor due Him." Daniel smiled broadly.

"Church, don't you realize that there is something about the name of Jesus? Demons have to flee. Depressed people have to get happy and sickness has to surrender to good health. Jesus, our Savior, conquered all of that when he rose from the dead and said that All

POWER was in His hands. We have that same power. He told us that we did. We can lay hands on the sick in the name of Jesus and they will be healed. We can call on the name of Jesus and every circumstance has to turn around for the good. Because of Jesus, we have liberty! We are free! He paid the price and all He asks is that we serve Him and love one another. We need to exercise our faith and know that He is ALL that we need! An old song says, Jesus Paid it ALL, all to him I owe. We owe it all to Jesus! The Lilly of the Valley, the Bright Morning Star and the Prince of Peace. He is no longer that baby lying in the manger. He is the Risen Savior, Our Good Shepard. When we hear his voice, we know it is He because He has bought us with a price and the price was His blood. Oh, glory to God! He is the reason for not only this season but for every season. Hallelujah!"

The church was again on their feet.

"Say Jesus!" Daniel shouted.

"Jesus!" the congregation returned thunderously.

"Something has to happen when you say His name! JESUS!" Daniel exclaimed. Some of the congregation had begun to dance in the middle aisle.

"JESUS!" Charla shouted as her hands flew up into the air. Her eyes were closed and she was saying the name of her Savior over and over again.

"My Lord!" Daniel said, shaking his head and thanking God for his Son. "All you have to do is say his name and by faith, things have got to change!"

"Thank You, Lord! Thank You, Lord!" Melina had begun shouting thanks.

"God, you are so good and we thank you! I thank you for allowing me to be used by you. Lord, so many things might have kept me from getting to this moment and to this day but thank You for the victory. You always cause me to triumph."

Daniel didn't care that he could be heard by the congregation. One day, he would share his testimony. He was overwhelmed with thanksgiving. He walked out into the aisle and embraced his mother. She was standing on her feet. The tears were silently streaming down her face. She was smiling jubilantly as she squeezed him back.

"Thank you, Jesus," were the only words that he heard.

Major remained seated but he admittedly couldn't deny a feeling that he couldn't explain bubbling inside of him. He tried to fight it as he looked around at the congregation. Everyone was running around the church, giving God thanks for Jesus or standing, honoring God with praise. He was in awe of the whole scene. His heart was stirring but he remained overtly calm.

"I guess that boy can preach!" he said and smiled in his brother's direction.

Baylor nodded as he stood clapping, giving God praise.

Major watched Daniel in his purple ministerial robe now standing behind the podium in the pulpit. Major remembered the dream that Daniel shared with them so many years ago. His mouth was now agape realizing that Daniel's dream had just come true.

The Son

Twenty Seven

*Behold, I stand at the door and knock: if any man hear my
voice and open the door, I will come in to him and will sup
with him and he with me.*
Revelation 3:20

Lila decided that she would clean up a little and
the first place she wanted to hit was Major's room. He
had been staying close to home for the last couple of
weeks and she found it odd because he was usually always
out and about.

She grabbed an old rag and Jubilee furniture
polish and started clearing off his dresser. He had the
same mahogany bureau and dresser since he was a
teenager. She smiled as she thought of the many times she
tried to teach that boy how to really clean and dust. To
this day, she believed that he knew how, but just like a lot
of men, acted as if they just couldn't get their brain around
the concept. Realizing that she had been hoodwinked, she
would enter his space once every month to do the job he
said that he couldn't.

She threw some strewn clothes onto the floor and
moved all of his loose change and colognes to the bed so
that she could get started. She noticed a piece of paper
coming out of a book that looked like it was a modernized
bible.

She picked up the book and turned it so that she
could read the title, New King James Student Bible.

What is this? Lila thought. "He is reading the
bible?" she asked aloud. The paper that was sticking out
simply read Romans 10:9.

Interesting, Lila thought.

She began the cleaning project and thought
nothing more of what she found until she saw a notebook.
It looked new. Inside there was one page written upon.
There were a number of scriptures that had been scribbled
down but only one jarred Lila's memory.

John 3:16; *For God so loved the world that he gave his only begotten son. Whosoever believeth on him should not perish but have everlasting life.*

She completed her cleaning of the dresser, bureau, and night stand and even cleaned the mirror with Windex. His items were neatly placed back where she'd found them but she wanted to be sure that he knew that she'd been there. She was sure this intrusion would speed up his pace in finding a place of his own. She made his bed and gathered all of his clothes and threw them in a pile in the corner. She didn't want to pick them up to place them in a hamper to have something fall out and give her a heart attack. She turned around and surveyed the room. It looked a lot better. She turned off the light and left the room, leaving the door ajar. She would talk to Daniel about what he thought was going on. She had no idea what to think. Major had been raised in the church, knowing the word of God but as soon as he became a teenager, his interest and adherence seem to stop cold. She wondered what caused him to renew his interest in the bible, specifically Jesus Christ.

Major knew that he had to do something but he didn't really know what or how. He knew that he had to come clean but felt that after all he had done, no one would believe him. Why should they? He'd been nothing but trouble. In the last few months he had tried to show that he could be a different person but it wasn't working. He was beginning to understand that couldn't he completely make the transformation without God. He knew that he could be a decent guy but he wanted to be more.

He wanted to be someone that he could be proud of; someone God could be proud of.

He didn't know how to handle what he'd found out about Daniel while staying at Anthony's. Instead of being vindictive and rubbing it in Daniel's face, he'd decided to keep it to himself.

The Son

That girl Eva knew she could run her mouth. He'd met her when he stayed overnight at Anthony's house the night everything hit the fan about his father's death.

Anthony was talking business with her and she noticed that he looked familiar and asked him his name.

"Why?" Major said cockily. She just wants to jump my bones, he had thought arrogantly. "I don't mess with white girls," he said and turned away without a second thought.

"Do you know a guy named Daniel Manders?" she inquired, unrelenting. "He lives in Wisconsin but grew up in this area.

"Yeah, he's my brother," Major's interest in the pale princess increased. He knew she was in deep and wondered how golden boy would know her.

"I got in a little trouble last year but it worked itself out," Eva said, laughing. She continued to look at Major but when he didn't crack a smile, she stopped. "He didn't tell you?"

"Apparently, not," Major said squinting his eyes. "Why don't you tell me the funny story?" he asked, his face becoming hard.

Eva, now reluctant, told the story of how she used Daniel and how he miraculously got off without even a blemish on his record. She, on the other hand was placed on probation but that was only because of some help from her friends who had contacts in Madison.

Major was shocked to hear that his "could-do-no-wrong" brother was in jail for possession and intent to sell illegal substances. He wanted to rub this in his face as soon as he saw Daniel. Even if he got off without even an ink mark on his life's file, he was still hand-cuffed and placed in a jail.

Major stopped and thought about this news. "This was why he came home. Wasn't it?" he audibly asked himself, knowing the answer.

"So you set him up?" Major asked Eva.

185

"No, it wasn't like that. I liked your brother. He was nice. I would get high in his bathroom and he wouldn't know a thing about it. I even kept a stash of the stuff that I wanted to sell at his place. He had no idea."

"He was just your little punk, huh?" Major said understanding now that Daniel was really the victim.

Disgusted, he turned from Eva, not even bothering to dismiss her.

The night Daniel found Major and took him back to their mother's house, he'd promised himself that he'd keep a lid on this information until he got a chance to talk to Daniel alone.

That had been months ago. Major couldn't air Daniel's business to anyone. It would be Major's little secret until Daniel found out that he knew. Major decided that he would never tell Daniel that he knew about the Madison incident.

Major placed his head back on the pillow, deciding to turn in and get to sleep early. He wanted to surprise everyone and go to church with the family. He felt the need to hear something that would help him make right decision.

Daniel and Melina were sitting on her sofa nestled together comfortably watching one of her favorite movies; *Devil In A Blue Dress*.

Melina loved Denzel Washington's portrayal of Eazy Rollins and always liked seeing Don Cheadle as Mouse. She wished that Walter Mosley's book, *Black Betty* would be made into a feature film as well.

Daniel seemed pensive all night. She caught him staring at her and smiling for what seemed like the longest time. She didn't think he even realized he was staring for as long as he was. When she heard him speaking to himself while in her bathroom, she shrugged it off, thinking that he was probably preparing for the youth class the next day and was inadvertently reviewing it aloud. Truth be told, he had been preoccupied lately and she was beginning to get a little worried about him. They had been dating for eight months and were becoming closer every day. It was funny how they had quickly fallen into step with each other. She knew him and he, for the most part, knew her. She knew that she loved him and he always told her that he loved her.

"Is everything okay, baby?" Melina asked looking up into the eyes that didn't always tell her what was going on in that head of his.

"I'm fine. I'm just enjoying this time with you, baby," Daniel said. He looked down at her and kissed her forehead. "I could get used to this."

Daniel seemed to jerk forward as if someone had pushed him from beneath the cushions behind his back. His countenance revealed a look of surprise and confusion and then it melted into a look of comprehension. He laughed and then breathed. Now, Melina was really worried.

"You sure you don't want to go out? We don't have to order the pizza," Melina said. Maybe he just needed to be out enjoying some fresh air, she thought.

"I was thinking about us and how I don't want to leave you anymore at night to go home," he said. Daniel sat up. His expression changed once again. He took her hand in his. "I'm so happy with you Melina. I knew from the first moment, that you were the one that I was supposed to be with for life."

Melina gave him a "yeah right" look.

"Okay, well not that first moment but it was certainly the next day. I just know that you took my breath away and I started loving you the first time we shared cheesecake on our first date at Mighty Plate." He stood up and pulled her up to stand with him.

"I prayed that *she* would be you and you are. You are the woman that I want to be my wife, to bring my children into this world and love until God takes us home."

Melina's eyes began to fill with tears and her nose began to tingle. This was a tell-tale sign that she was about to cry.

"You are my friend and once we are married, if you'll have me, you will be my only lover. I want you Melina and no one else."

Daniel lowered and kneeled in front of her. "I hadn't planned on doing this tonight but it has been on my mind. I don't have a ring but I just feel the need to cement this tonight. I know that I need you as my wife. Like you said, you are my helpmate." Daniel exhaled and then with liquid filling his eyes causing them to shine like the setting sun through painted glass, he asked, "Melina Rose Lawrence, will you marry me?"

Melina smiled and held Daniel's gaze. As she looked in his expectant eyes, she responded, *"Let him kiss me with the kisses of his mouth; for thy love is better than wine."*

"Song of Solomon," he confirmed

"First chapter, second verse," she said.

"I am yours."

"And I will always be yours," she said.

They kissed sweetly as their tears mingled with one another's. They laughed, feeling giddy and empowered at the same time.

The Son

Twenty Eight

But the natural man receiveth not the things of the Spirit of God; for they are foolishness unto him; neither can they know them, because they are spiritually discerned.
1 Corinthians 2:14

The house was alive with Lila's singing and Major awoke up with a strange feeling of expectancy. This was a new and unusual way to greet the day, Major thought. He sat up in his bed and noticed for the first time that his room had been touched up. He smirked and remembered that his mother would always make her way into his room every so often to keep the house up to par.

"Just in case something should happen to me, when people come to the house they won't find it in a state of disarray and dirty. At least they'll know that I tried to keep a clean house," she'd said on more than one occasion.

She would always say that to guilt her boys into doing their part. The line had never worked on Major but for some reason today, he felt a little ashamed that his mother had to come into his room at his age and clean up behind him.

As he walked over to the mirror, he noticed that the loose change was arranged neatly and his new bible, the one he had tried to keep a secret, was sitting on his dresser with the notebook under it.

"Get up, Major, we are having breakfast now because we are going to be leaving for church right after!" Baylor shouted through the slightly open door.

"Go ahead and eat. I'll jump in the shower and ride with you," Major shouted back.

There was silence and then the door opened just a little more.

"Major, did you say that you were going to church with us?" Baylor asked.

"I think getting to church today may do me some good," Major said and walked past him toward the bathroom. "Don't leave without me. I won't take long."

The astonishment the family felt when Major announced that he was joining them at church was nothing compared to Daniel's. He was in the middle of greeting the members when he stared at Major openly until the family found their seats. Major had visited before at Charla's request but surely under protest. It was obvious that he had come today of his own volition.

In an effort to focus his attention back on service, he nodded to the organist to signal that he could begin the song that started the choir processional. The musicians started playing *You are My Daily Bread*, recorded by Fred Hammond and the choir started walking in. Daniel loved the song. He knew that he couldn't sing like Pastor Cuffe but he started singing anyway. He looked up into the balcony and saw Melina smiling. He then realized that he sounded terrible. He laughed and continued to sing as they continued to smile at each other. She was even more beautiful as his fiancée. He strutted over to the choir director that was singing behind the standing microphone and handed him the wireless one. Donny took the microphone and smiled. Daniel retreated to the pulpit and stood clapping his hands as the choir, now in their places in the choir loft, began to sing louder and with more vigor.

"You are my daily bread, you are my living well, you are my present help..."

The congregation was standing and enjoying the song. Daniel's eyes traveled back to Major and at that moment Major turned and they looked at each other. Daniel nodded and smiled. Major, true to form, did not return the smile but nodded.

Major looked around the church. It was already packed. He lied to himself, not wanting to admit that he needed to re-evaluate his life now that the truth had been revealed about the reason why Naimond really left. He had been selfish all of his life; always thinking of no one but himself. He even tried to bribe his own father. He shifted all of the blame on Naimond, and then poor Daniel, who had nothing to do with the whole sordid affair. He'd been promiscuous for as long as he remembered and he couldn't remember any of their names. The woman that he really wanted, tired of his ways and wound up dating his baby brother. He had gained absolutely nothing. Trickery, lying and being deceitful had left him with a big fat zero and that is exactly how he felt; like a zero. He was living with his mother, didn't have a real job, no real friends and no one really thought much of him.

During the ride home, the night before Naimond went back to Portland, the brothers talked about God and what being saved really meant.

"It's just acknowledging that Jesus Christ is Lord. He died on the cross for your sins. Christ was without sin but because He loved us so much and knew that He was the only way you would be able to get access to God, he gave his life as the sacrifice. Because of that unselfish act, performed more than 2000 years ago, we now have access to everything that we need. We can have health, success and most importantly a friend that will never leave us or forsake us. He will always be in our corner even when we screw up. He loves us just that much."

Major, naturally understanding what Daniel just explained, still didn't buy it. He understood the logic behind it because he wasn't a dummy but he just didn't believe that he could have a friend like Jesus; after all that he'd done to his family. He just couldn't fathom that kind of forgiveness. He never felt like anyone was in his corner. Daniel was the good one, Baylor was the baby and Naimond was the eldest. He was just Major.

"Major, do you understand?" Daniel asked.

"I understand but how can I know that Jesus will intercede for me and help me if I decided to surrender my life to him," Major responded with a confused expression.

How can I simply turn over my life to someone that I can't even see? He thought. His mother, his dad,

Baylor, Charla and of course Daniel had done it, but how could they?

"We surrender our lives to Christ by faith. We believe that He knows what is best for us and He is always right. We always don't understand what He's doing, but by reading his word, the bible, we can have peace in knowing that what He decides for us is best. That's why it is so important that we read the bible because the world and even some so-called Christians will have you believing everything but what God says. Romans 1:17 says, *for the righteousness of God is revealed from faith to faith; as it is written, the just shall live by faith.* One can be saved, or become righteous only through faith. The relationship between man and God proceeds from Jesus. That is why you only have to truly *believe* in Jesus to be saved." Daniel stopped talking for a moment and looked over at his brother and tried to read his face. "Do you understand?"

"I get it. I knew all of this but the key is to have faith. That is the foundation huh?" Major said.

"That's it. We believe in Jesus Christ by faith. We can't see him but know that He is who we believe he is. The more I read His word and the more I seek Him and trust him by faith, I move from glory to glory. That is why I'm here today. Believe me, Major, I had my issues with surrendering to God but something happened that made it clear that I had to trust Him because I was totally screwing up my life," Daniel confessed.

The last statement struck a chord with Major. He was screwing up his life. He knew right from wrong but just thought it was too hard to make the right choice. He also remembered what Eva said and put two and two together. He knew that Daniel was talking about his run in with the police and how that in its own way resulted in Daniel answering the call to the ministry.

"Don't over think it, Major. Because I believe in Christ's resurrection, I put my trust in Christ. That's all I need to comprehend. We of course need to study, but that is all it takes really. The knowledge can't be grasped by the wisest brainiac unless that person accepts God's message. The bible says that those who reject God's message are fools." Daniel chuckled looking at Major. "If I know anything, I know that you are not a fool."

Twenty Nine
For I neither received it from man, nor was I taught it, but
it came through the revelation of
Jesus Christ.
Galations 1:12

A jab to the rib cage brought Major back to the present. The choir finished their processional song and Pastor Cuffe began speaking. Major looked over at his brother with a "what did you do that for?" look.

Baylor comprehending the non-verbal question, cocked his head in the direction of their mother who eyed Major sternly and nodded toward the pulpit as if she was telling him to pay attention. He immediately felt like he did when he was a kid. His mind often wandered during service and his mother probably read his countenance and knew that he was somewhere else. He obediently turned his head in the direction of Pastor Cuffe.

"Church we need to stop being lazy," Cuffe stated, nodding and looking skyward as if responding to an invisible directive. "We need to stop thinking that we can simply call on the name of Jesus for help and expect Him to respond if we are not doing what we are supposed to be doing. Are we really doing what Jesus asked? Have you told anyone about Jesus this week? Isn't that the work that he asked us to do?"

A couple of "Amens" sprinkled the air and Pastor Cuffe continued.

"We can know who God is, recognize how important He is and believe in Him but if we don't do anything about it, what good is it? We can believe in Jesus, sure, but what good can it do if we just keep it to ourselves and not share the good news? James 2:17 says, *even so faith, if it hath not works, is dead, being alone.* Our works show our commitment to God. Our loving service further verifies our faith. Our service is what? Caring for the sick, feeding the hungry, right? Okay, when we do that, are we sharing the word of God? Are we telling people about Jesus?"

The Son

Pastor Cuffe looked around. There were a few guilty faces that looked back at him. "Beloved, I am not asking you to brow beat someone, just tell them about Jesus. Remember saints, You are the light of the world. Matthew 5:16 says clearly to *Let your light so shine before men, that they may see your good works and glorify your father which is in heaven.* Most of the people of this congregation are supposed to be the lights of the world. We have to love our enemies; *a work*, we have to pray for them that spitefully use us or speak badly about us; *a work*, we must say I'm sorry, even though we feel as though we are not wrong; *a big work.* Our sole job as Christians is to spread the gospel of Jesus and live according to his statutes. Work mixed with faith spells Christian success. Don't get me wrong, you don't have to spend your whole day at church or join every church auxiliary to do work. Saying hello to someone in the grocery story and telling them about the Lord is a work that will not only spread the gospel but bring souls into the kingdom."

Pastor Cuffe paused and surveyed the congregation. "I want you to ask yourself this question. Am I living the way God would have me to live? Am I showing others that God is real by the way I help others or the way I go about my daily activities. Saints, someone is always watching you and he or she is making their decision about Christ by how they see you behave. Are we being the lights that we are supposed to be? Jesus told us that we are the salt of the Earth. We are supposed to add to flavor to this world aren't we?

The church laughed at the way Pastor Cuffe emphasized the word flavor.

"God is faithful. He will do what He said He would do. Can we say the same? Now this isn't a shouting sermon but I truly believe that we need to realize the importance of service and how our works speak louder than anything that we can ever say. There are people here that are not sure how to become a servant of the most

High God. They need to see Christ in you because you are the living epistles. God is working through you."

Pastor Cuffe stopped speaking and turned as if someone had tapped him. He then seemingly assessed the congregation. "There is someone here, right now, who is being spoken to by the Holy Spirit. They want to give their life to Christ because of what they have seen and heard. They have witnessed a person that has not only had the faith but has seen their works and all praise and honor has been given not to themselves but to God for every victory. They have not only begun to understand the logic but understand the spiritual aspect, knowing only God can do what they need done in their lives."

Pastor Cuffe walked down into the congregation and searched a few faces. Major lowered his eyes to avoid looking at him. He awkwardly pretended to look at his church program.

"God is calling you," Pastor Cuffe said to the congregation. "You may not be all that you want to be right now and you recognize that. God has placed certain people in your life that have been a walking witness of His goodness. You are seeking and seeking but know now that Jesus is the only answer. It's okay. We are all working out our salvation."

The choir began to sing "Just As I Am" and Pastor Cuffe started back up to the pulpit. The congregation started clapping as a young woman walked down the aisle. She was smiling as she stood at the front of the church. Pastor Cuffe, descending the stairs once again embraced the pretty, brown skinned woman. Her smile was truly genuine. She looked as if she had been set free. The joy that she displayed radiated to everyone and the entire congregation stood to welcome her.

"Welcome, my sister," Pastor Cuffe said to the young lady. "God be praised. What is your name, sweetheart?"

"Venus Carpe," the woman responded.

"Well, we are happy to have you join our congregation, Venus."

The congregation began to applaud again and Venus started clapping with the rest of the congregation. "Who told you about He Is Risen?"

"Charla Norris. She works with me and she is always talking about Jesus. I became so curious about her church after our many talks about Jesus, I had to come. I want to have the kind of relationship that she has with Christ and know Him as *my* personal Savior." Venus beamed at Charla, who was sitting with Baylor and the rest of the Manders family.

"Amen, Amen," Pastor Cuffe said happily. "I guess your light was shining really bright, Charla," he said with a heartfelt laugh. "Come on up here and embrace your sister in Christ and walk with her back to her seat."

The church again, applauded as Charla made her way to the front of the church and hugged her co-worker and friend.

"Praise the Lord!" Charla exclaimed.

Charla had been praying for Venus and she erupted with thanks because God had once again proven himself to be faithful. It was as if Charla sent a current to Venus because she started jumping up and down. Sister Mattie sitting in the first row jumped out of her seat and started shouting praises unto God. After that, it was all she wrote. People were experiencing the overflow of the Holy Spirit. Many simply rejoiced over the new addition to the kingdom. Pastor Cuffe just started walking up and down the front of the church with tears flowing.

Daniel saw this and smiled. To a stranger this would seem bizarre, Daniel thought to himself, but this is how it sometimes happens, he rationalized. He stood and started giving God praise.

Within minutes, the whole church was up and shouting. Pastor Cuffe felt the unction of the Holy Spirit and said, "There is another. Come on... Don't wait. Give your life to Jesus now. You can have the peace of the Lord for yourself. I know that you have hurt others but God loves you and will forgive you. You just have to ask Him and trust Him. He will fix everything. Believe it."

A spiritual fire had ignited in the balcony and the entire church was praising God.

Melina was crying and thanking God for all of the blessings and how He had delivered her time and time again. "You are so faithful, God. I thank you…"

Daniel knew it was the Holy Spirit speaking to his heart when he found himself walking toward Major. He loved his brother but had so many mixed feelings. He needed to release those feelings to the Lord and the only way to do it was to show his brother the love that he knew Major didn't think he deserved. That was a big *"work"*. When he hugged Major, he wouldn't let go. Major tried to retreat but Daniel held fast. He held on to him tight and kept saying, "I love you, man, I love you, man, I LOVE you, man, God loves you!"

After Daniel said **God** loves you, he could feel Major's shoulders and upper body tremble.
"I love you too, man. I love you too," Major said.

He stood back and looked at Daniel. "I'm so sorry. Forgive me," he begged, tears streaming down his face.

"You are my brother and I will always love you. God loves you too," Daniel said.
Daniel led Major to the altar and Major humbly kneeled much to his own surprise. Daniel kneeled beside his brother and lifted his hands in praise.

"I know and I am ready to give my life to Him, I want to be better than I have been. I finally get it," he said almost laughing. "I want God to show me how to be a true man of God, just like you." Major smiled as he quickly wiped tears from his face. "Jesus died for me, Daniel, for me. And I want to serve Him because He loved me so much. I believe that His word is true and that He will never leave me nor forsake me. I'm ready to do the work because I have the faith."

Someone was shouting Hallelujah behind Major and he suddenly realized that it was his mother. Lila had made her way into the aisle and was shouting up a storm. The Nurses Aid made a circle around her as she danced like nobody had ever seen anyone dance before.

Pastor Cuffe watched the entire church as they praised God. It did his heart good.

"Praise the Lord everybody!"

Thirty

Therefore we are buried with him by baptism into
death; that like as Christ was raised up from the
dead by the glory of the Father, even so we
should walk in the newness of life.
Romans 6:4

"I have a new job!" Major exclaimed as he entered his mother's house. He was feeling like he'd won the lottery. He walked into his mother's room and sat on her bed smirking in an effort to suppress the smile that wanted to make an appearance.

"I don't know how but it seemed to fall right into my lap," he said to his mother as she exited her walk-in closet.

"Now, you know exactly how it happened," she said, smiling at him. "And you know who you should be thanking right now."

Understanding exactly what she was saying, he nodded in agreement.

"So..." his mother asked, "what will you be doing?" Lila looked at her son with renewed pride. He'd been trying so hard to find a job. He had left his slinging and hustling behind and had enlisted the help of his baby brother, Baylor, to help him create a resume. It was not an easy task because Major had not worked legitimately for a number of years but they did it and he'd been submitting his resume everywhere. The game plan was to focus on his sales skills and work from there. She knew that he might have a hard time but had faith that her son would get a job that would help him financially.

"Well, Daniel was working with one of the teenagers at the church and one particular young man was having a lot of trouble in school. He didn't seem to be able to focus. Daniel took the young man under his wing and helped him out. He showed him alternative ways to do his work and stay out of trouble. I guess he shared the things that had worked for him. Well, to make a long story short, Daniel needed to drop the boy off at home for some reason. I guess he promised to keep a close eye on this boy and the parents took that opportunity to thank Daniel for working so closely with their son and said if there was anything that they could do for him by way of thanks, they would do it in a heartbeat."

"Okay, what does that have to do with you, boy?" Lila said growing weary from the story.

"Well, the father was a big executive at WNR. You know the radio station in Newark. They needed someone in their sales and promotions department that was a hard worker and that had a 'way' with people." Major said almost bursting at the seams.

"You do have a way with people, especially the ladies," Lila said, understanding now where the story was going.

"Daniel told him that he would get him my resume and the rest is history," Major said proudly, crossing his muscular arms across his chest. He rose from the bed and was standing against the wall looking like the cat that ate Tweety Bird.

"Well, I'm so very happy for you, son," Lila said and patted her son on his forearm as she made her way out of her room. She knew that he had begun to get a little discouraged. She had been praying along with the rest of the family that he would be blessed with a position soon. She could recall walking past his room to find him on his knees with his bible asking the Lord how he should proceed. She overheard him saying that he knew that God had not saved him to be discouraged and without a means to provide for himself. He asked the Lord for direction and more patience to wait for what was in store. Sure enough, God provided a career and not just a job for her son. He was a Promotions and Sales Rep for WNR and he was not far from home. Newark was just a hop, skip and a jump away.

"I'm proud of you, son," Lila said as she walked further into the hall. She stopped and turned to him. She walked back over to him and embraced her son. She was happy he was doing the right things. He was truly seeking God in every aspect of his life. It had only taken him six weeks to find a job. Some people have a much harder time. Thank God that he was not one of them.

"Thanks, Mom," Major said. "I've got to go and thank Daniel. Is he home?" Major looked at his watch and noticed that it was about six thirty.

"He's with her," Lila said. "Alex is going to Portland this weekend to visit Naimond and he is riding with Melina to drop Alex at the airport," she said in a sarcastic tone.

"Mom, what's up with you and Melina?" Major inquired.

"I'll let him tell you," she heard herself say. She didn't like the way she sounded.

Lila realized that she sounded like a spoiled child realizing that she had to share her toy. Why was that? She knew she needed to resolve that issue but hadn't been successful thus far.

I need to do better, she thought to herself. Well, he is *my* Danny, she rationalized, having a silent conversation with herself.

"Does Daniel have something to tell me?" Major said.

"Well, I guess it's no secret. He has asked her to marry him," Lila said. She felt her mouth turn into a pout.

"Why aren't you happy?" Major asked confused as to why his mother was behaving in this manner. "I guess she said yes."

"Of course. That was her plan from the beginning."

"Mom, you don't really believe that. She seems okay to me," Major said.

"Well, whether I like it or not, it's going to happen," Lila said, noticing that her happy mood was souring and she couldn't stop it. "Let's change the subject," she said as she descended the stairs.

"Well, I'm going out tonight," Major said

"Is that right?" Lila stated.

The Son

She hadn't reached the bottom of the steps. Surprised, she stopped and turned to him while on the final step.

"Where are you going?" It had been a while since he had been out, she thought. "Who are you going out with?" Lila asked impatiently.

"Well," Major stated tentatively, "Daniel invited me to go out with him. It seems that Venus, you know the woman that joined the church the same day I did, and Melina have become friends and they invited me to double date with them. That was why I was wondering if Daniel was home."

Lila didn't like this at all. So Melina was at the core of this. She didn't allow the anger that was brewing to become visible and kept it concealed for the moment. She put on a façade that said all was well.

"Well, you guys have a great time. Venus seems like a sweet child. Isn't she a friend of Charla as well?" Lila asked.

"Yes, she works with Charla."

"Will you see Baylor too?" Lila inquired.

"No. Charla had to work and Baylor decided to put in some more hours tonight so that he could have the weekend free," Major explained.

"I can certainly understand that," Lila agreed. She was happy that Baylor finally had his degree in Business. He opted not to attend graduation and simply have his degree mailed to him. Since then, he had been a working fool.

"Well, don't let me stop you. Go out and have a nice time," Lila said, waving Major away. "Go wash your behind. You want to smell good when you go out with Miss Venus."

Major laughed and kissed his mother. He ran back up the steps to get ready for his dinner date. He told himself not to have any expectations. He just wanted to laugh and enjoy time with friends.

Thirty One

*Favor is deceitful, beauty is vain but a woman that feareth
the Lord, she shall be praised.*
Proverbs 31:30

"I don't understand, Mom," Daniel asked. "What
is it about Melina that causes you to get so angry?"

Lila tried to turn her back to her son so he would
not see her tears. She couldn't believe that little 'so and
so' had wriggled herself into his heart so fast. Daniel was
moving quickly with his wedding plans and hadn't even
consulted her on most of them.

She thought that she had her baby back when he
stopped going over to Melina's house so often. He'd said
that he wanted to focus on his studies and the ministry.
She thought that she would have a chance to spend some
time with him in the evenings. At least he would be home
with her. On a few occasions, he'd been able to take her
here and there when she needed him. He was a good man
just like her Obadiah. That was short-lived. Now he was
telling her that he was going to marry that girl, *Melina.*

"Mom, please don't get upset," Daniel pleaded.
He walked around to face her and noticed tears on her
cheeks. He hated this. He knew that he'd found a good
woman. God had placed her in his life. Why couldn't his
mother understand that?

"Daniel, do you know what you are doing?" she
asked. This caused him to review his choices in women.
His most recent choices caused him to shift
uncomfortably. A flash of Eva's face caused him to
unnoticeably shudder.

No, I'm not going to let anyone talk me out of
marrying Melina. I can't let my past dictate my future, he
thought.

Daniel looked directly into his mothers glassy
eyes. "What has she ever done to you?" he asked.

"What has she done for you?" she countered. She
immediately regretted saying that. She reached for his

hand and he allowed her to take it in hers. That statement stung him because he knew that their relationship was pure and he loved her with every part of his being.

"We are getting married the Sunday before Labor Day," he said with finality.

"Where is she? Why isn't she here with you?" Lila asked.

"I'm right here." They both turned to the front door and Melina entered the room with a smile on her face. Melina's voice was soft but she made her presence known with a quiet confidence.

Daniel went to Melina and placed his arm around her waist.

Lila grimaced. "Do you really love my Danny?"

"Yes, Mrs. Manders…"

"Why?" Lila quickly added not allowing Melina to finish her sentence.

"He is a caring, God-fearing man. He is the one that I have prayed for. I trust him like I trust no one else. He loves the Lord and isn't ashamed to let the world know. I know that he will do right by me and any children that we have. He is what I want and what I need." Melina assertively issued her response while looking into Daniel's eyes.

He returned her loving gaze and kissed her on her cheek.

"You are a career woman, how are you going to handle being a pastor's wife? You are a sheltered girl from South Jersey; you are used to getting your way… I know your type, you expect my son to spoil you. You aren't ready to become a wife. You haven't even grown-up yet!" She hurled these words at Melina as she paced the floor. It seemed as if she was reading or reciting a script. Lila was heaving. Daniel could see her chest ascend and descend as she hurled each fabricated accusation.

"Mrs. Manders that is untrue. I don't know how you have arrived at those conclusions about me when you haven't really spent any time with me." Melina was trying to remain calm. Each word released was enunciated and spoken with exaggerated emphasis.

"Mom, Melina, I would like us to get together to have dinner so that we can calmly and rationally discuss any misconceptions one may have about the other. This wedding is going to happen. You two are the most important women in my life and I will not walk around on egg shells when I'm around the two of you."

"Daniel, I want you to understand this. Please know that I don't possess any ill-will toward your mother." Melina stopped and decided that she should speak directly to his mother. "Mrs. Manders, I respect you because you are the woman that gave life to the man that I love so very much. I love you with the love of Christ. That being said, as a woman of God and his wife to be, I will not be disrespected by you. You have nothing on which to base your apparent dislike for me. I would like us to be civil if we can't be friends. You must know in your heart of hearts that I do love Daniel and want to be his loving partner throughout this life's journey."

"Touching... very touching," Lila said. She lifted her hands and lamely applauded.

Lila couldn't believe herself. It was as if she was watching herself perform. She wanted to stop but she couldn't. The mad woman she'd become had taken on a life of her own.

"Stop it, mom. That is unfair," Daniel said. He couldn't believe that his mother was acting like this. She was a Christian and knew the Lord. How could she behave like a demon straight from hell? Daniel thought with shame.

"I love you, Mom, but I follow the word of God and I will cleave to my wife because she and I will be one."

Lila gasped unable to believe what she was being told.

"I will still honor you but Melina will be my wife and after God she will be first in my life. I won't want to hear anything negative said about her by you or anyone, especially when she has done nothing to deserve it."

"What does that mean?" Lila asked as her eyes allowed more water to be released.

"Mom, don't make me have to choose. I don't want to," Daniel said. His voice cracked and he began to walk to her. He loved his mother but she was being unreasonable and he didn't understand. He never knew his grandparents but wondered if they gave her even half of the trouble that she was giving Melina.

He looked over to Melina as a current of understanding passed between them. She nodded and slowly walked out of the front door. He didn't want to lose her. He couldn't.

Lila was speechless. She tried the tantrum and it hadn't worked. She couldn't believe that she was going to do what she had only slated as a last resort. It would certainly mean that she would dig a deeper hole of deceit for herself but at the moment, she didn't care.

She closed her eyes and placed her hand over her chest and began to groan loudly.

"Daniel, please stop," she whimpered. "I'm having trouble breathing. Please get me to the hospital."

Daniel yelled out to Melina hoping that she hadn't pulled off yet. He heard steps coming toward him.

"Hey, why is the door ..." Baylor didn't finish his question and immediately ran to where Daniel sat with his mother in his arms. "What happened?" Baylor asked. He immediately removed his suit jacket and kneeled in front of his mother.

"Mom, are you okay?" Baylor asked.

"I'll be alright," she said, "Daniel is here." Lila looked up at Daniel creating a pained smile.

Thirty Two

*If thou hast done foolishly in lifting up thyself, or if thou
hast thought evil, lay thine hand upon thine mouth.*
Proverbs 30:32

Daniel paced outside of the physician's office worriedly wringing his hands. He prayed that his mother would receive a good report from the doctor but didn't like the way she looked only thirty moments ago. All he could do now was wait and believe.

"What happened with Mom?" Baylor asked as he returned from parking the car. His eyes were darting from Daniel to the door of the examining areas nervously.

"She got excited," Daniel responded. He really didn't want to provide an in-depth explanation as to what actually happened. He believed that it would only result in more chaos.

"What got her excited? Come on Daniel, you are not telling me anything." Baylor was trying to remain calm but he was concerned about his mother and knew that he wasn't getting the entire story. He didn't tell Daniel that he saw Melina running to her car just minutes before he walked into the house to find his mother clearly shaken. Melina looked upset too.

"Come on, man," Baylor repeated.

Daniel exhaled, feeling exhausted and knowing that he couldn't keep this from his brother, motioned to Baylor with his head to move to the far left corner of the waiting room.

"I told Mom…" Daniel began.

"Mr. Manders," the nurse called across the room, "you can go back and speak with the doctor."

Daniel quickly closed his mouth and nodded to the unprofessionally loud nurse. He and Baylor made their way back to examining room. His mother insisted that they stop by Dr. Samuel's office rather than going to the Emergency Room.

"He will see me," his mother said confidently. "He always makes time for me." She smiled and directed Daniel to the physician's office located in Westfield.

Daniel acquiesced. Baylor, once arriving at the destination, pulled over on Broad Street in front of the large medical office building.

Daniel and Baylor walked into the sterile room. Their mother was sitting, seemingly comfortably on the examining table smiling as if all was right with the world.

"Praise God," Daniel said looking in the direction of his brother. Baylor smiled recognizing that it looked like their mother was okay.

"You both walked in here like the doctor said I was going to die," Lila said with a small chuckle. "I'm fine," she said. "Right, Doctor?"

"It seems that your mother had a minor anxiety attack but her pressure is fine now and her heartbeat, although a little elevated, is not anything that I would be overly concerned about," Dr. Samuel said in a soothing and reassuring tone.

Although Dr. Samuel had been treating her for years, Lila didn't think that he would really be able to tell that she had been faking it. She smiled again. She knew that she was wrong and a thin veil of guilt covered a part of her heart but it wasn't enough of a conviction to make her remorseful.

"You must remember that she is older and her pressure has always been a concern. She is on medication for her heart but this was just a minor flare up." Dr. Samuel walked over to place his hand on Lila's hand. He looked solemnly into Lila's eyes.

"You have to take care of yourself and refrain from anything that is going to cause you undue stress." Dr. Samuel smiled parentally as if trying to coax a child to behave. "Is that understood, Lila?"

Lila decided to play the part until the final curtain call. She obediently nodded her head and looked up at Dr. Samuel and said, "I will, doctor. I promise."

"Mom, are you sure that you are okay?" Baylor said. He walked over to his mother and helped her down from the table.

"Yes, Baylor, I'm okay. I just don't think that I need to be in the midst of confusion." She looked purposefully at Daniel. "You know confusion is not of God."

"I'm glad that you are doing better, Mom," Daniel said. He breathed a sigh of relief and kissed his mother.

Lila was a little peeved that her last statement was lost on him. She placed her hand on his face and hid her emotions. "I just want to get home and get in the bed to take a nap. It has been quite an afternoon."

Both of her sons nodded and thanked Dr. Samuel. He followed his patient to the front desk to see them out. Dr. Samuel was an old-school doctor. He raised an eyebrow and unbeknownst to Lila, the statement that she made about confusion and the subsequent look that she darted in Daniel's direction was not lost on him. He scratched his curly salt and pepper hair and wondered. He then placed her chart on the desk for the receptionist. His cocoa hands found their way into the pockets of his white coat as he wondered what Lila was up to. He'd known her for years and the quick recovery that seemed to occur as soon as she entered the examining room, made him a little uncomfortable.

"Take care of yourself Lila," Dr. Samuel said. "Son," he said and motioned toward Daniel, "make sure she takes her medication. I'm sure that she'll be just fine."

Melina was too upset for words. The liquid blinding her vision almost caused her to have to pull over. She couldn't believe what had just transpired. Her safe arrival home was nothing short of God's intervention. As soon as she pulled into her parking space, she released the hurt that she had been holding on reserve since leaving the Manders' home.

The day that had started so wonderfully turned into a nightmare.

"How could she talk to me like that? What did I do to that woman?" she screamed as she placed her car in park. She stared at herself in the rearview mirror wondering what she could have said when she was in Lila's presence. She replayed every interaction and there was absolutely nothing.

"God, if I'm missing something and if I did do or say anything to Daniel's mother, please reveal it to me," she pleaded. She really wanted to be sure that she wasn't the reason why the woman behaved like a raving lunatic.

"Daniel," she thought.

She began to cry again. She didn't want this to be an issue. He loved his mother but he had rightfully told Mrs. Manders that she would be first, after God. She was so proud of him and that made her love him more.

"I don't want to cause a wedge between Daniel and his mother Lord," she sobbed. "What should I do?"

She knew that it was the Holy Spirit that spoke to her heart in that moment. *Be still and know that I am God; I will be exalted among the heathen, I will be exalted in the earth.*

"Thank you, Lord," Melina said as fresh tears began to flow. She was now crying because she had heard from God and not a moment too soon.

During mid-sniffle, Melina's cell phone rang.

"Hello," Melina answered, her voice sounded as if she had a stuffy nose.

"Girl, no need to explain why you sound like you do. I've just spoken with Naimond. He called and asked me to stop by his mom's house because Baylor called him."

Melina couldn't help but smile. Alex seemed to have 'Melina needs a friend' radar.

"Alex, it was horrible," Melina explained.

"What was horrible? Naimond said that Mrs. Manders had an anxiety attack but never said what caused it," Alex stated. Her voice was raising an octave with each phrase.

"Oh, that's right. I am so sorry. You haven't heard," Melina stated apologetically, beginning to breathe normally again.

"Heard what?" Alex asked in a deafening soprano voice.

"Daniel asked me to marry me and I said yes," Melina said. A semblance of a smile made its way to her lips. After all of the drama, she could still smile about the thought of becoming Daniel's wife.

"What?!" Alex sang, impersonating an untrained Leontyne Price.

"Yes. I am sorry that I didn't tell you. You should have been one of the first people......" Melina was rambling. She sniffled and continued. "We went to Daniel's house and formally told his mother about our wedding plans and Mrs. Manders went ballistic. She is clearly against the marriage and the most disparaging remarks she made about me were... unreal."

"Girl, stop. I'm coming over," Alex said. She snapped her fingers when she realized that it was only 4:30 and wouldn't be able to get there until about 6:00. "Can you hold on until I get there?"

"Yeah, I don't want to stay in, let's go out to dinner and I'll tell you all about it."

"Good thing you took a half day today, Melina. You couldn't have finished the day the way you sound."

"You are right. I'll see you about six."

When Daniel, Baylor and their mother arrived back at the house, Major was waiting for them. He hadn't any idea as to why the house was empty and he was immediately concerned about his family.

"Where have you guys been?" Major asked no one in particular when the three entered the house and headed toward the kitchen.

Lila was so happy with herself that she made her boys stop off at the local *Stop and Shop* to pick up some ground meat and sausage so that she could make her famous lasagna. They tried to talk her out of it because she mentioned that she wanted to go home to lie down. She was relentless in her requests and Daniel and Baylor, not wanting to deny her anything, stopped and purchased what was needed to make the meal.

"Hi, Major," Lila said as she made her way around the kitchen once shedding her coat. She was pulling out all the necessary ingredients to make her lasagna the best ever.

Lila thought she would have skipped if she were alone, but since she had an audience, she would stay in character just a little while more.

"Not to worry, Major. I'm better. Just a little too much excitement. Dr. Samuel says that I should be fine if we behave ourselves." She quickly glanced at Daniel and this time he met her eyes. This time, her comment was not lost or overlooked. He understood immediately.

To test his theory, Daniel smiled and sat in one of the chairs. "It's all good."

Daniel turned to look at both of his brothers. "I am getting married."

"What did you say?" Baylor said.

"I asked Melina to marry me and she said yes," Daniel said smiling broadly. He loved saying that he was going to be marrying the woman of his dreams. Daniel used his peripheral vision and saw his mother turning her lips downward. Her scowl was obvious.

"Sons, give me an hour and I'll start dinner. I'm feeling just a bit light headed all of a sudden," Lila said as she made her way past all three men.

"Mom," Daniel said. He was on her heels as she slowly walked into the hall that led to the staircase. "I'm sorry that you are not happy about Melina and me but you have got to know that she will be my wife. The wedding is only six months away. I hope that you can come to terms with the fact that she is the woman that I have chosen. More importantly, I believe that she is the woman that God has chosen for me."

Lila turned to her special boy and her eyes filled with tears but she said nothing.

"Mom, you know how much I love you. If you love me as much as you say you do, you'll give Melina a chance. Get to know her. You'll love her just like I do."

Lila couldn't believe her son. She had no more words. Her heart felt like someone had torn it from her chest. Her sweet baby. Why couldn't he wait? Why her? What was the rush? She thought all of these things but uttered not a syllable.

"You know you ain't right, Lila." She heard the voice of Obadiah say. She shook her head violently trying to shut him out.

"Mom, are you okay?" Daniel shouted, still a little concerned about her health.

Baylor and Major entered the hall and saw that their mother's face was saturated with moisture.

"What is going on?" They both asked in a jumbled fashion.

Daniel turned to look at his brother and immediately, they understood.

Lila sat down in a chair against the wall and placed her hand over her mouth and said nothing. All of her shenanigans hadn't worked. She knew that she was wrong to behave in such a manner but...

Daniel began to pray that his mother would accept the plans that were underway to make Melina his wife.

"Please don't let this be a thorn in this family," Daniel pleaded. "Search your heart, Mom. Search your heart and if you find anything that shouldn't be there, ask the Lord's help and He'll remove it." He kissed her tear stained face.

His mother remained wordless as she watched her son walk up the stairs, enter his room and close the door.

Lila, not sure of what to do, stayed glued to her seat and refused to remove her hand from her mouth. She knew that if she did, she would scream.

The Son

Thirty Three

*Therefore being justified by faith, we have peace with God
through our Lord Jesus Christ.*
Romans 5:1

Daniel was initially torn and couldn't bring
himself to call Melina or even talk to her when she called.
He knew that he loved her and would marry her but he
needed to be by himself to talk to the Lord. He wanted to
hear from the Lord again that she was the one. He sought
the Lord but didn't receive what he thought was a suitable
answer.

He had not thought it wise to cease all
communication with Melina because his heart was drawn
to her. He thought about her constantly. She was smiling
at him in his mind's eye. Memories of her laughing at one
of his stupid jokes and cuddling on the couch brought him
some solace but he wanted to hear from the Lord so that
there was no mistake.

"Lord, I know that you sent me here to preach and
bring others to you but Melina... was she part of your plan
for me?"

Each night he prayed that prayer. Nothing else
seemed to matter.

Melina could tell that something was wrong.
Daniel finally confessed to Melina what the issue was and
although initially taken aback, she agreed that they should
both seek God for an answer. She told him about her
answer from the Lord but he had to get an answer for
himself. Only then, would he be at total peace.

Melina thought that any other woman would
become angry and call off the wedding. She wouldn't.

After talking with Alex, she understood the
connection between Daniel and his mother. Naimond
filled Alex in on some of the family history and how
everyone knew that Daniel had always been the apple of
his mother's eye. Naimond, never allowed the obvious
favoritism to bother him because he knew that his mother

215

loved him. It was just something about Daniel. No one knew what it was but nevertheless it was understood that Daniel, was the 'chosen' one. This obviously affected Major and although Baylor recognized it, he was the youngest and the baby so he wasn't too pressed about it. Daniel had been away in college and then working in Wisconsin so Baylor received all of the affection that would have been lavished on Daniel.

"I would just like to be able to have a woman to woman conversation with Mrs. Manders," Melina said.

"You mean a believer to believer talk," Alex corrected. "I thought she was saved? She sure isn't acting like it."

"She is feeling threatened and has just let the flesh take over," Melina said. "I know that she loves the Lord." Melina smiled unconvincingly at Alex. She prayed that Mrs. Manders would get on the good foot.

During the week, Melina prayed more than usual and stayed as close to God as she could. She didn't call Daniel. She wanted him to get the answer that he needed to receive.

Melina believed that she would benefit from the answer just as much as Daniel would. The answer that he received would confirm the word that she received.

The work week was hectic and she found that she was at peace. She didn't worry about anything. She knew that all things work out for the good for those who love God. On Friday, she received her first performance review in her new position and was awarded with a substantial increase. She was so thankful and happy that she instinctively called Daniel to tell him the good news. She'd forgotten that she was going to let him have his space.

"Hey there," Daniel said. He loved the sound of her voice. It always sounded like she was singing. He smiled without noticing until he turned and looked into the living room mirror to find that he was touting a 100 watt smile.

"Guess what?!?" Melina teased. Not even giving him a chance to speak she said, "Today I received my review and I received an unheard of 10 percent raise!" She screamed, "To God be the Glory!"

Daniel matched her enthusiasm and joined her in her praise to God. "Praise the Lord. My wife is rolling in it."

Daniel stopped abruptly and looked at himself again the mirror. "Did I just say 'my wife?" he asked Melina

She laughed. "You certainly did, Rev. Manders."

That was it, he thought. He confidently continued. "You are my betrothed and the one I want to spend the rest of my life with." Daniel felt the burden of indecision being lifted from his shoulders. He automatically felt lighter.

"Did you receive your answer?" Melina asked curiously.

"I had the answers all week but didn't recognize them as answers," Daniel acknowledged.

"What do you mean?" Melina asked, not sure of what he was saying. She needed him to spell it out.

"I thought of you all week. Your smile..., your voice..., the thought of you and I being husband and wife..." He stopped, chuckled and then continued, "Not in the biblical sense but being a couple dedicated to the cause of Christ. I was feeling so disconnected this week and it was because I have not talked to or seen you. I know that I need you, Miss Lawrence. You gave me the time that I needed to hear from God and no other woman would have been so kind and considerate with my request. I love you, Melina, please be my wife."

At that moment, the Holy Spirit allowed Daniel to remember a scripture that sealed the deal for him. He heard Proverbs 18:22; *He who finds a wife finds a good thing, and obtains favor from the Lord.*

"Thank you, God!" Daniel whispered.

"Did you say something, Daniel?" Melina asked.

"I was just thanking God for always providing the answers when we look to Him. Let's go out and celebrate," Daniel suggested.

"You're on!" Melina said. "I can be ready in an hour."

"Make no mistake Melina, this dress is absolutely gorgeous. Most importantly, it looks great on you." Alex seemed more excited about the wedding gown than Melina.

Cassandra was nodding enthusiastically. She was smiling and walking the perimeter of the gown. "You are going to be the most beautiful bride in history, since me of course."

They all laughed. Planning the wedding had been so much fun. Melina was sorry to see it all coming to an end. She couldn't understand why she heard so many horror stories about planning a wedding. She had only a few minor issues but everything was falling together so perfectly.

Only God, she thought.

To her surprise, Mrs. Manders had not been the obstacle that she originally thought she would be. She of course continued to be icily silent when Melina visited the Manders' home but she didn't directly interfere. Daniel arranged for her to have all of the necessary fittings. All of the women were getting their dresses made by a fabulous seamstress. Melina's mother even traveled up from Willingboro to meet everyone, except Mrs. Manders, in Irvington at the dress shop. Ms. Phoebe was a spirit filled woman who was also an impeccable business woman. The dresses were looking great and the last fitting was scheduled in two weeks.

The summer seemed to fly because of all the preparations. Daniel and Melina couldn't believe the deal they received on the reception hall. The facility was brand new. They would be the first couple to utilize it. Even before they saw the price, they agreed immediately on the place. It was the epitome of romance. The décor was reminiscent of a lavish, fairytale ball.

They decided against a DJ and hired a jazz band. The local favorite, Mesmerize, was their first choice and they were able sign them without a problem. The food for the reception was the reception hall's responsibility and the menu was the only difficult aspect to decide upon. Because they were both Italian food junkies, they went with all the Italian foods offered. They decided not to go with the veal parmesan for obvious reasons.

Daniel and Melina had a great time and were falling deeper in love as the summer came to a close. It was now August and it had been a hot summer, but neither seemed to mind.

Love was in the air. Baylor and Charla were becoming quite serious as were Naimond and Alex. Naimond was due in town the last week in August.

He hoped to be able to take a two week vacation away from his beloved paper. Alex traveled to Portland almost four times since they met and she always returned glowing. Even Cassandra's marriage was improving. Melina was happy that everyone seemed to be as happy as she was. She selfishly wanted this time of her life to continue forever.

She'd even mentioned to Daniel that she wanted this time of her life to continue.

He frowned and said, "How would I be able to make you my wife and turn you out girl?" He looked almost devilish. "You know we will have a honeymoon to remember. I promise, I will not disappoint."

"You better not," Melina laughed.

He kissed his wife to be and playfully smacked her lightly her on the backside.

"Oh see, none of that," she warned and laughed.

Thirty Four

*Let us hold fast the confession of our hope without
wavering, for He who promised is faithful.*
Hebrews 10:23

"What is going on?" Melina asked.

Daniel's shrouded light eyes told her something
was wrong but he quickly turned away not wanting her to
see through him. During the last couple of months, she
had become quite adept at reading him and at this moment
he could not risk that.

"Daniel, please talk to me," Melina said. She was
beginning to become uncomfortable.

"Melina, it's not good."

"Alright," she said, grateful that he was beginning
to open up.

"Mom informed all of us that she hasn't been
feeling well. She said that she went to the doctor on her
own and he confirmed that she has blockage in her heart
valves."

Melina ran to her husband-to-be and took him in
her arms. She felt for him. He truly loved his mother.
She had both of her parents alive and all he had was his
mother.

"What are the next steps?" she asked as she sat
down on the sofa pulling him down with her.

Daniel looked into her eyes. He could actually
feel the love she had for him. He exhaled and told her the
story.

"Well, Major said that he would look after her
after the necessary surgery but she insisted that I be the
one to look after her. Major reminded her that I would be
a newlywed and that it would be easier on everyone if she
would just allow he and Baylor to look after her."

Daniel looked down. He seemed to search the
beige carpet fibers for the rest of the story. He didn't want
to rehash the turn of events but knew that he had to.

"When the truth finally came out, we found out that there wasn't any blockage and that this was a feeble attempt on her part to keep me from marrying you."

"Why does she continue to do this?" Melina asked, rising to her feet and walking to the other side of the living room.

"Melina, the big problem is that she didn't realize how much her not wanting Major to take care of her hurt him. He seemed to be thrown by her adamant resolve that I be the one to help her and left the house two days ago. No one has seen him since."

"What?" Melina shouted as she whirled around to face him. "The wedding is tomorrow!"

"We all know that, Melina. It is not about the wedding, Melina. We have to find Major. He had just accepted Christ and got a good job. He was doing such a great job in trying the being the man that we all could be proud of and then Mom does this." Daniel's face went into his hands.

Melina wanted to go to him and comfort him but she couldn't. He was always letting his family dictate his life. Was it going to be like this after they were married?

"What do you plan on doing?" she asked, trying to lower her voice and regain composure. "Have you told Naimond?"

"I don't know what to do. He is not in the places we thought he'd be in and no one has seen him. He and Venus had been getting close and she said that he'd called her but didn't say where he was. She did say that he didn't sound like there was anything wrong."

"Again," Melina said, her voice trembling. "What is your plan?"

"What is wrong with them? Why am I always the one that has to make everything right?" Daniel asked no one. He asked the question but already knew the answer.

"Daniel, I think that you like being the one that everyone looks to for the answer. You like being the one to save the day," Melina said sharply.

The statement cut Daniel. "Why would you say that?" he asked looking over at her.

"You know why. As soon as something goes wrong with your family or as soon as your mother calls you, you put on your Christian Superman cape and feel the need to fly to the rescue."

She hadn't meant to let all of the words escape her lips in such an undiplomatic way but Melina was finally saying what she had always wanted to say. She stood, feet planted and arms across her chest, staring at Daniel awaiting his response. She'd had enough of his family. If it wasn't his mother, it was Major causing problems or the absentee brother that had been found. She breathed and felt the water behind her eyes. She was determined not to cry.

Although shocked by Melina's words, he understood why she felt the way she did and could not be angry with her for making him aware of what had obviously been buried in her heart.

"I'm about to marry the woman that was made for me by you, Lord," Daniel said looking up at the stucco ceiling. "Is this a test? Are you testing me to see if I'll do the right thing?"

As if he was unhappy with the answer he received, he turned to look in Melina's direction. His eyes became dark and his mouth opened.

"They are my family and I am obligated to help them. Just because you have run away from your family because they weren't ambitious enough for you does not mean that I should totally leave mine when they need me most."

His words, like daggers found their way to her heart, puncturing it with each syllable.

"I need you, Daniel," Melina heard herself say. She was pleading with him to understand how she felt. It was the day before they were to be one and once again she had to contend with the Manders family. "Do you understand that ever since you have been back they have called on you for everything? Major is a grown man and your mother should be ashamed of herself for pulling such a stunt."

Daniel stood at the mention of his mother.

"What Daniel? Do you think that God would want you to walk out on your wife to be?" Melina looked at him. She found his eyes. They returned to their normal nut brown hue. "Would God want you to turn your back on your commitment to me?"

Daniel opened his mouth as if he were about to speak.

"Daniel, you want to go and save the day but you have already shown them the way. Your mother knows better. What can you really do? I know that you want to postpone the wedding but I can't let you do that. Something else will come up and we'll be fifty before we can peacefully be made man and wife."

Melina, lowered her voice again as she walked closer to the man that she loved more than herself. "You have a responsibility to me. Major knows the Lord and knows how to contact us if he needs us. Your mother is another issue entirely. I'm going to be at the church tomorrow and I will be waiting there to be your wife. God has placed me here for you. I'm here for you." She took his face in her hands.

A faint knock was heard at the door. Melina went to the door to find Baylor, Charla and Venus.

"Come in," Melina said and allowed them entry.

"Daniel, we know that you have a lot on your plate with the wedding. Let us do some of the searching. You have to get ready to marry this wonderful lady," Baylor said. He winked at Melina. Melina smiled, grateful for his understanding.

"Some family you are marrying into, huh, Melina." Baylor said with a chuckle, sensing the need for levity.

Melina said nothing.

Daniel abruptly jumped to his feet. "I've got to go."

"Daniel, what do you want us to do?" Charla asked. She motioned to Baylor and Venus. They followed him to the door exiting the house as well.

"I don't know…" he said. He looked at Melina. The gaze lingered. She could see the war that was going on inside of him. His eyes told her of the hurt, disappointment and confusion that he was experiencing.

Daniel felt as if he was literally being pulled in two different directions. He knew that he had promised himself to this woman and shouldn't let anything come before her but she wasn't his wife yet and he had promised God that he would keep his family together. He loved Melina. He couldn't fathom life without her but…

Daniel's eyes once again held the woman that he knew that God had created just for him but he realized that he was needed elsewhere. Major was missing, his mother was not acting herself and he believed that he needed to at least make sure that Major was alright.

"Lord," he silently asked, "what would you have me do?"

He nervously placed his hands inside of his pockets and deepened his gaze into Melina's eyes hoping that she would understand what he had to do.

Melina couldn't exactly read what Daniel was thinking but she held his eyes and felt something in her stir.

She recalled a scripture that she had been meditating on throughout the summer believing that God would give her, her expected end. She embraced him and whispered in his ear, "*I am my beloved's and his desire is toward me,*" She kissed his cheek and closed the door.

The Son

The Wedding...

Thirty Five

*Looking unto Jesus, the author and finisher of our faith;
who for the joy that was set before him endured the cross,
despising the shame and is set down at the right hand of
the throne of God.*
Hebrews 12:2

"Cassandra, how can you say that?" Melina asked. Tears threatened as she looked incredulously at her friend. Her anger was increasing. Melina didn't appreciate being double-teamed by her mother and friend. She clearly had the wrong person back here with her. She should have asked Alex or even Neici to help her. She thought better of it and realized that those two were much better at crowd control. Things were getting tense and they were right where she needed them.

"What do you mean, 'how can I say that'?" Cassandra responded in like manner. I knew there was something about Daniel," Cassandra admitted. "I just couldn't place my finger on it. Don't get me wrong, Melina, its clear that he loves you, but he has always been running in two different directions because of his imagined allegiance to his family. You have even said that you were worried about how life would be after you were married."

Cassandra turned and closed the door completely and lowered her voice. "Don't you think that this is his way of saying that he has made his choice and that he has chosen to be everything to his family and not you?"

Cassandra didn't want to go there but she felt that as a friend, she should allow Melina the opportunity to examine the situation she now found herself in. In Cassandra's opinion, all arrows were pointing in the direction of the Manders family being Daniel's number one priority.

"He knows that we will be considered one once we are married and that he will place me before all others, including his family. Just because he honors his mother and tries to do right by his brothers, screwed up as they were, he never made me feel unimportant." Melina thought about the day when they announced their engagement to Mrs. Manders and how Daniel asked *her* to leave. Did he put his mother first then? She also remembered the time when Major was almost arrested on Christmas Eve while driving home from service. Granted, Major was not at fault but Daniel had to cancel Christmas dinner with her family in Willingboro after all of the preparation. It wasn't as if Baylor couldn't have taken Mrs. Manders to the police station to pick up Major's car. Major did feel horrible about the situation and the police did apologize profusely but true to form, "Super Daniel" had to be there to make sure everything was done decently and in order. Was Cassandra right?

"I'll admit, Cassandra, there have been instances where I have been made to feel insignificant but that doesn't mean that he doesn't love me or that he won't be here today," Melina said, believing that the words that she spoke would somehow cause Daniel to appear in the next few moments.

"Like I said, Melina, where is he?" Cassandra asked and lifted her arms into the air searching the room for the missing groom.

Melina turned to look at her mother and almost lost it.

An urgent knock on the door kept Melina from allowing the first of the tears that had been stored up for release to emerge from her perfectly painted eyes. Cassandra and her mother were making a very convincing case.

"Come in," Melina said, barely audible.

Baylor walked into the room. His face was unreadable. His ascot was missing and his vest was undone. His strides were purposeful as he walked up to

The Son

Melina. "Remember Naimond said that he wouldn't be able to make the wedding at the last minute?"

Melina nodded, not understanding why this was of any importance.

"He is on his way to the church. He should be here in twenty minutes. Can you postpone this until he gets here?" Baylor asked as the corners of his mouth teased with a smile.

"Why, Baylor?" Melina asked.

"Major and Daniel are with him. Naimond called Daniel early this morning and told him that Major was out there. Major was determined to bring Naimond to the wedding. He said he felt that if it weren't for him, Naimond would have never been living in Oregon and he really wanted to make things right. He just waited too long to put his plan in motion. His heart was in the right place."

"I thought that he was upset about his mother?" Melina asked. She nervously folded her hands and looked up at her mother as if Zenia could explain the whole state of affairs.

"He was but that didn't cause him to go off the deep end. The letter that she finally showed him, caused him to make up his mind," Baylor explained.

"What letter?" Melina asked.

"Naimond wrote Mom a letter the morning he left many years ago. In it, he told her that he knew that he wasn't her son and he said that he loved her but would never feel like a part of the family because of the lies. He explained that Major was a part of the problem but didn't say how and that the love that she showed him would never be forgotten. The letter said that he was going to find his people, his real people."

Baylor paused and looked at Melina and then Cassandra. "That broke Mom's heart. She'd never really forgiven Major for whatever his part was in causing Naimond to leave, although she never knew how significant it was. There always seemed to be a limit when it came to the love she showed Major after that day.

Major was determined not to let this day happen without having Naimond here. He felt that he had to do it. He thought it might help mend some fences." Baylor breathed and stated with a grin, "Everyone should be here shortly."

"Melina, did you hear Baylor?" Cassandra said.

Melina nodded. Although she was happy that Daniel was on his way, she was still a little angry at him for causing her to worry unnecessarily. Why hadn't he called? The story Baylor conveyed helped explain things but she was still a bit frazzled.

Melina, finding the mental strength to stand, reached for Baylor. "Are you sure?" She didn't know how to feel. Why had Daniel gone to pick-up Naimond? Wasn't there someone else that could have done that? Again, she felt as if her feelings didn't matter when it came to his family.

"Yes, they were calling me from the car. They were on Route 1&9," Baylor said. "Daniel knew that if he called you to try and explain the matter, it might make matters worse and he couldn't chance that. He believed that you would be here. He believed that you believed in him." Baylor was sheepishly grinning. He was admittedly a little worried as well and was relieved when he received the call from his brother.

"Melina, I need to speak to you alone," Zenia said. Melina's mother connected visually with everyone in the room and they understood that they needed to exit. Cassandra nodded and quietly left the study, almost tip-toeing behind Baylor.

Zenia's satin cranberry spaghetti-strapped gown was making its way toward Melina. Once reaching her destination, Zenia extended her hand to the chair to her right, noiselessly requesting that Melina sit down. Melina did as she was asked and Zenia took the seat next to her.

Zenia took her daughter's hand in hers and spoke softly. "Daughter, you don't have to do this."

"Mom..." Melina began.

"No, sweetheart," Zenia continued. "I know that you love him and believe in who he is, but does he believe in you and what you represent?" Zenia lifted her eyes. She looked through the window. The day was so bright and beautiful. This day should be just as bright and beautiful for her daughter. "If this is how it is going to be, you should really ask yourself if you want to be married to a man that has already shown you that his family will always be an 'issue' for him. I'm not saying that I think his loyalty to his family isn't admirable but they have been nothing but a thorn in your side from the beginning. To top it all off, his mother has already made it clear that you will be her adversary. Do you want to contend with that for the rest of your life together?"

"Mom, I can't worry about his mother and as for his brothers, they have made strides to become better. They don't lean on Daniel as much," Melina said, trying to defend her decision to still want to marry Daniel.

She hadn't said it aloud but she was going to marry him as soon as he walked into the church. God had made it very clear. She couldn't act like the children of Israel and continue to doubt God. He had made it clear and she would stand on His promises.

"Mom, Mrs. Manders is not my problem. I'm certain that God will take care of whatever her problem is toward me. I haven't done anything to that woman and she knows that. Daniel told her that once we are married we would be one and I have to believe him. I will be first in his life and second only to God." Melina kissed her Mom.

"I need to go and freshen my make-up. Could you please send Neici back here? She's with Alex."

Zenia lowered her eyes and uttered a prayer asking God to bless and safeguard their union. "Be happy, Melina."

As they embraced, the door opened and Charla entered the room. "Melina, there is someone who wants to have a few words with you since there has been an unscheduled delay." Charla's eyes were bright. She was clearly happy about something. As she neared, Melina could see that her eyes were like glass.

"With God, all things are possible. Remember that, girl," Charla said. She gave Melina's hand a quick squeeze and said, "You can come in."

Melina didn't expect a visit from this person. The beautiful dark burgundy and gold brocade dress that was adorned with gold buttons down the middle looked absolutely regal on Mrs. Manders. Her hair was upswept into an up-do that likened her to an African queen. The braided halo that encircled her bun was perfectly decorated with gold studs. Her make-up was star quality. Mrs. Manders entered and smiled warmly at Melina.

Lila completely understood Melina's loss for words. She was the last person that the child had expected to visit her, moments before the wedding.

"You are a beauty, Melina," Lila said genuinely.

"Thank you, Mrs. Manders," Melina responded. "Lord, please help me...," Melina whispered.

"Child, please don't look so stricken. I know that I haven't been behaving myself very well and I can certainly understand if you don't wish to allow me to say a few words to you."

Melina was silent.

"I'll take your silence as permission to speak," Lila said. She looked over at Zenia and smiled. They hadn't spoken during the entire planning stages of the wedding.

Zenia nodded in an effort to be polite. She didn't trust herself to say anything to the woman. Zenia hadn't had an opportunity to meet Mrs. Manders. Usually, the parents get the opportunity talk at the rehearsal and dinner. The rehearsal had been two days ago and Mrs. Manders decided that she couldn't participate. Daniel decided against a rehearsal dinner as well because of his mother's unpredictable conduct. Zenia was upset that Mrs. Manders had treated her daughter so cruelly but at Melina's request, she hadn't approached the woman.

"Mrs. Lawrence, I have to apologize to you and your daughter," Lila began. "Charla and I had a good conversation while we were waiting for the men to get here. It's funny, if it hadn't been for them being delayed, I don't think that we would have had an opportunity to talk to each other so frankly." Lila smoothed her dress and stared into Melina's eyes to ensure that she had her undivided attention. "I'm sure that Daniel told you about Naimond and his real mother Opal. Well, Opal is the woman that Obadiah's parents wanted to him marry. She was from what was considered a good family in our small town and they thought that she'd be an ideal match for him.

You see, I came from a modest upbringing. My father and mother didn't have much education and we lived on the land that they farmed. Sharecroppers are what they called my parents. I always loved Obadiah but Opal had the means to catch his eye. Opal, on the other hand didn't love Obadiah but knew that he was being forced to court her. He delayed it for as long as he could until the night that Opal found out that the man that she loved was moving to New York. She wanted to go, but the man wouldn't take her with him. He said he wanted a woman that had culture, a city woman. Opal was devastated and off she went to find Obadiah. Up until then, they were just good friends. Neither thought that they wanted anything romantic. Well you can guess what happened, Naimond.

Unfortunately, Opal died during childbirth but Obadiah convinced me that what happened between he and Opal was a mistake. He loved me. When he told his family, they hit the roof. I was trash in their eyes. Remember, Obadiah was their only boy. He was their pride and joy. I was just some non-shoe wearing farmer's daughter. They wanted something better for their one and only son."

Lila stopped and sat down in the chair that faced the sunbathed windows. She smiled. "Obadiah, stood his ground and told them that he was going to marry me if I'd have him. He said that he and I would raise little Naimond. His parents threatened to take Naimond but he did them one better. He and I eloped a month after Opal's death. They didn't know where we had gone. They found out though. Oh boy, did they give me grief. They saw me as the one person who took their baby away. They would come and see the baby and not speak to me or act as if I were not in the room. It hurt me deeply."

The smile faded from Lila's face as she remembered the way her husband's parents talked about her to other people, calling her trash. "These were supposed to be God-fearing, educated people." Lila shook her head. "What is crazy is that I have done the same thing to you. I have treated you exactly the way his parents treated me. I love my Danny and want only happiness for him. I know that my actions didn't show it but I love the Lord too."

Lila chuckled knowing that there wasn't anything funny about the way she had been treating Melina. "Charla helped me to remember that. I'm so very ashamed. Please forgive me," Lila pleaded with a contrite expression. "Daniel has always had my heart but I have to realize that you have his heart now and I must step aside. Child, you have done nothing to deserve the hell that I have caused." She stood and opened her arms inviting Melina to come to her.

Melina stood frozen. This woman had said so many horrible things to her. She had caused her to question her faith and the love that she had for Daniel. Who was to say that she wouldn't begin to show her behind again and act a fool a few months from now?

Melina turned her head slightly in the direction of her mother. Her mother's eyes said nothing. Melina once again replayed the events of the last months and all of the things that occurred that could have derailed her from getting to this moment.

The Holy Spirit once again made Himself known to Melina as she recalled a scripture in Ephesians 4:32. *And be kind one to another, tenderhearted, forgiving one another, even as God for Christ's sake hath forgiven you.*

The Son

Melina smiled with the love of God in her heart and embraced Mrs. Manders. Zenia, proud of her daughter, walked over and all three women embraced.

Thirty Six

*Hold fast the pattern of sound words which you have
heard from me, in faith and love which are in
Christ Jesus.*
2 Timothy 1:13

Alex burst into the room smiling from ear to ear.
She was holding Naimond's hand. He looked at everyone
in the room apologetically.

"Don't hold this against my little brother,"
Naimond said remorsefully. He took a few steps back as
Melina untangled herself from the embraces of the other
women. She stood in front of Naimond, smiling. The joy
that she felt was evident in her countenance.

"Wow!" Naimond said. "I'm sure that if Daniel
knew what you looked like, he would have left me at the
airport. You are breathtaking, Melina. I can't wait to see
Alex in that get-up when we get married."

Alex nudged him and giggled.

"I can't wait that much longer to make you mine.
You know that it is better to marry than to burn, woman.
Please make up your mind."

Melina grabbed Alex. "He's proposed?" She
whispered gleefully.

Alex nodded enthusiastically.

"Stop that gossiping, we have a wedding today!"
Naimond said, feigning impatience.

"You have some nerve," Melina said. "Aren't
you going to be the best man?" she asked.

"Because Major came to the rescue, Daniel
wanted him to stand with him. We are so proud of Major.
His methods were a little last minute and unorthodox, but
he came through."

Daniel stood at the front of the church feeling a
little lightheaded. He could feel the beads of perspiration
dancing around his hairline but refused to move. He
looked over at Major and nodded.

The Son

Major smiled broadly at his brother. He was the best man. Who would have ever guessed that he would be standing up with his brother on this day?

What a mighty God we serve, Major thought. He could feel his smile getting wider. He was glad that everything had worked out and that his plan to get Naimond here worked. It was a little shaky but all three of them were standing proudly with Daniel.

Major's eyes unconsciously settled on Melina's sister, Neici. She stood behind Alex looking like a glowing angel dressed in cranberry. He instinctively licked his lips.

The sound of organ music brought him back to the task at hand.

Pastor Cuffe patted Daniel on the shoulder and winked at him. Everyone stood and all eyes were on the vision of white that was making her way to the altar.

Daniel's eyes met Melina's as she approached him. He'd always been right about this woman. She was the most beautiful creature that he'd ever seen. She would be his and he would be hers.

He felt a nudge and turned his gaze from his bride. Major placed a handkerchief in his hand. Major motioned to Daniel to wipe his face.

Daniel touched his face and felt the moisture on his cheek. He had not realized that he had begun tearing at the sight of his woman.

He looked deeply into her eyes. She smiled at him and her beauty seemed to light up the room.

Melina had beaten Daniel to the punch. She'd started with the waterworks as soon as she laid eyes on him. Walking on the petals of roses, she held onto her father as if she might fall. Her eyes settled on Daniel and it seemed as though she lost the ability to breathe. He was hers. His desire *was* toward her.

God, you certainly know what you are doing, she thought. As she let go of her Dad's arm and took Daniel's moist hand, Pastor Cuffe began to speak.

"Let's begin with 1 Corinthians 7:3-4. *Let the husband render unto the wife due benevolence; and likewise also the wife unto the husband. She hath not power of her own body, but the husband and likewise also the husband hath not power of his own body, but the wife.*"

Daniel squeezed Melina's hand and looked into her eyes with all of the love that he had.

Melina received the unspoken message of love and smiled. She couldn't stop smiling.

Daniel then looked at his brothers: Baylor, Major and Naimond. He silently thanked God for their presence. God had used him to bring his family together and with His guidance, it had been accomplished.

Naimond told him on the way to the church that he had accepted Christ as his personal Savior. Naimond was laughing when he said that there was no way that he could be around Alex, Major, Baylor and his brother, "the preacher" and not be affected. The word of God is too powerful.

Now, all of his brothers knew Jesus Christ as their personal Savior. Daniel realized that because of Jesus, his entire family had a heavenly home. He knew that it was all Jesus but marveled at how God used him and Pastor Cuffe.

Daniel had to admit that he'd had his doubts about coming home. He didn't know what God had in store for him but realized that because he was a true son of God and sought first the kingdom of God, all other things had been added. God truly does reward those who diligently seek him.

Daniel believed that more than ever as he looked at the gorgeous addition. He was now beginning a new life with Melina, his bride, his wife, his gift from God.

About the Author

M. Ann Ricks is a graduate of Rider University and a former health insurance professional. She currently resides in Bear, Delaware with her loving husband and two beautiful sons.

The Son, is her second novel. She is working on her third project; *The Blood Done Signed My Name.*

2182279